BRACED *for* LOVE

Books by Mary Connealy

From Bethany House Publishers

BROTHERS
IN ARMS

BOOK ONE

BRACED for LOVE

MARY CONNEALY

BETHANYHOUSE
a division of Baker Publishing Group
Minneapolis, Minnesota

Published by Bethany House Publishers
11400 Hampshire Avenue South
Bloomington, Minnesota 55438
www.bethanyhouse.com

Bethany House Publishers is a division of
Baker Publishing Group, Grand Rapids, Michigan

Library of Congress Cataloging-in-Publication Data
Names: Connealy, Mary, author.
Title: Braced for love / Mary Connealy.
Description: Minneapolis, Minnesota : Bethany House, a division of Baker
    Publishing Group, [2021] | Series: Brothers in arms ; #1
Identifiers: LCCN 2020042393 | ISBN 9780764237720 (trade paperback) | ISBN
    9780764238215 (casebound) | ISBN 9781493430123 (ebook)
Subjects: GSAFD: Mystery fiction. | Western stories. | Love stories.
Classification: LCC PS3603.O544 B73 2021 | DDC 813/.6—dc23
LC record available at https://lccn.locgov/2020042393

Scripture quotations are from the King James Version of the Bible.

Cover design by LOOK Design Studio

Author is represented by the Natasha Kern Literary Agency.

21 22 23 24 25 26 27   7 6 5 4 3 2 1

This book is dedicated to my cowboy.
He's retired now, but he'll always be a cowboy at heart.
He'd have done fine in the Wild West.

ONE

evin Hunt came awake with a snap. A metallic clink. He didn't need to figure out more. He slid a hand over his little brother's mouth and felt Andy wake up instantly.

An inch from his ear, Kevin hissed, "Hide."

Not a word from Andy, not a question. Nothing but instant obedience. It made a big brother both mighty proud and sad. A shame the kid had learned such ugly lessons. Silence, fear, danger, death. Stay hidden. Move, move, move.

Ugly lessons they'd all learned well.

In the darkest night Kevin had ever known, he crawled on his belly around the campfire, its ashes burned down until they didn't even glow. The sky was a starless, moonless black mass. Not even a sliver of light.

Wind whistled with a mournful howl through the rolling hills and waving grass. The reminder that soon cold weather would return to push back the warmth that now ruled August in Wyoming.

Fighting for silence and speed, hoping the wind covered when he failed, Kevin reached Molly on the far side of the campfire. Even though she was his sister, she said it was improper to sleep by the men. It was a cool night, and Kevin regretted Molly held herself apart from her brothers. She'd learned her own bitter lessons, and holding herself apart wasn't all about being proper.

He felt more than heard her wake up and stir just a bit. She judged the silence correctly and maintained it without his covering her mouth.

Bleeding Kansas had taught them a lot. Even all these years later, they remembered. All that teaching might save their lives tonight.

Kevin whispered just louder than a breath, "Hide fast."

Molly was moving before he said the second word, Kevin right behind her. His brother and sister were no kids. Molly an adult woman of nineteen. Andy fifteen. The three of them were on their way west, abandoning the town that'd turned on them.

Kevin crawled after Molly, scraping on his belly like a low-down cowardly worm, and it burned him to retreat. He'd like to stand and fight, but he couldn't fight what he couldn't see.

Summer grass closed overhead, but it wasn't tall like the prairie grass back in Kansas. Still, it was tall enough to cover a person lying on their belly. The grass rustled as they crawled into it, but with the wind covering their movements, Kevin hoped whoever was sneaking up on their camp wouldn't notice.

If they could just be silent and stay hidden in the grass, they had a good chance of surviving this night.

He listened. His vision was keen in the dark, but it was useless tonight, so he relied on sound and smell.

He heard a clink of metal again and a faint creak of leather. The very fact it was so quiet alerted him. A faint jingle of a horse's bridle, but not close. A brush of footsteps. More than one person. Whoever they were, they'd left their horses behind, sneaking up.

Not native folks. There wasn't usually metal on their hackamore bridles. And if it'd been an Indian, Kevin doubted he'd've heard them coming.

He turned back, crawled to the edge of the grass, not sure just where he'd be visible should the clouds part and the moon shine down. When he'd gotten as close as he dared, he waited, breath held, wondering where Andy was now.

An explosion of movement came from the far side of the camp. Two dark forms silhouetted against a black night leapt into the clearing and fired an instant after they appeared. Their deafening guns poured lead right into the blankets where Kevin and his family had slept.

Kevin saw the flare of light that accompanied each shot. Smelled the gunpowder, sharp and acrid. One of the men roared as if he were more beast than human. Their horses, tied somewhere nearby, whinnied as the noise of pistols blared.

Kevin forced himself to stay still. Any movement could bring those guns around to shoot at him.

The guns clicked on empty chambers. Then silence. Kevin's hand went to his holstered pistol. He could get them both before they reloaded.

Weight hit his back like a load of sod.

"No!" Molly's hiss was hidden in the breeze, only a hair from his ear.

She was a skinny little thing and couldn't have stopped him. But remembering all he stood to lose if his bullets missed and they reloaded in time to shoot back made him release the gun and relax when he wanted to fight.

"They're gone!" One of the men kicked the blankets aside before kicking at the campfire. "It's gone stone cold. Are you sure this is where Hunt was camping?" A doubting Thomas who'd just told Kevin this wasn't a simple robbery.

Not two men sneaking up on strangers to rob them. No, these men were hunting Kevin. And he knew just who one of them might be.

"Yep, three of 'em," the other man replied. "I spotted them in Casper. Coming like we figured. Made sure they took the main trail west, straight for Bear Claw Pass, then I came for you."

Like I figured. Very few people knew Kevin was coming out here. Very few people would profit from his death. Only one in fact.

A brother he'd never heard of until three weeks ago.

Kevin owned a share of Wyatt Hunt's ranch. Or rather their pa's ranch. Pa had been dead for less than a month. Again.

Before he'd left Kansas, Kevin had torn down the memorial headstone they'd put up for Pa twenty years ago. Tore it down and smashed it to pieces.

"If Hunt set up this camp and left, then they're on to us. Let's git." Doubting Thomas whirled and strode back into the grass. His saddle partner hesitated for an instant, then went after his friend.

Kevin's fingers itched to go for his gun. Letting Wyatt Hunt ride away unscathed didn't suit him.

But shooting from cover in the dark didn't suit him, either. Kevin wasn't a killer. But folks killed who weren't . . . if they had reason enough.

It wasn't long before Kevin heard two horses gallop away. On toward Bear Claw Pass.

Murderers were waiting on down the trail west.

"Another half hour, I'd say, and the sun'll rise." Molly climbed off him and patted him on the back. "Could you see their faces so we can recognize them?"

"Nope, but I think I'd recognize their voices." Kevin rose to his feet. In a low tone, he asked, "Andy, you all right?"

"Yep, Kev." Andy emerged out of the grass.

The clouds scudded along, and for a second, the moon peeked out. Kevin made out his little brother. Andy was still a gangly boy, but he was getting his growing on and stood taller than Molly, near Kevin's six feet. He was all coltish awkwardness, as if he hadn't learned what to do with his long legs and arms. It struck Kevin that his little brother was close to the age Kevin had been when Ma had died, and Kevin had become the father of two.

Running one hand through his brown curls, Kevin looked at his brother and sister. Good-looking blonds. They took after their pa, while Kevin looked like Ma. No sign of Kevin's father anywhere.

And wasn't that just the truth.

"I wonder what that was about?" Andy dropped his gun into his holster.

Molly tucked her gun away, too. They'd all learned to sleep armed. Hard lessons for a fact.

"Probably my brother trying to kill me."

That brought silence to both of them.

Finally, Molly, a quiet woman, said into the black night, "Wyoming's about as friendly a place as Kansas."

~

Andy fetched their horses. Those men had been bent on murder, or they'd've taken the time to hunt up the horses. Kevin had them well-hidden away from the camp, but a thief would have searched for them.

Kevin, Molly, and Andy made short work of loading the three packhorses and saddling the other three before setting out. Those two would-be killers would stick to the trail and ride straight toward Bear Claw Pass, the town nearest the ranch. They'd figure Kevin and his family were ahead of them.

That didn't mean Kevin was going to be reckless. They moved along slowly, sticking to the trail, but he could smell the dust of the riders ahead. They must be galloping to kick up the faint trail.

In a hurry.

Must be trying to catch up to Kevin before he could claim his land.

Kevin didn't see any way not to go where he was going, so he moved forward, grimly hoping he wasn't riding his whole family straight toward death.

Well, not his *whole* family. Wyatt was family, too, he supposed.

Another brother.

Huh.

Hard to get used to that.

It wasn't a long ride west from Casper to Bear Claw Pass. But Kevin was sickened by what this ranch meant.

Worse than the almost certainty of a fight with a brother he hadn't known existed, it was the shocking, undeniable proof his pa was a cheat and a liar.

A son in Wyoming. An abandoned family in Kansas. Kevin had gotten a telegram from some lawyer in Kansas, telling him his pa—rather than being dead all those years—had owned a ranch in Wyoming. Kevin got a share. The only mention of a brother was telling him Wyatt Hunt, Clovis's son, lived there now. It added up to Pa leaving his family, taking up with another woman, and being a man with no honor.

Not something Kevin wanted to believe about his pa. Better to believe he died exploring the West. That didn't help Kevin's ma get food on the table, but being an explorer had a heroic, thrilling kind of lure. Kevin had understood why Pa had wandered off. Well, some days he'd understood. Other days he'd wanted to punch Pa right in the face.

Pa was no hero. He was a cheat. Old Clovis Hunt had a son with another woman while Kevin's ma was still alive.

That made Pa a no-account varmint. No lure in that to Kevin. Only shame.

Now the siblings rode along, all three of them paying sharp attention. Kansas had been a dangerous place the last years before the Civil War had broken out. Some said that Bleeding Kansas was the Civil War on a small scale before the big scale came along. And the danger hadn't stopped just because the war did.

They'd learned to sleep light, stay sharp, and hide away on short notice to escape renegade night riders thieving and killing in the name of their cause. And their cause was slavery, a free state, and abolition. In truth, outlaws used anything to justify their crimes.

The trail they'd been following widened just as the sun pushed back enough of the darkness to make out fresh tracks from two horses. Stretched out as if the horses were running. It didn't look like the riders had plans to dry-gulch Kevin and his family. They probably figured they'd do that later.

In the early light of dawn, Kevin saw a town ahead. It had to be Bear Claw Pass. Kevin had brought his sister and brother along to their new future. And now it looked like he was leading the two most important people in his life toward death.

TWO

"You've got to go." Winona Hawkins slapped both hands flat on the kitchen table she sat beside.

At the head of the table, Cheyenne jumped.

Winona knew her lifelong friend Cheyenne Brewster wasn't a jumpy woman in the normal course of things. But this was no normal day. And anyway, Win wasn't talking to Cheyenne.

"There's no getting out of this." Winona shoved her chair back, irritated beyond belief that they were so stubborn.

She understood why, but— "You're like an ox kicking against the goad, Wyatt. You're wasting time and energy better used for roping cattle." She added more gently, "And that's not like you. You're a man who accepts things as they are."

The betrayal of Wyatt's father had rocked Wyatt and Cheyenne.

Win had been there the day Clovis died, and she'd been there for the reading of the will.

Carl Preston, the lone lawyer in Bear Claw Pass, had come with news that still echoed in Win's ears.

He'd ridden up to the ranch house just as Wyatt, Cheyenne, and Win came back from unceremoniously burying Clovis

Hunt—away from the family cemetery so as to keep Wyatt and Cheyenne's grandpa from spinning in his grave.

Carl had taken a step toward the front door. "Let's go inside. I have to go over some details with you."

"You can just leave it, Carl." Wyatt had been so calm about the burial, good riddance about summed it up. Then he calmly handled this detail. "I'm sure Ma's wishes are all in order. She told us both how she'd split things up."

That earned a grim look from Carl that shifted between Wyatt and Cheyenne. "These aren't your ma's orders, Wyatt. They're your pa's."

Win's heart had stuttered a bit. She knew too much about poor men marrying rich wives and outliving them.

Wyatt frowned and looked sideways at Cheyenne. "Pa didn't own nothing I've heard tell of."

Shaking his head, Carl said, "That's not true. A man and his wife are co-owners of any property in the marriage. In fact, the man is the sole owner by law. Clovis Hunt came to me and wrote his own will after your ma died."

Win's stomach twisted. What low-down thing had Clovis Hunt done now?

Wyatt had gotten the door and held it while Cheyenne, Win, and Carl went in.

<hr />

"Brothers? What brothers?" Wyatt shoved himself to his feet.

"Your father, Clovis, left this land, the Rolling Hills Ranch, all the cattle, horses, bank accounts, everything, divided in three equal parts, or rather, technically, kept in one large part with three equal owners. It goes to you, Wyatt; a brother named Falcon, who lives in Tennessee; and another brother, Kevin, from Kansas. Your father explained things very clearly to me, and there's no other way to say this. It appears he was married to three women, a-all—" Carl cleared his throat—"all at the same time."

Cheyenne stood and turned from Carl to pace toward the window.

Win knew just what she saw. The beautiful rolling hills that had given the ranch its name. It was a landscape that looked out on a huge log barn, well-built corrals, the bunkhouse, the foreman's house, and the ramrod's house. This ranch had forty thousand head of cattle spread over fifty thousand acres, bought up by Wyatt's grandpa over many years, spending every penny and every bit of strength in his back to build his ranch and build a life for his only daughter and her two children.

Nothing like how Win's pa had gotten his ranch. The grand and lavish ranch house was built by others, and the land bought in one huge parcel, paid for with Win's ma's money.

Over here at the RHR it had been work. Years and years of work done by Wyatt's grandpa, Jacques LaRemy, followed by Wyatt's ma, Katherine, and her first husband, Nate Brewster, who were Cheyenne's parents. Then Nate Brewster died, and Katherine remarried and had Wyatt—who grew up fast and went to work, too. They'd poured blood, sweat, and tears into this ranch. Absolutely none of the work had ever been done by Clovis Hunt, who'd outlived Jacques and Katherine and, without telling anyone, altered the will his wife had left behind.

"And as instructed in this will, I immediately telegraphed another lawyer in Casper to inform him of your father's death. He'll contact your brothers and—"

"Don't call them that." Wyatt hammered the side of his fist on the desk. Carl jumped and quit talking.

Win's heart clutched as she waited for Wyatt to launch himself at Carl. Wyatt visibly struggled to get ahold of himself . . . and then his eyes went wide.

"What about Cheyenne? She was supposed to inherit the land from her father. Surely Clovis has no ownership of Nate Brewster's land."

Carl swallowed hard. "He does. I'm sorry. The law says any property brought into a marriage by a wife immediately becomes the property of her husband. Clovis never exerted any property rights over your mother's land, but according to the letter of the law, since the day they married, your father has been the owner of all Katherine Hunt's holdings, including those left to her by her first husband."

"That land was meant for Cheyenne."

Carl shook his head helplessly. "Intent doesn't override the law. When your grandfather died, his will left everything to your mother, but by law he really left it to your mother's husband. He, that is, Clovis, wasn't even here when your grandpa died."

"I remember that. He hadn't been around for years. Most of my growing-up years."

"He came around once in a while," Cheyenne said bitterly.

"Yep, and we were all mighty glad to see him go, which he always did." Wyatt began to pace the huge office.

"But it'll take time for letters to reach them, won't it?" Wyatt stopped pacing to look at Carl.

"The lawyer in Casper wired back before I rode out here and informed me he had clear instructions of his own. He sent telegrams to the towns closest to your broth—uh, that is, uh, your father's other sons. He was fully paid to hire riders to take the telegrams directly to their homes to make sure they knew of their inheritance."

"Fully paid with my mother's money."

"That's correct." Carl ran a finger around the collar of his white shirt as if it were choking him. "The brother in Kansas may know already and be heading here. The other one, the oldest, Falcon Hunt, lives in a remote part of the Blue Ridge Mountains of Tennessee. But included in the telegraph were precise directions to Falcon Hunt's home. Your father kept track of his sons and thought of everything."

Carl paused. "I'm not aware of the . . . condition of the other wives."

"Other *wives*, good grief." Wyatt paced faster, his fists clenched.

Cheyenne remained utterly silent, looking out. Win waited for her to start shooting. Cheyenne wasn't known for taking bad news cheerfully.

"It's possible your br—" Carl coughed suddenly, then continued. "That is, your—that is, Cl-Clovis's other sons may be bringing his wives—their mothers—here as well. In addition, they could be married men. They could have children."

Wyatt slapped himself in the face. There was an extended silence.

Carl didn't break it. Cheyenne kept staring out.

Win sure enough wasn't going to speak up.

Finally, Wyatt's head came up, his hazel eyes flashing fire. "I want you to find a way to break this will."

Carl's mouth pinched tight as he shook his head. "The will is finely and carefully drawn, including caveats that make it almost impossible for your father's other sons to sell—if they could be convinced to sell their parcels back to you. I wrote it up, but Clovis took it to Casper and had it gone over to make sure there were no weak spots."

"Cavee-what?"

"Caveats. What it comes down to is, if any of the three brothers sells his parcel within the first ten years of Clovis's death, the entire ranch must be sold, and Clovis arranged to donate the full amount, bank accounts and everything, to the state of Tennessee to build a monument to the Confederacy."

Win rubbed her mouth for a few seconds before she said, "Did he write the will before or after the South lost the war?"

Carl winced. "After, I'm afraid. About a week after Katherine's death."

Wyatt swept a hand wide. "That don't matter. My pa's other sons won't sell out anyway, leastways not for less than a fortune. They'll be like him. They'll come out here and move in like a pair of locusts, chomping it all down for themselves."

"I did have one notion."

Win started. Cheyenne turned around.

"What's that?" Wyatt asked.

"If your father had another *living* wife when he married Katherine, then he couldn't legally marry again. That would make his marriage to your mother bigamous. If that's the case, then he'd have no legal standing to inherit her land."

Wyatt—just told he might be the offspring of an unmarried mother—looked wildly hopeful. "What can you do to track this down?"

"Well, we can see if Falcon Hunt arrives with his Tennessee mountain ma. If she's living, then the will is void."

"And if she's not living, we'd need to know when she died," Wyatt said. "Not likely Falcon would aid in his own loss of the ranch."

"If he won't cooperate, I suppose we'd need to hire investigators of some sort."

Wyatt's mouth got tight, and he frowned at the lawyer. "I

guess we can pay for that out of my third of this ranch's bank accounts."

"Let's wait until Falcon arrives. His mother is the first marriage and possibly the only legal one. Once he's here, we'll know more. While we wait, I'll try and figure out how to handle things if need be. Finding investigators and such. We'll talk about it as soon as I have some advice for you." Carl left a copy of the will on the table and gathered up his satchel.

Win watched him go, left in the house with two very unhappy people.

But they didn't start raging.

Yes, the telegrams had gone out to Wyatt's brothers.

Yes, the ranch was in the hands of two strangers who might be as worthless as Clovis.

But those two things could be endured because, at least for now, they had hope.

And now the time had come to meet the brother from Tennessee.

Falcon was coming in on today's train. He'd gone to the lawyer in Casper. Apparently, he was instructed to do that. The lawyer sent him to Bear Claw Pass and wired ahead to Wyatt with the news.

"You. Have. No. Choice." Win could only say what was true even if it was the worst kind of dirty shame.

Wyatt Hunt was the same as a little brother to Win. A full-grown man, of course, but she had a hard time not thinking of him as a kid. A stubborn kid. She was tempted to give his ear a good twist.

Cheyenne was Winona's lifelong friend. They'd spent their younger years picking on Wyatt, and he'd done the same right back. It was hard to get out of the habit of growling at him. Bossing him around. Insulting him. Tormenting Wyatt was her favorite thing to do.

There was just no use for him acting like this.

"You have to go to town." Win tried to use small words so the poor idiot would listen. "It's the right and decent thing to do."

"There's nothing right nor decent about this ranch being stolen from Cheyenne. I'm mad clean through, and I don't have one speck of interest in making this easy for anyone else. Pa was a coyote, and we all knew it long before he died, but I never thought he would sink this low."

Win closed her eyes. She had to say it, and it caused her pain, dread really. But Wyatt was digging in his heels, and Cheyenne wasn't about to go to town. That was just too much to ask.

It made her sick to offer, but she forced herself to say, "I'll go with you."

Win was as torn up about this as her friends. Well, probably less, she hadn't had her whole life jerked out from under her feet. But the Rolling Hills Ranch felt like home to her, and losing so much of it gouged deep.

Even so, this had to be dealt with. If she had a quick image of grabbing Wyatt by the ear and dragging him to Bear Claw Pass, well, he didn't need to know that was how she thought of the little squirt. The little six-foot, two-hundred-pound squirt.

"But we've got to get on now." She gentled her voice to make up for her annoyed daydream. "The train is due in. The telegram said your brother would be on it. Wyatt, you've got to face up to this."

"I know. I know." He stepped away from the table and shoved his own chair back in. He gave Cheyenne an agonized look, like he was watching her be stabbed in the back. With a hard shake

22

of his head, he glared at Win. "You'll stay right beside me and keep me from swinging a fist?"

That was a hard promise to make when he outweighed her by near a hundred pounds. But she could promise to try.

"I'll stay by you and help you get through this." She knew how bad it hurt. She'd known betrayal in her life, and she had the hardened heart to prove it.

Wyatt's eyes burned into Win's. He showed all the signs of anger, but the truth was, he was hurt right to the center of his heart. Not as bad as Cheyenne, but bad.

No one expected a father, even a worthless father, to be such a low-down sidewinder.

THREE

When we get to town, we'll find someone who knows Wyatt Hunt." Kevin studied the trail. He could see the little town ahead. Along the trail there were no trees, no rock piles, nowhere for a pair of dry-gulchers to hide. Away from the trail, there were mountains all around, but right here, the trail was a treeless, grassy stretch.

He looked on west to see majestic mountains rise up, studded with outcroppings of rock and thick with forest—there was nothing like this back home.

It struck him as a new and interesting way to live. It'd be hard work learning the ways of those mountains. And that wasn't including killers on his trail. Somewhere ahead of them were two back-shooters who'd very likely come at them again.

"We'll find out where the ranch is," Kevin went on. Then they'd have to ride out of town into that rugged land. Plenty of chances to lie in wait out there.

"Are we going to tell the sheriff what happened last night?" Andy had ambitions to be a lawman, leastways he did this week. Talking to the town sheriff would thrill him.

Kevin thought it over. "Might be a good idea to talk to a

lawman, just so someone besides us knows an attempt was made on our lives."

"It's Wyatt Hunt's town." Molly said out loud exactly what Kevin was thinking. "The lawman might not be real interested in outsiders accusing a local man of attempted murder."

"We can try, then we'll ride out to his ranch." Kevin gave his head a good shake. "I mean *our* ranch."

He looked left at Molly, who gave him a stiff smile. She was such a subdued young woman. She liked her books and her schoolmarm work and keeping the house up for Kevin and Andy. She'd been courted by a young man who'd seemed nice to Kevin but who had rejected her when they'd gotten word of Clovis Hunt's death.

The young man wasn't nice enough to marry a woman born to a man and woman who weren't legally married.

Kevin knew what was at the root of her quiet ways. And he knew she was afraid of what might escape her mouth should she ever speak freely. That was the way of dark secrets. She'd gotten in the habit of thinking her words through very carefully before she spoke them. And because of that, a lot went on in her head, or leastways he thought that was what was behind her quietness.

Then Kevin looked at Andy, whose eyes flashed with excitement. He was glad Andy didn't bear the burdens Kevin and Molly shared.

"Let's pick up the pace." Andy kicked his horse into a slow trot, gathering speed as the packhorse behind him slowly moved faster. They'd sold everything they could before they left Kansas. They had decided to take only essentials so they could travel fast and light. They'd buy whatever was necessary when they reached their new home.

The mountains rose higher as they rode on. Soon Bear Claw Pass came into sight. An ugly little sore of a town that looked like a scar on the beautiful rolling mountains and valleys.

There was a train track that reached toward them. It was lost in the grass, and Kevin hadn't noticed it until he heard the distant chug of a train. As the noise got louder, a whistle blew.

The tracks headed through town, and Kevin saw them curve into a gap. It was a deep break in the foothills that looked mostly natural. There were jagged edges to a rock wall that looked like a swipe taken by a mountain-sized bear. That must've earned the town its name.

"Good," said Kevin, "there'll be people getting on and off the train, loading and unloading mail and supplies. Folks to see us riding into town alive and well. Witnesses. I'll make sure it's known that we believe Wyatt is a danger to us, and I'll make sure Wyatt knows I've told folks what he did."

And then Kevin would spend the rest of his life sleeping with one eye open.

Bear Claw Pass was quiet enough, except for the chugging train. It was pulling to a stop as Kevin reached town. He headed straight for the station. He wanted to be around people. He guided his horses to a hitching post by the train station, swung down, and tied his horse. His sister and brother handled their own mounts easily. The packhorses were left strung out behind.

Kevin walked up on the wooden platform as folks spilled out of the train. A dozen people or more. A conductor stepped out carrying a mail sack. A man working at the depot stood in an open window with a ledge in front selling tickets.

Kevin smelled the steam and the burning coals and the press of sweaty bodies in the warm August weather.

The rasp of the freight-car door sliding open sounded through the rumble of voices and the dull thud of footsteps as the engine chugged and the water spilled into the train tanks.

A man with a heavy satchel stepped out of the train car. He wore a wide-brimmed hat with a flourish of bright feathers on one side of a red woven hatband. It looked like everything on him was handmade. The hat was pulled low over his eyes. Swinging down to the platform, he turned slightly so Kevin only saw him from the side.

"Pa, is that you?" Kevin couldn't stop the words. His heart lurched with love and longing. And rage. For one heartbeat, he leaned forward, reaching out. Either to give his pa a hug or strangle him, Kevin wasn't sure.

The man turned. Raised his eyes to meet Kevin's.

This wasn't Pa. Of course it wasn't.

But the man looked so much like Pa it tore at the lonely place in Kevin's heart that had always wanted to see his father again.

After not seeing him for twenty years.

After knowing he was dead.

Twice.

But this wasn't him. This man was Kevin's age, maybe a little older. But he had Pa's eyes. Kevin's eyes. For all that Kevin looked like his ma, he'd had eyes she'd always said were his pa's. Eyes that burned with a strange light brown shot through with stripes of gold. Hazel she'd called them.

Kevin squirmed with shame that for one second, he'd sounded like a hopeful, abandoned child. He fought to get the embarrassment under control.

He shouldn't want to see Pa again. He should feel neither hope nor anger. He should be disinterested in knowing the man who'd left him and Ma behind so long ago.

His still-twisting stomach was full proof he hadn't really

forgiven Pa for abandoning him and, even more, for not dying years ago. And worst of all, Kevin still loved Clovis Hunt . . . at least when he didn't take time to think about what a coyote he was.

They'd gotten a letter with the news he was dead twenty years ago. That's when Ma had put up the memorial stone.

And now, just a few weeks back, a telegram. Another death notice.

Kevin was glad his ma had died not knowing she shouldn't have married again.

Pa had been out here apparently married to another woman.

"I ain't no one's pa, mister." The voice. The twangy Southern accent. Kevin had very few, very vague memories of his pa. But this man had the exact tone of voice and accent Kevin remembered from his betraying, lying, abandoning father. And this man had a trail-savvy look to him that reminded him of Pa.

"Of course you're not." Kevin tried to sound casual to cover up the rush of love and hate he felt when he thought he was seeing his pa again. "You must be Wyatt Hunt. I'm Kevin. Your . . . your . . ." He had to force the words out. "Your b-brother from Kansas."

Your brother you tried to kill.

Kevin's jaw tightened. But why would Wyatt Hunt, whom Kevin was coming to see, be getting off the train? He lived here in Bear Claw Pass. And the men who'd tried to kill him were ahead of him on the trail, not coming from behind on a train.

The man's golden hazel eyes blazed hot as a blacksmith's forge.

"I ain't Wyatt Hunt, neither." The man's voice was gravel. His hands were work roughened, as were Kevin's. But Pa's voice. Kevin didn't even know he remembered Pa's voice until he heard this man speak. This was Pa over and over again. "I'm here to *meet* Wyatt Hunt."

There was a long pause. Too long a pause. Finally, with narrowed eyes, the newcomer said again, "I'm here to meet Wyatt Hunt, my brother."

Kevin straightened away from the man. "If Wyatt is your brother, and he's my brother, then . . ."

"Kevin, are we going to talk to the sheriff?" Molly interrupted.

Kevin could barely hear her over the roaring in his ears.

"I reckon we're all three brothers." Clomping boots on the train station platform accompanied the new voice, one with a Western drawl.

Kevin turned. So did the man from the train.

They faced a tall, lean man with overlong brown hair clamped down with a Stetson.

No sign of Pa in this man except . . . yep, there were those same eyes.

Kevin's head was spinning. The wire that'd been brought out from town said Kevin had a brother. It'd mentioned Wyatt Hunt. There'd been no mention of *two* brothers.

Molly must have missed the exchange between him and the man coming off the train. She slipped a hand nervously into his. "Kevin, which one of these men is your brother?" Molly drew the attention of all three men as she looked uncertainly between the two strangers.

Kevin edged closer to her. He was ruled by his instincts to protect her, then he turned his thoughts away from why. Nothing he wanted to remember.

Then Andy came up by Molly.

"I'm Wyatt Hunt." The man with the clomping boots tugged

his Stetson as if in greeting, but nothing in his expression was welcoming.

"So y'all need help buryin' pa?" the man with the Southern accent asked. "I'd be glad to tamp down the dirt hard enough to break both his legs."

FOUR

he only thing that stopped Win from using her heavily laden reticule to beat Wyatt for putting her in this awkward spot was knowing he'd finally found the grit to show up here. Win had promised to get him through it. And there was absolutely no doubt that he needed help.

From a pace behind Wyatt, she stared at the five frozen people while she waited for the rapidly emptying station platform to clear. The two men had Wyatt's striking hazel eyes and could only be the Sidewinder's sons—that was a name for Clovis she and Cheyenne used. But who were the other two strangers? Just how many parcels was this ranch going to be split up into?

Win needed to break up this standoff. She took the mighty bold step of putting herself in the middle of it.

"I'm Winona Hawkins. Welcome, well, no, not welcome really." It struck her that there was no reason to be other than completely honest. "You're not *welcome*, but you're here, and Wyatt can't think of a single way to be rid of you, so—" She jerked one shoulder. "You've made it to Bear Claw Pass, Wyoming. Wyatt has his wagon, and I've got a second one. We were expecting considerable belongings."

Her eyes slid to the man with curly brown hair. She extended her hand, hoping to bump him free of his frozen shock. "You must be Falcon?"

The man flinched and glared at her. At least he'd moved.

"Kevin Hunt from Kansas."

Ah, he could talk.

He reluctantly reached out, and they managed a handshake.

She turned to the other man. He resembled Clovis Hunt so completely it made Win's stomach hurt. "So you're Falcon Hunt, then?"

The man's jaw was so tight he didn't speak, only gave one nod of his head.

Well, fine, she didn't want to chatter away with them, either.

She turned to the young woman with Kevin. His wife maybe? "And you are . . . ?"

The woman looked almost painfully reserved, but she eked out a shy smile. "I'm Molly Garner, Kevin's sister. They were told years ago that Clovis was dead." Molly hunched her shoulders sheepishly. "Ma remarried and had Andy and me."

With an awkward gesture to the half-grown boy behind her, she said, "This is my brother Andy. When we found out our ma and pa weren't legally married it cast us in a bad light back in Wheatfield. We decided if Kevin had a third of a big ranch out here in Wyoming, he could find a place for us on it, so we came along."

Andy nodded. More inclined to silence like the other men.

"Well, let's get your things unloaded from the train and onto our wagons."

"Thank you. We didn't ride on the train." Molly gestured behind her, and Win saw the heavily packed horses. "There isn't much. We had a small cabin. We sold it, left the furniture, and

34

brought our clothing and such. Kevin had some tools we were able to pack along."

Not wanting to even look at the man, Win forced herself to face Falcon. "Molly can show me their things, but what about you?"

Falcon, still tight-jawed and hot-eyed, said, "I ain't got much. My bedroll. A satchel. Figured to buy a horse here in town. I'll do that and follow along after your wagon. Don't need no ride. Don't need to wait for me, either. I can track you. Once I get there, you can show me my part of the ranch. I'll move onto it. Then we're done with each other."

Win was surprised so many words came out of the man's mouth.

"If only that were possible." She took Molly's arm, then laid a firm hand on Andy's back and shoved. "Let's go." She led them off the station platform, leaving those three growling men behind.

Or at least Falcon was growling, and Wyatt had sure been growling since they'd buried the Sidewinder and read his will. Kevin hadn't had much to say. But what he had said seemed at least somewhat calm. That probably wouldn't last.

"I'll bring our horses over to your wagon," Molly said.

The three of them made short work of getting the horses ready to ride.

Molly said quietly to Win, "How long do you think they'll stand there glaring at each other?"

"I'm going to go kick all of them in the backside and get them moving. We're burning daylight."

"I'll come along."

Win held up a staying hand. "I'd just as soon you didn't. I'd like us to be friends, Molly. I may have to do some real kicking, and I'd as soon you don't see me in a temper."

"Think carefully before you risk befriending a woman whose parents weren't legally married," Molly said with heavy sarcasm.

"Wyatt's ma was married before Clovis. His big sister is named Cheyenne, and she's my best friend. She's no kin to Clovis Hunt, just like you aren't. I've known Wyatt all my life, and it appears his folks weren't properly married, either. If I can be friends with a woman whose little brother isn't from a legal marriage, then I can be friends with you."

"Go get my brother, then, if you can move him."

They both turned to look at the men still staring at each other in a tense triangle on the platform. Like three gunslingers squared off at high noon.

"We'll have lots to talk about," Win added, "whether we want to or not."

She made her way back to the triangle of cranky men. And honestly, she didn't blame them exactly. Two of the brothers had been tossed a big old shock when the news of their father's death reached them. And Wyatt had lost a huge chunk of his ranch, along with land that should have been his sister's. From what she'd overheard, Kevin hadn't even known there was a third brother until Falcon had stepped off the train. Win had no idea what the lawyer in Casper had told the two surprise brothers, but it looked like he'd left out a few important details.

Yep, shocks like you'd get from a bolt of lightning.

Striding up the platform stairs, she waded into the shootout before real lead started flying. She stood smack in front of Wyatt and sank her claws into his arm.

"Ouch, let go." He tugged to get his arm loose and failed. She had his attention.

"Get in your buckboard and lead the way home."

36

Wyatt glowered at her like the old friend he was, but he didn't move.

She kicked him in the shins with her nice pointy boots.

"Ouch!"

"Go." She pointed toward the steps and beyond to where his team stood hitched to his wagon. "Now."

Wyatt's expression turned sullen. "If I take them home, then they're gonna set right in to stealing my grandpa's ranch."

"It's done. The Sidewinder already stole it. It's none of their fault. Stop glaring at them and go." She kicked him again.

With a furious look at his two brothers, he turned and clomped away.

Next, she turned to Kevin. She had to admit Falcon, with his almost eerie resemblance to the Sidewinder, scared her a little. Clovis Hunt had been a big strapping man but also a charming, handsome man, who could talk the birds down from the trees or tempt a woman to take a bite right out of an apple. And who, it appeared, had no difficultly talking three women into marrying him.

Despite the resemblance, Falcon showed no such gift of charm. Win found that to be a relief. He looked hard and wild and dangerous. She'd never risk kicking him, afraid of what his reaction might be. Instead, she decided to handle Kevin next. A man who brought his family along on a long journey rather than abandon them to their fate, as his father had done.

"Your sister and brother tied their horses to my wagon and are riding with me." She pointed. "Go."

Kevin gave her a look of unsettled confusion. She took his arm and drew him toward the steps. He balked, but then, as if he didn't want to fight with a woman—which she appreciated—he came along.

As they reached the steps, she tugged Kevin to a stop, then turned back to Falcon. She was far enough away from him to dare speaking to him.

"The ranch owns plenty of horses, reckon you own a third of them. Buying a horse in town's on the stupid side. You can ride along with me, if you've a mind, or buy your horse or come afoot. If none of that suits you, you can stand on this platform glaring until you starve to death. No one here will mourn you."

She faced forward in time to see a grin break across Kevin's sunbrowned face. They headed for the wagon together. Before they reached it, she heard Falcon coming—which made her walk faster.

FIVE

'm not sleeping outside in the Rocky Mountains. Not when I've been invited to stay in a nice house with a proper bedroom." Molly had a heavy satchel over one shoulder and her valise in the other hand.

"And I'm not sleeping under their roof." Kevin had stopped her from just following that woman right into the house. A woman who'd kicked Wyatt, insulted Falcon, and dragged Kevin to her wagon.

Winona. Strange name. But a pretty woman. A beautiful woman, honestly. A little thing, an inch or two shorter than Molly. Her hair had escaped from around the edges of her blue calico bonnet. What he could see was as shiny brown as well-varnished oak. It was inclined to curl. She had blue eyes that sparked when she smiled, when she scolded, when she kicked, when she threatened Falcon.

Kevin found her the most likeable of the people he'd met so far.

But that wasn't saying much.

"And don't you forget Wyatt Hunt might've tried to kill us

39

last night," he hissed quietly to his sister. He didn't want Win to hear.

Silence stretched.

"Couldn't you just sleep with one eye open like you said before?" Molly sounded like a woman tired to the bone of sleeping on the ground.

"I'll share a room with you, Kev." Andy gave the house a longing look. "I'll lie up against the door."

Kevin studied the house. It was about the nicest one he had ever seen. Two stories, log and stone, tucked into a fold in the earth, with mountains rising up to the west. Heavy woods lined those mountains—*No, those rolling hills*, Kevin thought with a snort. The name of the ranch made him wonder because he was looking at some mighty big mountains. If these were rolling hills, what were they comparing them to?

The house was set so the woods and hills would block the cold north winds in winter. A knowing man had picked this spot to build.

Through light clouds, Kevin saw the sun reaching for its noontime height. It had been less than an hour's ride from town on a slow-moving wagon. Falcon came along, riding in the back of the wagon. Kevin and Andy rode horseback leading their packhorses. Molly sat on the wagon seat beside Win. And Wyatt rode alone in the other wagon.

It'd been a quiet ride.

Win had mentioned when they reached the beginning of the Rolling Hills Ranch. They'd ridden in from the east, through a beautiful herd of black cattle spread across the land. Thousands of them scattered over vast acres. Each cow branded with the ranch's initials. The letters were pressed together, and the first *R* backward, so it looked like two *R*s with a dash between them.

Kevin thought of his few cows back in Kansas and how he'd considered bringing them with him. It'd've been a six-critter cattle drive. Instead, he'd sold them to add to their short supply of cash. The thought of showing up out here with those few red-and-white spotted cows made his cheeks burn. He tugged his hat low over his eyes so no one could see.

If the facts stood, a third of all this was his. Including the house. Kevin could hardly tear his eyes away from all of it.

He'd come from a humble home. Ma's eighty acres, then later his eighty, were torn out of prairie sod. Those six cows, counting the two spring calves, were raised for milk and meat. The calves barely came along fast enough to keep ahead of their needs.

Molly's money from the school was their only real cash coming in outside of Kevin's annual wheat crop. Otherwise they'd lived off the land. A few acres of corn to feed the cows, a big garden, and some chickens. Kevin had worked hard at back-breaking labor all day every day to carve out a living. No man alone could really handle one hundred and sixty acres, but he broke new sod every year, always expanding, then racing to keep up with the planting, weeding, watering, harvesting. And he'd been satisfied with his life. He'd never be a rich man, but he fed himself and his family. He figured that was enough for anyone.

They'd've even survived losing Molly's income, though when she started work a year ago, making thirty dollars a month for nine months out of the year, times had gotten easier for a fact.

But when they inherited this land. Or rather, when *he* inherited it, because certainly nothing was left to Molly and Andy, the sinful nature of Molly's and Andy's births had come to light, thanks to a loudmouthed telegraph operator.

Molly's being fired was an injustice that'd burned Kevin

bad. But nothing could stop the school board from their hasty decision. Doors were closed to them. Molly and Andy shunned.

Their choices were to keep to themselves or leave. And they had nowhere to go but here.

Kevin thought of the ugliness they'd left behind, and despite the cold welcome, he was glad to be done with Kansas.

But that didn't mean he was sleeping under the generous roof that had sheltered his father while Kevin and his ma struggled. Molly could sleep here if she was allowed. Andy too. Kevin planned to sleep under the stars. He'd find out which acres were his and build a cabin for himself, though how to build a log house was a mystery. He'd had a sod house, then later a board house from wood shipped in on the train. But he'd figure it out before cold weather came. Until then, he'd let God shelter him. No roof necessary.

Wyatt had taken the team to the barn, but Kevin waited for a chance to tell him his home was of no interest. Even more, he waited for a chance to accuse Wyatt of trying to kill him. He was real interested in looking the man in the eye when he braced him with it.

For now, Kevin followed along with his family, and if Wyatt Hunt didn't let those two sleep inside a house Kevin owned one third of, there'd be a ruckus that might just level these mighty rolling hills.

~

Win realized no one was with her when she stepped into the house and held the door. She looked behind her at the grumpy folks she'd brought home. She honestly didn't know whether to comfort them or smack them on the head.

Win shouldn't even be here. But she was a woman of her

word, and Cheyenne had made her promise to come back and stay a few days. She had a room at Parson Brownley's, but school was out of session during branding, so she was staying here to help out. It was no hardship. She always came out to help with the cooking during busy times of the year. Mostly she just came out here whenever she could because she dreaded going home to her pa and didn't have the courage to just tell him she knew what he'd done. Instead, she made excuses. Work in town. Work at the RHR. Anything to keep her from having to live at home.

Cheyenne was a miserable, angry woman these days. More deeply hurt than anything, but it tended to come out of her in wild ways. Win had to protect her from whatever madness might overtake her. Like shooting the two unexpected Hunt brothers. Or digging up the Sidewinder and killing him again.

When she was idle, which wasn't often, Cheyenne knitted. The house had knitted blankets in every room. It didn't fit with the tough outdoor woman, but she said that tying knots in thread unknotted her brain.

Branding was taking every waking hour now, but in the weeks right after the Sidewinder's will was read, Cheyenne had knitted a blanket with stitches so tight it'd keep out wind. Oh, who was Win kidding, it'd keep out rain.

Win turned back to assess the newcomers. Molly was the closest to nice, but she was quiet, almost withdrawn. Soft-spoken. She'd said she'd been a schoolmarm. How had such a meek woman managed to keep order in a school?

With a sigh of impatience, she went back to Molly. She'd get them all inside eventually.

"Come in." Small words, short sentences. That worked with some of her more stubborn students. "I'll put on a meal." Win rested a hand on Molly's arm. She looked at Kevin, then glanced on past him to Andy. Falcon stood apart from them holding all his earthy goods in a satchel and a bedroll.

"Come in, all of you. There's a hitching post. We need to have a long talk."

"We'll unpack our supplies in the barn and be right in," Kevin said. "Molly, go on in if you want."

Win jabbed a finger at a small house between a large log barn and a low-slung bunkhouse. "If you men want your own rooms, take the ramrod's house. Ross Baker, the ramrod, took off to see his family in Texas a couple of weeks ago. His pa is ailing. The Rolling Hills Ranch has as many hands as they can hire right now because they're branding, but Wyatt didn't replace him, because he hopes he'll come back. You two"—she looked between Kevin and Falcon—"can figure out how you want to share it, or we can make room in the house. We'll have to hope Wyatt and Cheyenne will let you stay in there."

"Who's Cheyenne?" The gravel in Falcon Hunt's voice was so like the Sidewinder, Win shuddered. Cheyenne was really going to hate this one.

"Wyatt's big sister. His ma was a widow with a daughter when she married your snake of a pa."

"Andy, come and help me unload things in the ramrod's house." Kevin turned to Falcon. "Come along if you've a mind to. It's a bigger house than the one we had at home. You don't need my invitation, but we're happy to share it."

Falcon nodded but didn't move.

"I'll soon have a meal on. There'll be plenty for everyone." Win hated to be sociable, figuring Cheyenne and Wyatt would be annoyed, but honestly the food was one-third these folks'.

Kevin took two of the horses, each with a packhorse strung

behind. Andy took the other pair. They headed for the tidy little house no one was using.

Win guided Molly to the big house. The already quiet woman looked after her family as if she could hardly bear to be separated from them.

But she did bear it. She came along with Win, and they went up the stairs to the ranch house.

Win noticed Falcon moving slowly toward the ramrod's house. Wyatt came out of the barn from putting up his horses and wagon. He stood in the doorway and watched his half brothers without drawing any notice to himself.

He sure as certain didn't offer to help them unpack.

SIX

$\mathcal{K}$evin and Andy made quick work of settling into the ramrod's house.

Kevin wondered what in thunder a ramrod was.

Falcon had come in, chosen one of the two bedrooms—the smaller of the two, but Kevin didn't say thank you.

Falcon dropped his bedroll on the floor, took a small fur bag that looked to be made from a skinned critter of some kind out of his satchel, and walked back out without speaking.

Molly appeared at the door a short while later and said, "The meal is ready. Please come in and eat with me."

She swallowed hard. "I've been talking to Win. No sign of Wyatt or Cheyenne. Win says they won't be in to eat. She makes them sound like decent folks who were done mighty wrong by your pa, Kev. I don't think Wyatt would try and kill you."

Kevin decided he'd go eat just because Wyatt wasn't there. He wasn't going to hunt up Falcon, either. He looked like the kind of man who could feed himself.

They all three walked over to the big house. Kevin hesitated to go in. He felt like he was taking more than a simple step. To go into this house forced him to admit what a low-down coyote his pa had been. Not just to leave them or to apparently marry before and after his ma, but also to live out here in luxury while letting his wife and child do without, fighting to scratch a living out of the Kansas dirt.

In the end, Kevin's hesitation was all foolishness because that's exactly what Pa had done, and there was no sense pretending otherwise. Staying outside didn't change a thing and only let dusty air into the house as Molly held the door open for him.

He stepped into an entry room with coats hanging in a neat row. A few pretty bonnets. A fancy, new-looking Stetson.

None of them wore a coat, it being a warm August day, so they went straight into the kitchen. The room was full of the smell of savory beef and fresh baked biscuits. Win was setting a big roast on the table.

She gave them a doubtful smile. "I think it'll just be the four of us. Cheyenne always helps with branding. Wyatt, too, of course. They'll eat around the chuck wagon. I saw Falcon walk away, and there's no sign of him returning."

From the look of all the food Win had prepared, it was clear she'd expected everyone to show up for mealtime. Or maybe not *expected*, but rather had prepared herself for that.

Win and Molly dished up the rest of the food. Kevin's mouth watered at the warm, delicious smells. It reminded him they'd had campfire fare for days and no breakfast at all.

"What's your connection to the place?" he asked Win as he approached the table. It reminded him of the Bible story about going to the head of the table and, when a more honorable man arrives, being sent to the foot of the table in shame.

He had hesitated, not sure if the foot of the table was right, either. That seemed like two places of honor. With no wish to be shamed and no idea what to do to invite it or avoid it, he sat down along the side of the table, and no one invited him to do anything else.

Win set a large bowl mounded with fluffy white potatoes on the table. As she straightened away, she turned and flashed a polite smile at someone behind Kevin. He stood and turned, wondering if Wyatt and the mysterious Cheyenne might have found time to come in, or if Falcon had returned.

Instead, a smiling man, well-dressed and smooth-looking, reached for Win and slid an arm around her waist. She let him and continued with the polite smile, but Kevin saw something beneath the smile. A glimmer of strain, or maybe a better word was *endurance*. Win endured the arm.

Of course, Kevin could be making all of that up because a spark of something strange flashed through him. He'd never felt it before. Maybe just a desire to protect any woman from a stranger. Although this man was obviously not a stranger. Kevin felt the desire to protect Molly all the time—and it didn't feel like this.

He fought down the urge to step between the two, to keep the man's hands off of Win, and waited for the smiling and hugging to end. He never for one instant considered turning his back on the man and sitting back down.

"Pa, I want you to meet Wyatt's brother."

"Half brother," Kevin corrected. *Pa, huh?* He still didn't like him.

The man reached out and caught hold of Kevin's hand firmly, then brought his other up and clasped the back of Kevin's hand. It felt friendly, sincere, trustworthy.

Kevin didn't believe a single one of the things that handshake made him feel. He had no good reason why, and yet he'd survived the Civil War in Kansas by trusting his instincts.

"Kevin Hunt and his half siblings, Molly and Andy. This is my pa, Oliver Hawkins. We own the ranch on past the RHR."

He shook hands with Molly and Andy, too. Better'n a hug at least.

"Welcome to the Rolling Hills Ranch." The man went straight to the head of the table and sat. No one told him to move, though Kevin was tempted.

"I've been around enough to know what a turmoil Clovis's last will and testament has wrought." The man had a way about him. He spoke up, made broad hand gestures. Was quick with a big toothy smile. It reminded Kevin of someone, but it was a vague, unclear memory.

It'd come to him.

Meanwhile the man kept yammering. "And I know Wyatt and Cheyenne enough to doubt you've been told much of what's going on."

Molly set a bowl of corn on the table, shifting the roast beef platter to make room. The shift was deliberate. It was now closer to Kevin than Oliver. Kevin met her eyes, which glinted with humor. It struck Kevin that, though Oliver was at the head of the table and doing all the talking, welcoming them to the ranch, for Pete's sake, this was Kevin's house. Leastways a third of it was, and that was a whole lot more than Oliver owned. It was Kevin's table. Kevin's food. His initial hostile reaction to old Oliver here only got more solid and sure.

He did his best not to let it show.

"I knew your pa, Kevin."

Kevin wanted to walk out. He wanted to toss the man out of the chair at the head of the table. He also was wildly curious about Pa. Instead of doing something rude, he forked a slice of meat off the platter and listened. He had a hunch Oliver didn't need anyone else to talk.

"He was a charming man. It doesn't surprise me he talked Katherine into marrying him."

"That's Wyatt's ma," Win added as she set a plate of biscuits on the table, then settled in straight across from Kevin. "There's a painting of her in the front room, over the fireplace. Her first husband was a scout for the wagon trains and the army. Nate Brewster was Cheyenne's pa. When he died, she married Clovis and had Wyatt." Win added with considerable venom, "And then Clovis vanished and left Katherine to raise his son alone. I suspect you know what that's like, Kevin."

"I do indeed." Kevin's grim response echoed with anger.

Silence fell over the table, not even broken by that talkin' fool Oliver Hawkins. They all paid rapt attention to the food. The roast beef was a little charred, but then they might've been late to the meal. The mashed potatoes were tasty except for the lumps. The gravy went with the lumpy potatoes pretty well. There was a big dish of corn that looked like it'd been cut off the cob just this morning. And the biscuits seemed to be overly brown on the bottom and a little doughy inside. Win had been in a hurry to get the meal on, so Kevin didn't fault her for any of it. And it tasted mighty good without the trail dust. The ball of butter and a pretty glass dish of red jam, heavy with some kind of berry, were perfect.

As the plates were cleared, Win got up and fetched a square of gingerbread. The smell was familiar. Ma had favored making it when they could afford ginger and molasses. Win added a small pitcher of sweetened cream, and they all had a serving.

Oliver went back to talking. "When Clovis came into the country, we all thought he was a lot like Nate. He knew the trails and loved wild country. It was the most natural thing in the world for Katherine to fall in love. They married too quickly. Her pa, well, he thought the sun rose and set with her. When he was against the marriage, none of us paid much attention. Katherine was a fine cattle rancher, but headstrong and couldn't be stopped. Her pa eventually accepted Clovis. And then, when Wyatt was little more than a babe in arms, Clovis said his feet were itchy, and he needed to see some new country. Off he went and no one saw hide nor hair of him for a year. After that he'd wander through, stay awhile, then head out again."

"I wonder if he married any more women?" Molly said quietly.

That brought dead silence to the table.

Finally, Kevin said, "If he did, he probably didn't have more children, or they'd've been here moving onto the Rolling Hills Ranch right along with the rest of us."

"Well, your pa once told me he'd been to—"

"Excuse me, Oliver." Kevin pushed his chair back. "I can't take a lot of stories about my no-account pa right now."

Oliver sputtered and Kevin stood, planning to make his escape. "Win, you said Wyatt and his sister are working on the branding. Where can I find them?"

"They'll be busy and not in any mood to—"

"I don't expect to take much of their time." Kevin cut her off just like he had her father. "I need to be told what land will grow a crop. I'm a farmer not a rancher. I aim to find some land that's not studded with rocks and build a cabin near it. All Wyatt has to do is point. Now, where is he?"

Win gave him a narrow-eyed look, then she pointed.

It seemed she wanted him to ride south, past the barn. Kevin figured he could find a herd of cattle and a herd of men.

And if he couldn't, at least he wouldn't be sitting in here listening to fond tales of his dear old pa.

SEVEN

*K*evin, wait." Win rose from the table. "I was just being foolish when I pointed, after what you said about Wyatt pointing. I didn't even point the right direction. They are branding about ten miles to the south, and west, and a little bit north, around a canyon mouth hidden by a rock fall and . . . well"—she looked at her father—"can you show him?"

Oliver rose from the table looking mighty friendly but regretful. "I really don't know where they are, either, Winona. I just came over to say hello to the new family. But I've got my own branding going on back home. I shouldn't have taken this hour, and I sure can't take two or three."

Win knew that wasn't true. Not exactly. Oh, it was true he probably didn't know where Wyatt was, though there were only a few regular gathering places for branding, and most folks around knew that about each other's ranches. And he did have his own branding going on, but it wasn't true he was too busy. Pa stayed to the house. He let his cowhands do the hard labor while he ordered them around and kept the books.

He looked at Win in some way that seemed strange, false.

She couldn't quite figure out what her father was thinking. But she knew him well, and it was a good chance he was thinking something odd. Pa always had strange notions.

"You take him." Pa looked at Molly and Andy. "Would you mind cleaning up after the meal while Win helps your brother find Wyatt?"

"I don't need a trail guide," Kevin said, slamming out the back door.

Win scowled after him.

"Help him find his way, Winona," Molly said in her reserved way. "We'll straighten the kitchen."

"Best be getting on." Pa left out the front of the house. Few people came and went that way, but Pa always had.

"Thank you, Molly. Kevin might be able to find them. There's a decent trail, and it's freshly traveled, but there are a lot of trails." She shrugged. "I'll ride along with him."

She hurried out. Kevin was slowed by his unfamiliarity with the barn, so Win got herself saddled and ready to go by the time he was.

"I don't need a caretaker."

"Fine. Stay here." Win reined her horse around and rode out of the barn, calling over her shoulder, "I'm riding out to where they're working cattle. Maybe I'll see you at—"

Then he was beside her, looking irritated. That seemed to be the usual way of things with him, so she didn't let it concern her.

"Are you living here?" Kevin asked the question out of the blue. He'd asked what her connection was to the Hunts earlier, then Pa had shown up and derailed the conversation. Taken it over like he always did.

"I—I am living here . . . temporarily. I'm helping with summer work by tending the house. I sleep here until branding is done or school comes back into session, which is usually about the same time because everyone is branding. Then I go back to living in a room that the Bear Claw Pass school board built on to Parson Brownley's house in town. I eat with the parson and his wife, and the school board pays a fee for that, but I have some privacy in the added room, and the family has some privacy from me."

Kevin didn't respond, but she didn't mind talking. It was everyone else around here that seemed to have a problem with it. Except Pa of course.

"The RHR has a chuck wagon and bunkhouse cook. But I make breakfast and supper for Wyatt and Cheyenne, and do laundry, mending, and cleaning for them. I've got a month off school so my students can work at home. I'm idle at home because we have a housekeeper. I could work alongside Mrs. Hobart, but she handles the house fine without me. And Cheyenne's such a good friend. I'm glad for a chance to spend time over here."

That was true as far as it went. "So I've gotten in the habit of coming to the RHR to help. I've been doing it since I came back from finishing school."

A silence settled between them, broken only by the clopping hooves, the creaking saddles, and a cry of birds in the nearby trees.

Talking about herself was boring. They had a stretch of time right now. It'd be best used to tell Kevin what was going on. Before she could start, Kevin broke the silence. "Katherine, that's Cheyenne's ma, right?"

Win nodded.

"And she inherited the land from her father?"

"Yes, she was Jacques LaRemy's only child. Katherine also inherited land from her first husband, who's been gone since before I moved out here as a child. Nate Brewster owned a big stretch of land right next to Cheyenne's pa. Katherine wasn't just a rancher's daughter. She was a big landowner in her own right. And once Nate died, she worked alongside her pa—as she had since her ma died when she was young.

"Katherine was a better cowhand than most men. And she raised Cheyenne as she'd been raised. I got sent back east to school while Cheyenne stayed out here busting steers."

Win couldn't help grinning. Kevin's serious expression lightened a little. "My fine book learning and finishing-school manners are of little use out here. All Cheyenne learned at her grandpa's and ma's sides made her well-suited to this life. I'm pretty useless."

His serious expression lightened a little more. "A family's gotta eat, and someone needs to prepare that food. Seems like you're mighty useful."

Win was surprised by the bit of warmth she got from Kevin speaking kindly of her food and usefulness.

The trail rose along a hillock, and as they curved around a pile of boulders, a rock slide ahead covered a narrow trail. There were plenty of hoofprints going down the slope to avoid the talus slide, but it was treacherous.

"Let's get down and walk our horses around that slide." Win dismounted without waiting for him to agree.

He must've agreed though, because he got down, too. The trail was narrow and steep, so she led her horse along ahead of Kevin's and thought again of how nice it was to be appreciated.

When they were across the slide, Kevin asked, "Do you mind

if we just walk the horses for a while? There's trouble ahead of us, and trouble behind us. This is the first moment of peace I've had today."

"I'm not looking forward to you talking to Wyatt, even less Cheyenne. Sure, let's walk awhile. There's plenty I can tell you."

Before they could pick up their conversation, another slide ahead blocked the trail. Again they had to go down the slope, and circle around the bottom of the slide. They were just about across it when a tumble of the fine rocks rolled under Win's feet.

She fell backward with a shriek.

She landed in Kevin's arms with a thud, his strong arms bearing her weight easily.

He looked down with real concern in those hazel eyes, and she thought of moments when he'd looked to his younger sister and brother. Checked on their well-being. He was a kind man.

"Are you all right? You didn't turn an ankle, did you?"

Win lifted and twisted first one ankle, then the other. Then put her weight on both. She realized she was enjoying being held in his arms and gave her ankles plenty of chances to pain her, but they never did.

With a smile, she said, "I'm fine."

A brown curl had fallen across his forehead. It nearly dangled in his eyes. She brushed it back. Then, with her hand still in his hair, their eyes met, and she froze, unable to look away.

A longing she didn't understand stirred inside her chest.

He lowered his head, then turned aside, letting her go. "What am I doing? This is madness," he mumbled to himself.

Win had felt that strange madness, too. She shook her head to clear Kevin from her muddled thoughts. She caught her horse's reins and started back for the trail. Wanting to get away from him.

No, not wanting that at all, but knowing she had to.

They mounted up again, and when the trail widened, they picked up the pace. Win tried to move fast enough to leave Kevin behind for a spell. By the time he'd caught up to her, she had control of herself again.

"Whatever that was, we can't let it happen again." Win glanced at Kevin. "It's a betrayal of my friends that would ruin everything. We have to forget that ever happened."

"I agree."

That hurt her feelings, which was ridiculous.

Then he reached across the distance between their horses. She hadn't realized she was riding quite so close to him. When he touched her hand, she had to look at him. Almost afraid of what she'd see.

"I agree that can't happen again." His hand tightened on hers. "But I doubt very much I'm going to be able to forget it."

With a final gentle squeeze, he let go of her and got back to watching the trail. "There's a lot of trouble between my family and your friends. I'm going to tell them I want a slice of land. Not a full third. For heaven's sake, I owned one hundred and sixty acres back in Kansas, and it was a full, hard day's work to tend what I owned."

"You'll get a mighty big slice."

"No." The word blazed with anger. "I don't want a mighty big slice. I want land that'll grow a crop. That means maybe near a stream, not covered with rocks or pitched on the side of a mountain. I have no idea of the boundary lines, but if Wyatt will just give me a nice patch of ground, I'll build myself a cabin big enough for Molly, Andy, and me. He could maybe give me a few head of cattle. I had six back in Kansas, and that's enough. I don't need any more'n what I can milk and raise up for beef. Then I'll get out of Wyatt's way. He can pretend I don't exist, and I'll do the same for him. You think Wyatt will take time off from his branding to point me to some good land and a stand of trees to cut for lumber? I brought my own ax."

Win was shocked. Deeply shocked. And a little sad for Kevin. He was just as hurt and confused by this stupid inheritance as Wyatt was.

"If you talk to Wyatt like this, I think—I hope—he'll calm down and help you out. He's so upset to find out he lost two-thirds of his ranch, but even worse is Cheyenne. Their ma left it divided between 'em. In fact, because the division was so even, she left her pa's ranch to Wyatt and her own ranch to Cheyenne. But Clovis Hunt came along after Katherine died. I suspect he heard she'd died, and that brought him running. And he's her lawfully wedded husband, even if he was a sidewinder. Turns out by law, he gets the whole thing no matter what she wrote in her will, because a man owns whatever property his wife brings to the marriage or gains during the marriage."

"When he died," Kevin said unsteadily, "it should have gone back to the division Katherine had set up, but it didn't."

Win saw Kevin swallow hard. He knew why it hadn't been divided according to Katherine's wishes. It was because of Clovis and his two surprise sons.

"We have no right to a single acre of this land," Kevin said. "It wasn't Clovis's to give to us. I left my home behind in Kansas and can't go back there. I thought I was being generous to only take one hundred and sixty acres, but instead I'm a thief. I—I can make sure he gets the money those acres would cost me, but I don't have it now. He'll have to wait awhile. I can't homestead again off the RHR because a man only gets to claim one homestead, but I'll give the bulk of my third to Cheyenne."

Then a dark expression came over Kevin's face, and Win had no idea what he was thinking, but he had something eating at him.

His words were right. If he said them calmly to Wyatt, that might solve some of the problems here. One-third of the problems.

"Let's hope Wyatt decides to listen instead of coming after you with a branding iron."

Kevin scowled at her. He wore no hat, and his brown hair was a mop of untidy curls that were ruffled by the wind. Its healthy shine made it seem as if his hair was happy, even if he wasn't.

A shout sounded from ahead, around another curve, another rolling hill, another stand of trees. They heard the lowing of a herd of stirred-up cattle, the loud bawling of calves. Smelled kicked-up dust.

"That's them just ahead," Win confirmed. "Do you want me to go in first and try to calm him down?"

"No, I'm interested in getting to know my baby brother without a woman standing between us."

That stung Win's feelings a little. "I might've been between you, but if you'll recall, it was Wyatt who got kicked in the shins."

"I'll keep up with you just the same. Brother Wyatt is going to have to stop pouting and wishing his brother was dead."

Win whipped her head around. "What? He never said that. He's furious with Clovis and with you, too, I'm sure. But he's a reasonable man. He knows none of this is your fault, nor Falcon's fault. He'll calm down."

"It's been near a month since Pa died. He's had time enough

to calm down." They rounded a huge fall of rocks, and the cattle and cowhands came into view. Kevin added quietly, "And time enough to plot."

His voice was low enough that Win wasn't sure he meant for her to hear him. Win had no idea where that statement came from, and there was no time to ask.

EIGHT

*K*evin was a farmer for heaven's sake. Some people might think farming and ranching were the same thing. Farmers and ranchers know better. He'd never even been on a ranch before.

Now he was witnessing his first branding, and he could only make out mayhem.

Noise, motion, running, fighting, bellowing. And that was just the people.

The cows and horses made it a whole lot worse.

From the middle of fire and dust emerged his brother.

Kevin made himself call Wyatt his brother. He had to get used to it.

Wyatt looked tough and capable. Strong and smart. Kevin considered himself all those things, too. But in his own world, not this one.

Wyatt was looping a long rope into a circle as he walked out of the dust. A step behind him came a tall woman, beautiful and filthy and with a rope of her own.

Win had said Katherine's first husband was half Indian, and Kevin could see that since he'd been told, but he wouldn't have thought it otherwise. The woman had a long, dark braid hanging over one shoulder. It was of a color with Wyatt's. She wore brown britches, also a match for Wyatt's, with chaps and a long-sleeved blue cotton shirt and a red kerchief tied around her neck. She was a woman dressed for a man's work, and it was clear she'd been right in the thick of a rough job.

None of the other dozen or so men gave her scandalous clothing a second look. They must be used to it.

Not a stitch she wore was feminine, but she had a womanly shape, and no one on earth with one working eyeball would've mistaken her for a man.

The two of them were talking. Wyatt laughed. The woman whacked him with her rope in an easy way that spoke of life-long friendship.

His sister, Cheyenne, had to be. She was one of the most beautiful, but oddest, women Kevin had ever seen.

When she came closer, he saw she had black eyes. They looked up, saw him, and the black turned thunderous. She said something Kevin couldn't begin to hear over the ruckus, and Wyatt's gaze came to lock on Kevin's. The friendly smile he'd had talking to his sister turned to a scowl.

Kevin saw Cheyenne's focus shift to Win, and the thunder turned to quiet clouds, like a woman who was hurt, betrayed.

Wyatt lengthened his stride toward Kevin. Cheyenne slowed. Wyatt shot a look at her, said something, and Cheyenne came on with him.

Kevin was determined to be reasonable. He understood why Wyatt might hate him. But enough to send night riders to kill him? He'd grown up in a time where Kansas and Missouri were running their own small Civil War before the big one started up. He'd thought all that was behind him. Now he had to be friendly to Wyatt when he wanted to plow a fist into his gut.

Wyatt tugged off his gloves and tucked them behind his belt as Kevin dismounted. Win got down, and they held the reins of their horses. She stood almost too close to him. She'd offered to go in without him and try to get Wyatt ready for a talk. It seemed she was still feeling protective of him. It pinched his pride a bit. At the same time, it seemed really nice of her.

They met a fair distance from the noise of the branding. Cows mooing. Men shouting. The whip of ropes, the crackle of the fire, the smell of horses and cattle. The air tasting of dust. It all swamped Kevin. But he found he liked it. And he would've liked to ask about it, learn. But these two had no look of being willing teachers about them, and Kevin kept his questions to himself. The four of them stood with Kevin in front of Wyatt and Win facing Cheyenne.

"I don't want to waste your time." Kevin jumped in, hoping he could reach some peaceable understanding with his possibly murderous brother. "Pa as good as stole your grandpa's and your ma's land from you and your sister."

Cheyenne's lips formed into a grim, straight line. She looked like she had her teeth clenched so hard that they might snap off.

"You're Cheyenne, I'm sure. I'm Wyatt's brother Kevin from Kansas."

She gave a tight nod but didn't speak. Sure as certain didn't say "welcome to Wyoming."

"Win explained the will to me. It's clear my pa—our pa— stole it." Kevin saw no reason to claim Clovis any more than Wyatt had to. "Hang the legalities, he stole it from your ma and gave a big old chunk of land to me and Falcon that he had no moral right to. I want no part of that."

Wyatt reacted as if he'd been slapped with something wet and cold. Maybe he was waking up to not blaming Kevin for all this. Maybe he was regretting sneaking up on a camp and shooting into blankets.

Maybe he wouldn't feel quite so bad now about missing.

Maybe he'd cancel any plans he had to try it again.

"I have no wish to fight with you, Wyatt. Neither do I feel any great need to be a brother to you. We're strangers and sharing the blood of Clovis Hunt is probably the worst thing we could have in common."

Wyatt didn't speak. Instead, he slung his lasso over his head and under one arm, then pulled his gloves from behind his belt. Held them in one hand and slapped them against the other. Probably wishing it was Kevin's face . . . or maybe Pa's.

"I'm a farmer. I want farmland. I know not all land that grazes cattle is good for growing crops. Especially out here where a lot of the land is stony. I only have to look around to see it can grow a good stand of grass to feed cows, but it's not good for much else.

"What I'd like is for you to point out on this ranch—*your* ranch—about one hundred and sixty acres of good, fertile land, out of the one-third that's supposed to be mine. I don't know if there's a way to cancel out Pa's will, but—"

"So far I haven't found a way," Wyatt snapped.

Nodding, not surprised, Kevin said, "Pa's crafty enough and dishonest enough to be married to three women at the same time. I'm sure he can get his land theft done all tight and legal. I can pay you a fair price for a small plot of land whether we want to call it buying the land or not."

"You can't just give the land to us." Wyatt slapped the gloves a little faster, a little harder. "Pa fixed it so that if one brother wants to pull out, the whole ranch has to be sold and the money used to build a Confederate statue."

That shut Kevin up for a few seconds. "Well, then, even if I own the land, I can stand aside. There's no need to do any legal will breaking. But it'll be yours. Between us, we'll know that, and I give you my word I'll never try and impose a claim to it. I don't have the money to buy the one hundred and sixty acres today, but I could pay it over time."

"I'm not going to let you buy land you already own."

"I . . ." Kevin searched for a way out of the convoluted mess. "I can't sell it, but maybe I can I trade it. If I could swap my one-third of the ranch for a half section of land, that wouldn't give you, Cheyenne, your full one half, but you'd have nearly one-third, and that's gotta be better'n nuthin."

When he didn't get any response from the pair, Kevin continued, "I've got no means to start up somewhere else. I've already staked a claim to a homestead and proved up on it. I can't do that a second time, and Andy and Molly are too young to homestead. If we live here until Molly is twenty-one, then she could homestead elsewhere, and we could give you the one hundred and sixty acres back. If it was just me . . ."

Kevin stumbled over the words, remembering those outlaws. Maybe one of them Wyatt. He considered Cheyenne and her manly ways. Could the second outlaw have been a woman? Two would-be killers shooting into the blankets with no care to who slept where. They wanted Kevin, but they were willing to kill Molly and Andy, too. Was that their plan, or were they just vicious in making sure they got Kevin? It burned him to be nice to these vipers.

And yet there they stood, grim and unhappy as if they were the injured parties.

Kevin forced himself to go on. "If we could, we'd just go, and leave you to this stupid ranch." Kevin felt his temper slip.

He was a reasonable man, but no one would deny he had a temper that slipped loose now and again. Ma had blamed his temper on her own. He'd inherited it from her, she said. But Ma was a mild-mannered woman. Probably how she'd gotten talked into marrying two coyotes.

He cleared his throat and swallowed hard on his temper. "Right now, I don't have anywhere to go. I don't know Wyoming. I don't know how to farm on a mountain. I am hoping you'll see your way clear to pointing me toward some fertile land, if there is such a thing on this ranch. If there's any choice, we could settle on the farthest corner of your . . . what is it . . . fifty thousand acres?" His voice snapped on those words. Fifty thousand acres and here they were, furious to share it. Greedy, lousy, wealthy ranchers.

Wyatt kept slapping those gloves. Kevin bit down on his temper.

Cheyenne whacked the side of her leg with her lasso. "Listen, you son-of-a-sidewinder, you stole my land, and I'm supposed to be grateful that you give some of it back to me? Keep your stupid charity."

"Now, look here—"

Cheyenne whirled around and stormed back to the branding. Yep, she might be able to shoot someone.

Kevin felt his fists clenching. Wyatt was sullen. Probably trying to decide if he could live with this, or if Kevin and his family would be better off dead.

To keep from swinging a fist, Kevin said, "Talk it over between yourselves. Let me know when you've come to a decision." He went to his horse, mounted up, and turned to ride away.

"Wait! Stop, Kevin."

It sounded like saying *Kevin* almost injured him. But Wyatt had something to say. Finally.

Kevin turned his horse and waited.

Wyatt slapped his gloves one more time, then he said, "I know a place. A good place, I think. To the west. Far enough away we can put some space between us, and I'll—I'll—" He seemed to have to force the next words past his lips. "I'll help you get a cabin up. You and I can start building it today. We've got plenty of men to finish branding and—"

"I don't need or want any help." Kevin needed help real bad. The buildings were mostly made of logs, and he really had no idea how to put up a log house. Chop down some trees and . . . that was the extent of what he could figure out.

Wyatt jerked one shoulder. "Cheyenne's mighty upset and I don't blame her. And whatever blood ties I share with you, *Cheyenne* is my sister, and my loyalty is to her. But—" He swallowed hard, and it looked like it burned him to say it. "But I think you're being real decent about this, Kevin. Better'n me." He looked over his shoulder at his sister roping a calf and the other cowpokes staying out of her way. "And a whole lot better'n her. Let me show you the place."

"I'll ride along with you two." Win mounted up. "In case you get to pounding on each other, I can toss some cold water on you or kick you in your backsides."

Kevin thought for the second time that she was the most likeable person so far.

NINE

"Didn't you say you went to some school back east?" Kevin asked as they rode.

Win wondered what Miss Agatha would say about her threatening men. She might forgive it when it was Wyatt, her old friend. And after all, Kevin was Wyatt's brother.

Miss Agatha would understand.

"Yes, St. Louis. Miss Agatha's Finishing School for Young Ladies."

"And are you finished?" Kevin asked.

Wyatt snorted.

Win didn't dignify the question with a response.

"How long ago did Pa leave you?" Wyatt asked.

Kevin didn't seem to much like talking about his pa. "A long time. Molly is nineteen. Her pa came along shortly after we heard my pa was dead."

"How'd you hear that?"

"I was five when Molly was born, so I only know what Ma told me. She grieved for him. Loved him. Believed he was dead because she thought he'd've come back to her if he could have.

Finally, she got a telegram. I never saw it, so I'm not sure what it said." Kevin was silent for a stretch. Then he added, "I reckon Clovis sent the telegram himself."

They were riding three abreast with Win on Wyatt's left and Kevin on his right. She leaned forward to look around Wyatt, and said, "My personal nickname for him is the Sidewinder."

Kevin nodded. "Sounds about right."

"And you never heard from him again?" Wyatt held his horse to a fast walk as if he wanted to be able to talk. "Never knew about Falcon or me?"

"I found out there was a third brother when I walked up on the train platform and asked Falcon if he was you." He shook his head as the horses kept their brisk walk. "I do have a few memories of Pa, so he stayed around for a few years. I wouldn't have said I could really picture what he looked like, but I was struck by how much Falcon looks like him. Sounds like him."

"Dresses like him." Wyatt held his reins loose in one hand.

"Hopefully he won't act like your pa," Win chimed in. "That'd be a relief."

"I wonder where Falcon took off to?" Kevin shifted in his saddle.

"Maybe he's gone. Maybe we'll never see him again," said Wyatt. "Maybe he does act like Pa."

Wyatt's gloved hands tightened on his reins, and his horse tossed its head. Wyatt noticed what he was doing and relaxed. He patted the horse and spoke quietly to it.

Win knew there were few cowpokes surer on a horse than Wyatt. Cheyenne was one of those few by just a bit. Wyatt refused to admit it.

"Pa wasn't around here much." Wyatt kept patting his horse.

"He married Ma, and it didn't take her long to realize he was a no-account. He had no interest in helping on the ranch, nor learning a thing about cattle and horses. He'd go hunting and not come back for weeks, but he was here more than gone at first. That's what Cheyenne told me. Then he took to disappearing for months at a time. Then he'd come through once a year or so. I liked him well enough. He was a big, smiling, charming man who was nice to me. But no one else paid him much mind. It took me a few years to quit letting it hurt when he disappeared . . . and to quit being happy to see him. When he came here, we all just waited, ignoring him as best we could, until he went away again. Things were better when he was gone."

"We thought my sister and brother were born out of wedlock since it turned out Ma was still married to her first husband when she married her second." Kevin spoke of the second husband with a strange tone, as if he hated that the other man had existed.

"But when I learned there are *three* brothers and realized that Falcon is older than me, I knew it was me who was born outside of marriage—not Molly and Andy. Ma's second marriage is all legal and in order because she was never really married the first time. The shame the townsfolk showered down on Molly and Andy should have been for me."

Kevin twisted in the saddle to glare at Wyatt.

Win hoped there wasn't going to be a fight. Something was chawing on Kevin. It was natural he'd be upset by all this. But there was more. Win didn't know whether to fear what he was toting around inside or to respect him for keeping it to himself.

"That makes you born in sin, too, Wyatt. Falcon is the only one with a real marriage under him."

"We're not sure of that," Wyatt said. "My lawyer has been

digging around, and it sounds like Falcon's ma died when he was only half-grown. If she died before Pa married my ma, then their marriage is legal."

"Leaving me the only baseborn child of our misadventurous pa?"

Wyatt looked at him and rolled his eyes. "Nothing Pa did is any of our fault. You're the exact same amount of illegitimate as I am. Falcon might come from a legal marriage, but it seems to me being a legal child of Clovis is as much to be ashamed of as whether our parents were married right and tight. Being his son is a shame because his blood flows in our veins, and there's no getting rid of it."

"But there is living above it," Kevin said. "Living a better life than the one he did. Being hardworking and treating a wife and any child born to her with respect and love and faithfulness."

Win quietly said, "Those are words for anyone to live by. No matter who your pa is."

The bitterness in her voice surprised her. She didn't even know his words upset her as much as they did until she heard the tone in her voice. The men were so focused on each other she hoped they didn't notice.

Then Kevin's gaze slid to her. He'd heard it all right.

She was thinking of her own pa. And all of this uproar caused by a difficult father reminded her that her pa and Clovis were friends.

Clovis had very few friends around here. The town was small. The ranchers all knew each other. And Wyatt's family was too well-respected for anyone to be friendly to Clovis.

Except her pa.

Pa liked him, and Win knew it was because they were of a

kind. Given to broad arm gestures and talking a bit too loud. Full of jovial stories. Some that, while appearing to be jokes, cut at people and offended and insulted them.

Win's pa was apt to say, in a joking voice, some terrible thing about her. She was a poor housekeeper or a clumsy rider. He liked to eat her meals and talk of the coming stomach pains. He did it all with a big smile on his face. If she dared to object, he'd say, "I was teasing. I didn't raise you to be so fussy."

Which was yet another way to insult her.

"This is the place." Wyatt gestured to a rushing stream that had cut steep banks. The water curved along the corner of a meadow. The water ran fast and looked deep as it tumbled with a fresh, rumbling sound over stones smoothed over hundreds of years.

Win was glad to tear her thoughts away from Pa's unkindness. "I've never seen this before." It was a long stretch of open land. There was waist-high grass, waving in the gentle breeze. Bright green and lush. It was surrounded by woods, and the hills didn't rise up for a couple of hundred yards. "This must be the stream that winds through the southeast corner of Pa's ranch."

"This one flows into that stream, and they both end up in the Colorado River a long way south. There's a waterfall just past those trees." Wyatt pointed to the far end of the meadow. "And the stream gets wild after that so don't fall in. The trout get through, but it'd kill a man." Wyatt pointed to where the stream vanished into a heavy stand of woods.

"You think this is fertile soil?" Kevin swung off his horse.

"You can tie your horse to that rail over there. I come here to fish sometimes." Wyatt dismounted and led the way. "The ground is unusually black. It's a nice smooth meadow. Not many rocks sprinkled over the ground. I've never tried growing a crop, mind you, but I think someone could. You could graze cattle on the land this fall and winter and start farming in the spring. There's a feed store in town that'll sell you seed for corn or wheat. They can get whatever else you want to plant shipped in, I reckon."

Nodding, Kevin walked forward into the flat of the grassland and crouched. He reached for the grass, then, to Win's surprise, reached on past it to dig up a handful of dirt.

When he lifted it, she was struck by how dark it was. She didn't spend much time thinking about the color of dirt, but even she could see that this was different. It looked rich somehow.

"We can talk about the boundaries of the land," Kevin said. "This clearing here is less than one hundred and sixty acres, but it's plenty. I can plant corn and wheat on this side of the stream and put six cattle on the other side. I might even dig irrigation trenches to water my crops."

"Or, Kevin," Wyatt said quietly, "I could give you a goodly number of cattle, more than six for sure, and you can just ranch. I'd help you learn the way of it. This land will grow a crop, but it's ranch country out here. A man can make a living running a herd of cattle."

Kevin rose to his full height. That's when it struck Win just how tall he was. Not that she hadn't noticed, she just hadn't thought much about it.

Kevin seemed somber. He seemed protective of his sister and brother. And he was more serious about life than his easy manner might indicate.

"I might do some of both. Tear up a little soil and plant it. Run some cattle on the rest."

"It's just a sliver of what's really yours." Wyatt sounded grim, like he had to force himself to say the words.

"What are the boundaries of the land? Am I on the edge of

the RHR here? If there's unclaimed land nearby, where Molly can homestead, we might make an easy move right off your ranch. I don't want land Pa stole from you and your sister."

"I've got a map in Pa's office. We can get it out tonight, and you can have a look if you want to see the layout of the ranch. But no, this isn't near the boundary lines. And on west of here is the Hawkins Ranch, Win's pa's place, so no unclaimed land that way. But I've heard this kind of black soil grows crops the best. I'd have to think on if there's another patch like this anywhere. None this nice come to mind."

Kevin stared at his boots as if they held the meaning of life, then he turned to look Wyatt in the eye. He stared hard, like he was trying to read Wyatt's mind. Wyatt didn't notice because he was studying the land, but Win sure did.

Finally, Kevin said, "Someone tried to kill me last night."

Win froze. Wyatt whipped his head around.

"They weren't there to rob us. After they shot into all the blankets, we heard them say they knew it was my camp. We survived because I heard them coming, and we slipped away before they opened fire. They spoke of me, but they were happy to kill us all. Me and Molly and Andy."

"You need to go to the sheriff."

"I was going to. Then I ran into two brothers in town and got taken right out to the ranch. No time to talk to the sheriff. And no sense talking to him most likely. He's not apt to take my word over someone local."

Silence stretched, broken only by the wafting wind.

A splash drew Win's eyes to the stream. A silver trout leapt high and dropped back beneath the surface.

"You think I tried to kill you?" Wyatt said in a voice she'd never heard before, cold and mean and dangerous.

The silence stretched again.

At last Kevin said, "You can let that make you mad, if you've a mind. But I don't know you, brother. I don't know anything but that you're the son of a wastrel and a cheat. A thief and a liar and a betrayer."

A red flush of pure rage rose on Wyatt's face.

"Same as me." Kevin's words cut off the worst of Wyatt's fury. Kevin shoved his hands into the back pockets of his brown trousers. He didn't seem to want a fight, but neither was he running from one. He saw Wyatt's anger and didn't back down an inch.

Same as me. Kevin was including himself in that insult.

The truth stung like a nest of yellow jackets. For both of them.

Through a jaw almost too tight to move, Wyatt said, "It wasn't me."

"And how can I be sure of that? You're the one who gains the most if I'm gone."

"If it'd been me, you'd be dead," Wyatt said through clenched teeth.

Win closed her eyes. She resisted the urge to go kick both of them. Step right between them. She didn't think anyone was going to open fire, but she expected a fist to swing any second.

"Well." She clapped her hands twice.

Both men jumped and turned to glare at her. She was glad she'd gained their wrath because she was pretty sure neither of them would punch her.

"I'm glad we got that cleared up. I've noticed something eating at you, Kevin. Now that we know what it is, we can get you to the sheriff and turn this over to him."

"And you can't sleep out here until we get to the bottom

of this." Wyatt sounded disgusted, as if his plan to get one of his brothers out from underfoot was thwarted. "If someone attacked you, then they may try again. You can't sleep out in the open. You're staying in the ramrod's house until we get a cabin up."

TEN

isten, little brother." Kevin sounded like a big brother, and he oughta be able to. He'd been in charge of his little sister and brother for a long time. Ever since Ma had died. Longer even, because through all the terrors of Bleeding Kansas, Ma's new husband had been worthless. Either drunk or gone.

Ma was a hard worker but not a strong thinker, not a woman able to fight well to save her children's lives, or her own. That'd fallen to Kevin from the time the little ones were born.

Wyatt turned to him. He looked him straight in the eye. Wyatt was a lean cowpoke, his muscles coiled and taut from long hours fighting cattle, horses, and weather. "There ain't much little about me."

Kevin smirked. He wished this man would take a swing. Kevin really needed to punch someone. "I'll stay at your ramrod's house, but I'll do it because I've got common sense, not because you're ordering me to."

Wyatt rolled his eyes. "I didn't mean it that way. I meant . . . it'd be a good idea if you did. I had no intention of hog-tying you and dragging you back to the ranch tossed over a saddle. Do as you please. I'd advise you to stay close to a strong building with a good field of fire. And I think it would be for the best if your sister and brother stayed, too."

Kevin could hardly punch the man for advice, now, could he?

With a hard jerk of his chin, Kevin said, "Much obliged for the invitation. We'd prefer to stay until we can get a cabin up."

"And until you get to the bottom of who shot at you," Win said. "If this happened last night, and you rode straight for Bear Claw Pass, then whoever did it is close around."

"I know that." Wyatt gave her a heated look, like he was calling her stupid. "That's why I told him to . . . I mean, that's why I *invited* him to stay at our house."

Kevin shoved Wyatt's shoulder. "No call to talk to a woman like that."

"I know. I think of her as another bossy big sister, and sometimes I get to acting like a pestering little brother with her."

Kevin had a pestering little brother so he knew the type.

Win stepped between Kevin and Wyatt and gave Kevin a shove. "I'm friends with his big sister, and it's my favorite hobby to torment Wyatt, and he pays me right back. We've always been this way to each other. Don't come in here and act like Wyatt isn't a good and loyal friend."

Kevin looked over Win's shoulder at Wyatt, who rolled his eyes. For one second, Kevin wanted to smile at his brother.

"I'll accept this stretch of land with my thanks and make payments until we own it free and clear . . . and we won't bother telling any lawyer about it. We'll get to building as soon as we can and get out of your hair. For now, I'll let you get back to your branding."

Kevin still wasn't sure about Wyatt. He sounded innocent, but Kevin didn't know him well enough to be sure. There were folks who could look you right in the eye and lie without blinking. He knew it well. He hadn't been around to see his own father be such a liar, but he'd seen it plenty with Stuart Garner, Ma's second husband. Or her only husband, seeing as how Clovis hadn't legally married her.

And Stuart Garner was a liar before the Lord. Every breath he took, every word he spoke, was a lie. And when the drink was on him, the lies were bigger and told with even more style.

Wyatt said, "I've got another week of backbreaking, soul-crushing work, then things ease off a little until we do the fall cattle drive. This year we were going to take the cattle to Denver, but it's not a good time to be gone. If you can wait until after branding to start building, I'll help you, and hopefully with a crew out here of salty, range-hardened cowhands all working together, no one will try and shoot you." Wyatt turned to untie his horse and muttered, "Even if you are an insulting, muleheaded sodbuster."

Wyatt swung up on his horse, so Kevin didn't grab him and start punching. Instead, he mounted up, Win a second behind him. Kevin reined his horse to follow Wyatt.

"See that trail over there?" Wyatt asked.

Win and Kevin nodded.

"I'm heading back the way we came to where we've got the cattle rounded up. If you follow that trail, it'll take you to the ranch."

Win turned her horse that way.

Wyatt called over his shoulder, "Don't get him lost, Win. I sure enough need all the brothers I can get."

Kevin couldn't quite laugh. His whole life was just too upside down. But he was tempted, and he appreciated the lightness of it.

He and Win rode out. Wyatt was heading down a well-trod

path, but Win led into a dense woodland on a trail mainly for game.

"Someone really tried to kill you? Last night?"

"Yep." Kevin ducked a low-hanging branch. "Do you mind if we lead our horses through this? The branches almost close over our heads, and in some spots they're lower than that."

"Good idea. Wyatt must've taken this trail to that trout stream. But I've never been on it before. It doesn't look like anyone rides it much."

Once they were walking, Kevin told her what happened and what those men had said.

"And you thought Wyatt tried to kill you?"

"I had one idea for a name of someone who didn't want me showing up out here. Honestly, the only name I knew."

Win led them on in silence. Kevin figured she was ordering her thoughts to scold him for his evil doubts about his honest, decent, and fine brother.

"I can see how you'd suspect him."

That surprised Kevin enough he stopped in his tracks, but his ambling horse nudged him forward with her nose, and that got him going.

"I appreciate that."

"The only thing is, Wyatt, along with Cheyenne and all the cowhands, has been working from before sunrise until after dark for the last two weeks. And I'm getting up before him and Cheyenne so they have a hot meal in their bellies before they start the day. Based on how far you say you walked before the sun came up, I'd say I was serving a meal up at the RHR at the same time you were getting shot at."

"Listen, Wyatt seems like a decent man. I'm not about to take his word for much, but truth is, he probably didn't do it.

And according to you, he's got a dozen cowpokes who were working right at his side when he would've had to be hours away. It's possible he hired someone to waylay us, but it's a tricky thing for a man to hire killing done. Known gunmen are around, I suppose, but most men wouldn't know how to find one of them."

The heavy woods were so different from Kansas with its treeless plains that rolled gently for miles in all directions. Here the limbs were weighed down with leaves. He smelled pine and damp, rich soil. Bushes flowered and some held berries. The day was warm, but in the shade with a breeze, it was cool.

"It's beautiful here. Thank you for taking me. I'd've probably never found my way back to the ranch."

"The limbs are still low overhead." Win eased her horse to the side of the trail. "But I think you can walk up here beside me." She stopped her horse, and Kevin came alongside.

"I think we need to talk." She picked up her walking again.

Kevin thought of those moments they'd shared on the trail heading for Wyatt and his branding.

"What are you going to do about those men?"

What men? Then he thought of being attacked in the night. He almost smiled to think of where his mind had gone, as opposed to where hers had.

But no smile was quite able to slip free. Her quiet question fit with the heavy woods and the low light.

Kevin heard a rustling in the trees, and a doe popped out of the woods right in front of them.

Win's hand came out and stopped Kevin. The two of them and the horses stood motionless as the doe looked at them with soft brown eyes wide with curiosity. She showed no fear. Maybe she'd never seen a human before. Then a fawn—its back and sides covered in white speckles—stepped with the grace of a dancer out of the brush beside her. The doe turned and walked down the trail in front of them.

Win and Kevin stood there, her hand on his arm as they watched the pair. The wind blew softly. The leaves of maple and oak fluttered. Stones covered with moss lined the trail. Heavy evergreen bushes and prickly scrub brush filled in every crack between the trees and stones. How had that deer walked through there?

When the doe and her little one rounded a curve and disappeared from sight, Kevin whispered, "Let's go up to where she came out."

They advanced a dozen yards or so, and Kevin saw a trail that made this one look like a well-traveled road. "We could walk down through there. But the horses would never make it."

Win smiled at him. "I'd've never recognized that as a trail without that deer to mark it."

"I want to follow it," Kevin said. "I know we can't, but I have an urge to leave this bigger trail and just see where that leads. I wonder if I'll ever have a chance to do something so foolish."

He thought of Falcon dropping his bedroll on the floor of the ramrod house and walking out. A man with no fear of getting lost. No fear of finding a trail to follow. And nothing to stop him from following it. No family—if he didn't count two brothers. And he most likely didn't.

"One of the lessons my finishing school taught in American history was the story of Daniel Boone," Win said. "I remember him saying, 'I've never been lost, but I was once bewildered for three days.'"

Kevin laughed. "Maybe that's how it is for someone who follows a new trail. Wanders in a new land. They really can't be lost because they don't know where they're going. And they may find the trail ends, and their way blocked, but then they turn back and find another way."

He looked at Win. The most likeable person he'd met since he came out here. The most civilized, too.

By far the prettiest. Of course, Cheyenne was pretty, too, but Win had her beat, and she was sure enough better looking than his brothers.

"To get to my school, I took a stagecoach across Wyoming and Nebraska, then south to Missouri and across to Saint Louis. When I came home, all those years later, I rode the train."

Kevin felt the pleasure of the moment fade. "Do you mean you left and didn't come back at all for years?"

Win shrugged one shoulder as if to say it was nothing, but Kevin couldn't believe that.

"With such a hard trip, it was unthinkable to come home for the summer, and the school was set up for students to board."

"What about your parents?"

"Ma died bringing a new baby when I was five. The baby was never born and died with her. Pa said she'd lost a son, too, after me but before that child. I think he was bitter that he'd never had a son and blamed Ma." She added quietly, "And me."

Kevin clenched his jaw to keep from saying something rude.

Win looked up, and the sadness he saw in her made him ache. "I stayed over here at the LaRemy place quite a bit."

"Wait, Laramie? You said that name before, but I didn't think on it. The town Laramie and Fort Laramie are named for Cheyenne's grandpa?"

Win shook her head. "Not Laramie, LaRemy." She accented different parts of the word, but Kevin thought it was awful close to *Laramie*.

"Jacques LaRemy. He has a lot of family history here, and some say the fort and the town of Laramie were named after Wyatt and Cheyenne's grandfather. He was an old fur trapper. He'd gone back east and married and was bringing his wife and half-grown daughter, Katherine, west on the Oregon Trail. His wife died, and Jacques had no heart to go on searching for a better life. He decided to drop out of the wagon train and stay here. One of the trail guides, Nate Brewster, was half Cheyenne Indian. Nate Wild Eagle Brewster. Nate said his people wouldn't allow LaRemy to stay—not without someone to smooth the way. So he stayed with Katherine and her father. Nate Brewster was a young man and sweet on Katherine, or so the story goes." Win smiled.

Kevin could see she loved the romance of it. It struck him with a hard tug of pleasure that in this rugged life, with all the uncertainties around them, a pretty woman could still enjoy a love story.

"Nate talked to the native people, and Jacques was wise in his behavior to them. Jacques had a few head of cattle being driven along with the wagon train, and he just stopped here and settled in to build a ranch. Nate settled beside him, and the two of them were good partners and fast friends, building an empire together. When Katherine was old enough, she and Nate married, and they lived alongside of her pa. After Nate died, she married the Sidewinder, and that brings us to Wyatt. After my ma died, for a time I lived here more than with my pa. Cheyenne and I tormented little Wyatt until it was a wonder he didn't try to strangle Cheyenne and me every time he saw us."

She laughed at that, and Kevin decided he needed to stay out of whatever the friendship was between Wyatt and Win.

"Jacques and Katherine were well suited to this life. My pa is much younger—a few years younger than Katherine. He came along later, when it was more settled and much safer. He didn't want me growing up like Cheyenne. He thought Katherine was mannish, and she was raising Cheyenne in her image." The pleasure faded from Win's eyes.

Kevin could see how it hurt Win to have her father looking down on people she loved.

"With Ma gone, Pa had little choice and let me live over here most of the time. We muddled along until the earliest age they'd take boarding students back east. I was ten when he took me there to live. I came back when I was eighteen."

"Eight years without coming home." Kevin's heart hurt to think of an abandoned little girl.

Nodding silently, Win said, "It was hard, but I settled in and loved Miss Agatha. I helped out, especially in the summer when almost all the children were gone. I cooked alongside her and helped her clean the school. I went to the shops with her, and after a few years, I started grading papers for the younger students and even filling in when a teacher was ailing or gone for some reason. Coming back here to be a schoolmarm was the most natural thing in the world."

Kevin reached up and rested a hand on her upper arm. "I'm sorry you got sent away. Your pa probably didn't know what else to do. Especially if he objected to taking you out to work with him. I know you love Cheyenne and love this whole family over here, but your pa probably thinks more like regular folks."

Win gave him a sad smile. "Raising a daughter as a cowhand isn't the usual way of things, but it makes good sense out here."

"I can't say I find a thing wrong with it."

Rustling startled Kevin, and he turned to the forest, expecting to see another deer. The rustling stopped, and Kevin looked down at Win. "I think we scared that one away."

She smiled and nodded. He realized he'd slid his arm across the back of her waist when they'd turned. Now she stood, pressed gently against his side. And he was too close.

Kevin knew little of women. His ma had frustrated and confused him.

He'd worked hard back home all his life. And he'd never taken the time to step out with a woman. Win was something new in his experience. A fresh wonder in a life that had changed so suddenly.

She looked at him. Her snapping blue eyes blinked. They reminded him of that graceful doe. She'd let her bonnet fall down her back. It hung by its strings, and her hair fluttered in brown curls where it had escaped from the knot at the back of her head. One curl blew across her face, and Kevin brushed it back, then found his hand resting on her soft cheek.

He felt something, a pull as if she were a magnet. He'd never known a man could be drawn to a woman like this. He leaned down. She didn't pull away. In fact, she stretched up.

Another rustle, this one louder, then the crack of a cocking gun.

Kevin's head snapped around.

ELEVEN

*G*unfire split the air as Win tackled Kevin. He hit hard as the gun blasted again and again. Win ended up on top. He realized she'd knocked him over. She'd reacted to the danger faster than he did. Even as he figured it out, he was rolling to put his body between hers and the gunman.

All the hard training from surviving Bleeding Kansas fired up. He crawled toward that almost-invisible deer trail. Win was clawing at the ground, scrambling as fast as he was. In fact, she was ahead of him now and grabbing his elbow to urge him faster.

The woods swallowed them up. The gunshots shredded the scrub brush around them. The rich pine scent was poisoned by the smell of gun smoke.

The horses reared. One gave a shrill whinny. They charged down the trail after the deer. The shooter paused briefly as the horses ran past.

Kevin and Win kept low, crawling on their bellies. When the shots started up again, Kevin thought they were going wide. Whoever was shooting might not realize there was a winding trail in here that would lead Kevin and Win away.

Kevin got to his feet, crouched low, and helped Win up. Clutching her hand, Kevin moved forward fast.

She was heavier than he'd expected. Clumsier.

Stupid thought. Rude.

She'd been running and diving, dodging, fighting for her life just like him, and she'd saved him. He might not seem all that graceful to her, either.

The gunfire stopped.

Was their attacker coming? Was he reloading?

Kevin picked up speed. He was almost dragging Win now. There were branches hanging low over a trail as narrow as a deer hoof.

They had to stay low, and they couldn't get any real speed. Then Win pitched forward, and she would've landed on her face if Kevin hadn't had such a tight grip on her arm.

She stumbled again, and with a bit of headroom for the next stretch, he swung her up in his arms and ran.

To where? How far?

"Do you have any idea where we're—" He looked down. Win's eyes were closed. She hung limp in his arms. That's when he saw the blood on his arm. She'd been shot. She fell because she'd passed out. He stopped so suddenly he almost fell over.

He had no idea where this trail led, but he sure couldn't go back the way they'd come. And the horses were long gone. Whatever he did would have to be done on foot.

He needed to see how badly Win was hurt. What could he do to treat the wound?

He heard footsteps pounding through the woods behind him.

He had to keep moving. And he had to stop and make sure Win wasn't bleeding so badly that to keep moving would kill her.

To try to give himself some space, he picked up speed. It all reminded him of his childhood. Of night riders coming through, shooting anyone they found.

Kevin had dug the cellar hole in their house, behind a cupboard he'd built for the purpose of hiding it. They hadn't told Molly and Andy's pa that it was there. He went out with the night riders many times. His vicious friends wouldn't have attacked their buddy Stu's house, but there were lots of dangerous men roaming the night. Kevin and his family had learned not to trust anyone. They'd learned to be sly and sneaky. They worked hard to learn how to get underground fast. If someone broke down their door, they'd find the place empty.

Kevin especially had learned to act fast and sure. He found a ruthless edge, and he stayed on it for years. And he'd learned to let the Lord give him inspiration. When he was in a tight spot and pouring out prayers for God's protection, he'd learned to listen to the whisper of an idea.

God spoke in that still small voice—not even a voice really. But a notion would come to him, and one came to him right now. Almost like a lantern light in the dark, he saw another trail open up, crossing this one. So faint that Kevin, with no experience in forests like this and under terrible pressure to run, should never have noticed it. But it was visible to him in a way that seemed as if God had guided him.

Kevin dodged onto the faded trail. He paused to look back. Was he leaving tracks? With a sickening twist to his stomach, he searched for a trail of Win's blood. He didn't see any, though his shirtsleeve was soaked. Fighting for silence, he charged on down this new trail, bending low to duck drooping branches, until his body was nearly curled around Win.

Win seemed too light in his arms. As if the weight of her soul was leaving her body. But it might be that he had the strength of rage and fear lifting him up.

Listening as he ran, he heard the man pursuing him pass the trail Kevin had taken. If they lost the gunman, he could see to Win.

Almost as quickly, the footsteps were back. The man after them had seen that Kevin's trail ended. Whoever it was, was very good.

Finding every ounce of speed, Kevin knew this might be the end. He braced himself to take a bullet in the back and prayed God would somehow protect Win.

Wild thoughts darted through his head. He should have written a will, something to protect Molly and Andy.

He never should have stopped to talk to Win when they saw that deer.

He shouldn't have gone to see Wyatt. Could this be his brother? He'd ridden off in another direction, but who was to say he couldn't have circled back? And hitting Win might've been an accident.

All of this raced through his mind as he tried to find a way to save Win and himself. Kansas had taught him how to think fast. Fight for his life.

He could tuck Win into the undergrowth, then set up and wait. Kill whoever was after them. The thought sickened him. He'd hoped after the war to never have to make kill-or-be-killed decisions again. And yet here he was.

Studying the edges of the trail, he saw big trees with saplings filling in the spaces. Between the saplings, the woods were clogged by the thick brush and broken-off trees until they were impenetrable. He had to find a spot to duck through to get out of sight—and there was nothing.

Finally, he saw a gap barely large enough and took it. He jumped over a downed tree, fought through a gooseberry thicket, and dropped to the ground. Gently setting Win down, he drew his gun and turned.

The thudding footsteps came on.

Without one whisper of warning, Falcon materialized at Kevin's side, his gun drawn.

A ghost.

A shiver went down Kevin's spine as he glanced at him. Falcon spared him a look, then focused on the trail.

How had he gotten here? How had he silently moved in this dense forest? Where had he come from?

Kevin turned back to the trail just as the footsteps coming at them slowed from a run to a walk. Then the footsteps ran again, this time back the way they'd come. Whoever was after them must have been smart enough to notice there were no running footsteps in front of him. Smart enough to know someone could lie in wait.

Falcon eased forward with silence equal to how he'd appeared. He looked over his shoulder. "You see to her. I'll go after whoever shot her. Get back on that trail where you left the horses. Keep going forward. I tied your horses up down the trail a ways. That trail will lead you to the ranch house. It's not far."

Kevin looked down at Win. "We should both—" He looked up.

Falcon had vanished.

Kevin felt another cold shiver rush down his spine as he was tempted to believe he'd imagined his big brother. Ignoring his rattling thoughts, he settled Win on the forest floor and rolled her to her stomach. She groaned and he almost did, too. He pulled a knife from a sheath on his belt and split the back of her shirtwaist. First, he smelled the blood. Then he saw two creases across her shoulder blades. The bullet hadn't gone into her body, and the cut wasn't deep enough to have touched her backbone.

Heaving a sigh of relief, he used his knife to cut a slice off one leg of her skirt and made a pad of cloth. Pressing it to her back, he held pressure on the wounds. Time passed like a ticking clock.

The need to get her back to the ranch house, get her to a doctor, finally took over from his fight to care for her here on the ground. He hoped it'd been long enough when he cut another strip off her split skirt and bound the bandage tight, wrapping it around the outside of her shirtwaist.

With every ounce of gentleness he could muster, he rolled her over. Win's face was bone white. But her breathing was steady, and the bleeding had stopped. For now.

He pulled her into his arms, positioning his right arm so he kept pressure on her wounds, then carried her back to the trail.

He turned in the direction Falcon had told him and soon found the horses. Win's eyes opened as he untied the reins on both critters, thinking one would just have to come along or not.

"Kevin, what happened?"

"You've been shot."

She blinked her dazed eyes.

"I'm getting on my horse to carry you back to the RHR."

"Are we safe?" Her voice was weak, addled.

"Yes, Falcon came along, and he's chasing the man who shot you. I didn't see who it was."

"Someone sh-shot me?" There was a break in her voice as if she might cry. If not now, then never.

His stomach twisting, he had to admit, "I think you got in the way of a bullet meant for me. It'd be a big surprise if there were two killers out here, one after me, another after you. I'm so sorry. Do you remember knocking me down? You must have seen something."

He juggled her into one arm, and he dragged himself onto the horse's back. Shifting her weight, he got her balanced across his thighs and clucked to the horse to head out.

"I do remember. I'm shot?" She was having trouble understanding in the midst of pain and confusion and being toted around.

He looked from the trail to the blue eyes in her ashen face. The pain in them made him want to find the man who'd shot her and tear him apart with his bare hands.

"It's a crease. A mean one but not dangerously deep—it cut both your shoulder blades. The bullet must have clipped you as you were knocking me out of the path of it. We'll get you back to the house and tend your wounds." He swallowed hard. "You saved me, Winona." He held her tight. "You saved my life. Thank you."

She managed a weak smile and rested her head on his shoulder. Sounding a bit like her sassy self, she said, "I did, didn't I?"

"Yes, you did." He found a smile in the middle of the madness. "Molly's had some experience tending wounds. So have I."

Experience tending wounds. That was a mild version of events.

"She'll help me bandage you up. I'll fetch your pa, he'll want to—"

"No!" She grabbed the collar of his shirt in one fist. A flush of color bloomed on her cheeks. "I don't want him to know if we can help it." Her dazed vision cleared as she held tight enough to strangle him.

"Why not?" The trail ahead widened, and he urged his horse into a trot, then a canter.

"He might make me go home. I—I don't want to be over there. I stay either here or with Parson Brownley in town when school is going on. I never stay with him." Her expression changed as she looked at him. He knew she was remembering how close they'd been before the gunshots.

Her pretty blue eyes locked with his.

For a second, despite everything, he thought of that almost kiss. Thought about making it more than almost.

Before he could act on that wayward thought, he emerged from the trees and saw the house ahead.

As they galloped straight into the ranch yard, he said quietly, "I won't go for your pa without your say so."

"Thank you." A faint smile curved her lips, then her eyes fluttered closed.

TWELVE

evin, what happened?" Molly didn't wait for an answer. Fool question. Time for that later. Instead, she went to work. It was all so familiar.

"Where's she hurt?"

"Shoulders—bullet wound."

Molly gasped.

Kevin shook his head. "It's ugly, but she'll be all right if an infection doesn't catch hold. A crease across her back. The bullet didn't go in, just cut her skin. Her spine wasn't hit. I got the bleeding stopped—I hope. But it was bleeding hard."

Andy grabbed everything off the table to clear it.

Molly rushed ahead of Kevin. "Facedown. I need to see what happened."

She shoved the chairs aside. "We need bandages. Andy, look through the cupboards here, and, if you need to, tear the whole house apart. They're bound to have something."

"I'll get a basin of hot water and a cloth." Kevin rushed to the water well on the cast-iron stove. Molly heard the clatter as he snatched up the basin they'd used at the noon meal to wash up. There was a ladle hanging on the wall.

Molly trusted Andy and Kevin to find what she needed and pulled the back of Win's shirtwaist aside. She went to work removing Kevin's rough bandage. He had it tight, and when she pulled aside the edges of the pad of cloth he'd used to press against the wound, she saw the nasty cut, but the bleeding had mostly stopped.

"I have to stitch it up," she said as Kevin reached her with a steaming basin of water. He set it down on a chair seat beside the table and bent his head to look at the wound.

"Do you think you can find a needle and thread?" She spared a look at her brother. He was upset, but as always, he was doing what had to be done.

"I'll find them." Kevin was gone in a flash.

She should call after him to look in Win's room and Cheyenne's. Likely they had sewing supplies. But Kevin would know that.

Molly wrung out a cloth in the hot water and began cleaning the mess, looking for bits of dirt or threads from her shirtwaist, which might cause the wound to become infected.

A groan from Win stopped Molly from working on the wounds. The blood had mostly washed any bits and pieces away. All Molly had to do was wait for her brothers.

To get down to Win's level, Molly sat on the chair next to the one holding the water basin.

Win turned her head to the side and met Molly's eyes. "How bad is it?"

"It's not too bad. It'll need stitches, there's an ugly cut across both your shoulder blades. But wounds on the surface like this rarely get bad infections. And I don't see anything cut but skin. No muscle involved. You're going to be hurting for a while, and you'll have a very interesting scar, but you'll heal."

Win closed her eyes as if to block her vision of the near future and the stitches that needed to be set.

"Should I send to town for a doctor? Is there a doctor in Bear Claw Pass?"

Win shook her head as best she could with the right side of her face pressed firmly to the table. "Not one who's known for a steady hand. Fond of the drink, is our doctor. I think Cheyenne has stitched up a few cuts."

"I'm planning to do it. I know the way of it. You can trust me. Kevin is hunting right now for needle and thread."

Win, already pale, went pure white. Molly hoped she'd faint dead away and sleep through this next bit.

"Do you want me to send for your pa?"

Win jumped. She pulled her arms up and pushed as if to sit up.

"Stay down there. You're white as milk. If you sit up, you'll end up collapsed on the floor."

"Don't send for Pa. Kevin promised he wouldn't."

Patting her on the shoulder, careful to avoid the bullet crease, Molly held her in place. It wasn't hard, the poor woman was out of strength.

"If Kevin promised, then his word goes for me, too." Molly wished Win wasn't alone with strangers. "How about sending for Cheyenne and Wyatt? Cheyenne could hold your hand and distract you."

"We're halfway through the afternoon, aren't we?"

There was no clock to be seen anywhere. "I think more than half. You've been gone for hours, and the sun is getting low in the sky."

"They'll work until dark, but the days are long. I don't want to interrupt them."

Molly leaned close to her, almost nose to nose. "You've been shot, Winona. That's important. They need to know, and when they get here later, don't you think they'll wish they'd known sooner? They'll want to come running to be with you."

Win swallowed hard. Molly could see she was tempted. She really did want someone here with her.

Except, could Kevin find his way back to the branding?

Molly heard footsteps thundering on the steps. That sounded like Andy coming. "We'll get on with fixing up this cut and see what Kevin thinks about riding out for Cheyenne."

A barely visible nod was the only answer Molly got. Molly pulled a cloth over Win's back to shield her.

Andy came in. "I found a good supply of bandages. They have a closet upstairs with everything we need."

"Thank you." Molly gave her brother a smile. He was too grown up for his age. He'd never had much of a childhood. They'd all had to grow up hard and fast.

"You shouldn't be in here now, Andy. I have to expose her back, and it's not fitting she should have men looking at her when she's uncovered."

Molly could see he was curious and eager to help. But he didn't voice a single protest. Instead, a pink flush colored his cheeks. He nodded and nearly ran out of the room. It was a reminder of how young he actually was.

Molly rinsed out her cloth and once again bathed Win's back gently. Her clothes were soaked in blood, likely ruined, as were her underpinnings. She was living here. Surely, she had a change of clothes.

Molly opened her mouth to shout for Andy to go to Win's room to find a nightgown or something just to give him a job, make him feel needed. But she snapped her mouth shut. She couldn't have Andy pawing through Win's clothes.

She felt bad about casting Andy out, but clothes for Win? That was all for later. They were a long while from worrying about that.

THIRTEEN

*K*evin came down the stairs. He rushed into the kitchen with a small bundle in his hands. "Here's a needle and thread."

Win's eyes were closed, and it looked like she had fainted again. His stomach twisted with worry as he thrust the supplies at Molly.

"You should get out. I just sent Andy away. It's not right you should see her so uncovered."

"You need a second set of hands, and I'm not leaving."

Molly stared hard at him, then seemed to accept him at his words. "All right. Keep this just like . . ." She held the edges of the open wound closed.

Together he and Molly worked carefully on Win's back. It made Kevin sick to see her hurt. As Molly finished the stitching, Kevin finally felt like he had a moment to talk. "Whoever shot her was almost certainly trying to kill me, Moll."

Molly gasped, but quietly. It shocked her to hear it, but she was a woman used to being shocked and used to handling things while madness roared around her.

"She saved me. She saw something. She must have. I asked her about it on the ride in but . . ." Kevin shook his head and went on. "It has to be the same person who attacked us on our way to Bear Claw Pass."

"They'll try again," Molly said. Their gazes met across Win's prone body.

Molly took the bandages Andy had found and formed two pads, one for each stitched-up shoulder blade. The cuts weren't terribly long, three inches maybe. And with the blood bathed away and Molly's tidy stitches, they weren't as horrible to look at.

But those threads, those tight black threads, were the beginning of lifelong scars. Something for Win to carry with pride. She'd acted with courage and speed and saved Kevin and herself. But still, it was a burden to know how violence could explode into any life.

Molly's scars were all in her heart.

"Wyatt took me to a place I think we could build a nice house." Kevin changed the subject. "He's no farmer, but he thinks the soil is good there. I saw it and agree."

"Where was Wyatt when you got shot?"

Grim silence stretched between them. "Surely he's not such a fool that he doesn't care if Win is in the path of his bullets?"

Molly shook her head as she wrapped bandages around the pads covering Win's stitches. "I'd say he's not, but then, if he's a killer, he might not care all that much who he kills."

"I accused him of attacking us."

That jerked Molly's gaze up to meet his. "Do you think it was wise to let him know we suspect him?"

Kevin hesitated before saying, "He convinced me it wasn't him. Then he rode off back to the branding, and Win took me on a different trail that was a direct path back here. He knew where we'd be, and the attack came from behind. But no." Kevin shook his head. "No, I can't believe he'd risk shooting Win. He treats her like a big sister."

Then he remembered the most mysterious detail of his story. "And Falcon showed up."

"Well, we saw him get off that train this morning. He couldn't have shot up our camp last night."

"Nope, and anyway, I could hear the man coming after us when Falcon showed up beside me." He looked at Molly and couldn't stop a tight smile. "He just appeared there."

"Appeared?" Molly finished binding the wound.

"Like a ghost that popped up in complete silence."

"Where is he now?"

"He went after the man trailing us." Kevin told her the details of the attack. Molly listened as she adjusted the bandage until she was satisfied with it.

"You know we're good at slipping around," Kevin said.

"We had to be."

There was another tense silence between them. Then Kevin went on, "But we're not a patch on him. I can't quite believe he could move with such complete silence on a ground covered in twigs and dead brush and leaves. It's impressive. I'm hoping he comes back in here soon dragging along some varmint he caught, even if it is Wyatt Hunt."

"It's not Wyatt, for heaven's sake." Win, her voice groggy, woke up to defend her friend.

Molly leaned down so Win could see her. "We've stitched you up. I'm going to your room to get a nightgown or something for you to wear. I don't want you to put on anything tight."

Win told her where to find the clean clothes and tried to

roll to her side, but Molly pressed firmly on the tops of her shoulders. "You're not decent if you sit up. We had to cut the back of your shirtwaist open."

Win dropped flat on her front and turned to glare at Kevin. "You shouldn't be in here."

Kevin was so glad to hear her talking that he managed a smile. "I know. But you've been modestly covered, and Molly needed help, though she tried to toss me out."

"I'll be back fast. Don't let her up." Molly darted out of the room and went thundering up the stairs.

Win clutched the remnants of her shirtwaist to her chest.

"Your shirtwaist still has the sleeves on it. Molly covered you except right where she was working." He pulled a chair around so he could sit in front of her. He wanted to get down low enough she didn't have to tilt her head up one bit more than necessary. "There, now I can't even see where you're bandaged."

When he saw her ashen face, he wanted to hold her, but instead he said, "I trusted Wyatt when we talked about the men who came into our camp early this morning."

"Have you only been here one day?" Win asked. "It seems longer."

Kevin gave a tilt of his head. "I'll admit it's been a long day."

He thought of how he'd almost kissed her out in that forest. That wasn't right, not after knowing her less than a full day. What had come over him?

Then he thought of how she was alone in this house with a pack of strangers. She needed someone here for her. Someone she knew. "I'd like to know why you don't want me to go for your pa, but considering my worthless pa and even worse Molly and Andy's pa, I'll allow as to how fathers are sometimes

110

trouble. I think I should ride out to get Cheyenne. It's nearing suppertime anyway, so she at least could come in so you'd have her company."

"Do you think you can find them?"

Kevin hesitated as he went over the winding route they'd taken out there. He was a man who studied the land and looked to his back trail. But he had to admit he wasn't used to mountains, and he'd spent the ride considerably distracted by Win. "I'll find them."

Win nodded silently. "I'd like her here. I expect Wyatt will come with her if you tell them I was shot. And they'll probably work until dark if you don't go. Cheyenne has been on a tear since we read the will. It's a busy time of year, and good thing, or she might've knocked the whole house down just so she'd have to build a new one to keep her distracted from what the Sidewinder did to her."

"He was a poor excuse for a man." Kevin studied her, judging if she'd pass out again. She was probably awake for good now. As long as she stayed on the table.

"He was that. And you say your ma's second husband was worse?"

Kevin shrugged. "She weren't no judge of men, that's the hard truth."

Molly came in. "At least Clovis had the good sense to pretend he was dead. My pa wasn't so helpful. He insisted on staying with us."

"When he wasn't out terrorizing folks in the night, to keep them from voting to abolish slavery," Kevin added. "Even though he had no slaves and never had. He just liked the terrorizing."

"You go, Kevin. Win should have Cheyenne or Wyatt here.

111

And tell Andy to stay out while she changes. I don't want her to try the stairs yet."

"I can wait if you want and carry her up."

"Go on," Win said quietly. "I'll be fine, and once I'm decent, maybe Andy can support me well enough I can move into a chair. I think I'd as soon stay down here for now."

Kevin stood, and Win's hand reached for his and grabbed hold. He didn't know if she'd planned that, but he liked the way she felt, solid and strong.

She said softly, "Whoever shot at you might still be out there. Ride careful."

~

"Wyatt, Cheyenne! Win's been shot."

Kevin might as well have thrown dynamite into the crowd of cattle and cowpokes. Nothing could have hit harder.

Cheyenne tore out of a cloud of dust, straight for a bareback horse.

Wyatt had a calf at the end of his lasso. He dropped the rope and charged for his horse.

Kevin spoke loud enough for Cheyenne to hear. "She's not hurt bad. She's been doctored. But she needs someone with her."

Cheyenne swung up on her horse and rushed at Kevin. "Where is she?"

"At the ranch—"

She was gone, bent low over her horse's neck. Wyatt was astride, and he took off after Cheyenne. Kevin kept up. Well, he kept up with Wyatt, there was no catching Cheyenne. They raced across the rugged ground. With his jaw tight, Wyatt turned to give Kevin a burning look.

"How bad?"

"A couple of bullet creases."

"She got shot *twice*?"

Kevin explained as fast as he could talk over the sound of thundering hooves. "Molly sewed her up. She'll be fine. The wounds aren't even deep enough to suppurate." He hoped. "But she's gonna hurt for a while."

"Sewed her up? How long ago did this happen?"

"Not long after you rode away." Kevin couldn't quite keep a suspicious tone out of his voice.

Wyatt reacted like he'd been snakebit. "Are you accusing me of shooting an old friend?"

Kevin didn't answer. He didn't think it needed saying.

He wasn't accusing. But he couldn't help but think there was one man who would profit greatly from his death.

One man.

Then he saw Cheyenne ahead. Riding with unbelievable grace. As tough as any man. Good chance she was as decent a shot as any man. And there she was, riding like the wind. Had she been at the branding site when Wyatt got back? Was she truly worried for her friend? Or did she just now realize her bullet had gone wild? Not questions he wanted to ask.

Kevin's gut told him neither of these two were killers. He thought of the way those footsteps had come after them. Definitely a man. And it was one thing to accidentally hit Win, another to come after Kevin and Win the way that man had. Those men last night hadn't cared if they shot and killed Molly and Andy, but today, if it was Wyatt who attacked them, he'd've never come chasing after them, because if he found them and Win saw him, he'd have to kill her, too. Or trust that she'd keep her mouth shut about murder. Nope, he didn't see Wyatt and

Cheyenne as cold-blooded killers. Oh, maybe in a fight for their lives, but not cold-blooded, premeditated murder.

And Kevin trusted his gut. But not all the way. He'd hold back on putting his complete trust in anyone here at the RHR for now.

FOURTEEN

Win wasn't sure how she was going to manage her life for the next little while.

A person spent a fair amount of time leaning back. Every chair was going to be a torture chamber.

She could sleep on her stomach, but she didn't prefer to. And even here stretched out on the tabletop, unmoving, she hurt plenty. It wasn't just leaning back, it was standing or twisting, bending—oh, who was she trying to kid, it hurt to breathe! It hurt to think!

She'd waited until Kevin left, judging Molly to be more easily handled. Or at least she was only one person to handle. She convinced Molly she wanted her clothes, not a nightgown.

Once Molly went back upstairs to swap the nightgown for a dress, Win sat up, slowly, carefully, dangling her feet over the edge of the table. Her head swam, and the edges of her vision darkened. A rushing sound filled her ears. She grabbed the table, afraid she might topple off. Fighting doggedly for consciousness, her vision slowly cleared.

By the time Molly was back, she felt sure she wasn't going to faint again. Not counting today, she'd never fainted before in her life.

She knew women back east who seemed to relish being delicate. They talked of fainting as if they did it once a week. She'd taken some pride in knowing she wasn't such a weakling, and it annoyed her not to be able to lay claim to that prideful boast anymore.

Her chin came up. Getting shot and passing out didn't count as fainting. Not by her measure. She decided she'd keep on thinking of herself as tough.

With Molly's help, she got dressed. Molly had brought a riding skirt and a loose-fitting shirtwaist. They got the ruined clothes off and the new ones on right there in the kitchen, of all scandalous places.

"Andy," Molly called, "you can come in now."

Andy came in, and Win noticed he was a look-alike with his big sister, and the two blue-eyed blonds had no resemblance to brown-headed, golden-eyed Kevin.

Win was unsteady, even with Molly's strong arms supporting her. "Can you please turn that chair right behind you, the one tucked under the table? Flip it around so the back is against the table, then I can straddle it, and sit with my front against the chair back."

Andy quickly did as she asked before coming to her other side.

"If I start to collapse," Win said, "please do your best not to sling an arm around my shoulders."

Andy grimaced.

"We'll be careful," Molly said. "I don't want to do any more stitching."

Win gingerly slid her feet forward while Molly and Andy steadied her. Her back was on fire with pain, and her vision narrowed again but not as badly as when she'd sat up. As it cleared, her thinking got some better, too. "I'm not up to wrangling calves."

"I'd say that's fair." Molly sounded pretty sarcastic.

"But my pa never let me learn to do that, so it's not a problem." Win sat, grateful for the split skirt.

After a moment of letting the pain ease, she said, "Before Cheyenne comes, can we get the bloody clothes out of here?"

Andy collected the pile from the floor.

"Don't take them away yet." Molly rushed for a large basin and filled it partway with cold water. She brought the basin to the clothes and dunked the much-worse-for-wear things.

"Give me a minute with them, Andy, then can you take this basin to *my* room not Win's. You saw the one I'm staying in, didn't you?"

"Yep, right across from Win's. Your satchel is in there."

Nodding, Molly said, "I want to get the blood stains out before we leave them to soak. The skirt will be all right, a dark color like this won't show stains easily. But the shirtwaist is light enough I need to try and clean it up now. After it has soaked awhile, I can try mending the shirt. The clothes look terrible, but maybe I can fix most of them."

"Thanks, Molly. I can scrub my clothes and see to the mending."

"I'm sure you can. I'll get you a needle just as soon as your hands stop shaking." Molly started the clothes soaking. She scrubbed them gently, dumped the pink water, then scrubbed again. Finally, after a few more times, the water poured out clear.

Andy headed out with the clothes as Win studied her trembling hands.

"Thank you, Molly. My main concern was to get all these

bloody clothes out of here before Cheyenne came in. I don't want her to see them. She's going to be so upset."

"Shouldn't we help you up to your room? Hide you same as we're hiding your clothes? You're pale as milk and mighty shaky."

Win crossed her arms on the back of the chair and plopped her chin on her wrists.

"I *am* shaky. But no, I don't want to go to bed, not yet. I want to be sitting up, looking as solid as I can manage when Cheyenne comes in. She's going to be wild with fear. Furious. Looking for someone to attack. Me being up and dressed will help us stop her from tearing the whole ranch apart searching for who did this."

"Would you like some water? It will help you regain your strength."

"Yes, thank you."

Andy came into the kitchen as she said that. "I'll fetch her a drink." He got the glass from the cupboard by the dry sink and ladled water out of a bucket.

He brought it over, and as she drank it, it bathed her throat, which she just now realized was desert dry.

She took a desperately long drink.

Molly jumped for the glass and pulled it back. "Not too much. Not fast."

Win grabbed for the cup, desperate from the sudden thirst. Molly got it away from her just as Win's stomach twisted. She feared she might cast up everything in her belly. Fighting for control of her swooping stomach, she stopped grabbing for the cup until things settled down.

A long while later, or maybe it just seemed long, Molly offered her the cup back. "Drink all you want, but drink it slow. A sip, then make sure it settles, then another sip."

When she felt able, Win took another drink. Just a bit this time. Being much more moderate, she finished the glass.

Andy took it back and refilled it, then set it on the table within her reach.

Molly came with a slice of bread on one of Cheyenne's china plates. "Getting some food in your belly helps, too. Eat it even more slowly than you were drinking. You may not feel hungry, but you've got some work to do building up your blood again. You lost plenty of it."

Win figured she needed her strength. She reached around the chair back to get the bread.

Glancing at Molly, she said, "Stitches? How to drink and eat after an injury? Where'd you learn so much about healing?"

"Ma," Molly said.

"The war." Andy spoke at the same instant.

Andy gave Molly a surprised look. "When did Ma need stitches?"

"No, the war, you're right. Ma . . . fell once."

Win noticed her hesitate.

Molly's eyes shifted in such a way Win knew Molly was lying even before she talked. She turned away from them and walked to where she'd left the bread uncovered before she went on talking, now with her back to them. "I—I stitched her up. She talked me through it. First time I did it."

"I don't remember that." Andy frowned. "But I barely have any memories of her. She died when I was—" He hesitated. "I was three or four, I think."

"You were five, Andy. I'm surprised you don't remember her better, but I've noticed you don't." Molly wrapped the loaf of bread with an oversupply of care and said no more.

Win's imagination took off, and she felt a flood of questions rushing to be asked. She stopped herself from asking a single one of them.

Instead, she faced the pretty plate with the slice of bread. "Wyatt and Cheyenne will be back here at a run, I imagine."

Looking at Andy, she asked, "Can you set the table for a meal?" Her gaze shifted to Molly.

"I've got the bone stewing from the roast beef at noon. I figured to make up some beef stew." Molly caught Win's urgency. The need to make things appear normal.

It struck Win hard. Molly saying she'd learned doctoring from stitching up her ma. Molly smoothing over Andy's confusion. Now Molly understanding about how to keep up appearances. Act as if things were normal. It all seemed to hint at some hard lessons learned that she had taken to heart. Lessons she'd hidden from her little brother.

It gave Win plenty to think about as she sat here eating bits of bread.

"We ate all the potatoes at the noon meal," Molly went on, acting as if preparing dinner was all she had to do. "I'll peel more and get them in the stew to cook. Then I'll make some biscuits. We can have a meal waiting for them when they come home." First though, Molly came close and rested a hand on Win's wrist. "How bad does it hurt? Is there an icehouse? Ice can take the pain and swelling out of a wound. I could—"

Win turned her hand so she could hold Molly's. "I haven't said thank you yet. Thank you for tending my wounds. I'm sorry for all you must've gone through to learn the skill, but it was a blessing to me today."

She gave Molly's hand a tight squeeze, and their eyes met. "You have a friend in me, Molly, if you need one. Well, whether you need one or not. Yes, my back hurts terribly. Yes, the RHR has an icehouse. But I don't think that's called for. At least not yet. I expect Cheyenne and Wyatt to come in here in a panic, which will turn quickly to anger because for Cheyenne, lately everything turns to anger."

Win shook her head, dreading how upset they'd be. Then she thought of that bullet and how close it had come to cutting through her backbone. She was mighty upset herself.

"If we have a meal ready for them and they can see me sitting up, ready to join them for that meal, maybe they'll think instead of racing out of here looking for war."

Molly gave Win a doubtful look. Which meant she was already getting to know Wyatt and Cheyenne.

Molly squared her shoulders and, with a nod, set to work acting normal. Andy was soon at her side mixing up biscuits. A handy young man.

Watching them and feeling useless, Win sat there, straddling the chair, hurting like her back was on fire and wanting a little war herself.

FIFTEEN

fter telling Wyatt about the attack, Kevin thundered the rest of the ride in dusty silence. The pair reached the ranch yard in time to see Cheyenne charging from the barn to the house. Andy was at her side, so he must've met her when the horse galloped in. It was probably the only reason she'd taken the time to put up her horse.

Wyatt and Kevin took that time, too, though they were quick about it.

Wyatt rushed toward the house and took the three back steps in a single bound. By the time Kevin got there—and he'd been pushing hard himself—Cheyenne was examining Win's back, and Wyatt was holding both of Win's hands, peppering her with questions. Kevin caught sight of Andy leaving the room. No doubt sent away with regard to modesty. Molly pulled biscuits out of the oven while a thick stew bubbled on the stove.

"I'm fine, Wyatt," Win insisted.

"Where were you? Where exactly did—"

"I can answer that, Wyatt." Kevin strode to the table. "Don't push her. She needs to take it easy."

He caught hold of Win's hands and yanked them, almost for sure too roughly, out of Wyatt's grasp.

Win narrowed her eyes at him, but there was a thread of relief there, too. She didn't want Wyatt and Cheyenne so upset.

"Get out of here, Kevin. You too, Wyatt," Cheyenne snapped. "You can't be in here when I'm doctoring her." She had the back of Win's dress open.

Mercifully, it buttoned down the back. She didn't have to cut it open like Kevin had, and judging from the way Cheyenne looked, she'd've done it.

A storm brewed and flashed as Cheyenne and Wyatt squabbled. Win protested their care, and Kevin chimed in with Win to explain about the shooting.

When Cheyenne was satisfied that there was nothing more for her to do, she started bullying Win to go up to bed.

Kevin tried to get them to leave poor Win alone.

Molly kept busy off to Kevin's side, getting the meal together with quiet skill. Taking care of everyone else.

Finally, Win was decent. The table was set. Wyatt was calm enough to wash up—Cheyenne had at least washed her hands before she looked under Win's bandage—and Andy was allowed back in.

"Molly, you did good work on those stitches," Cheyenne said.

Still looking pale, Win added, "Yes, she did. Thank you, Molly."

"It's a hard thing to have a needle set to your skin," Molly said as she brought the last of the food to the table. "I don't expect thanks. I was glad I was here and had the knowledge."

That seemed to bring everyone to silence. Kevin wondered if anyone else could say that they were glad they were here, together. Once she thought of it, could Molly even honestly say it?

Then Wyatt said, "It was good that you were here, Molly. I'm no hand with stitches. I've set a few in a cow before, with about five cowhands lying on her to keep her still. Win probably wouldn't have appreciated my methods. Thank you."

"I've done that kind of doctoring for the hands and for Wyatt and even myself once," Cheyenne said. "I don't seem to be improving with practice."

"We've had more than one cowhand ride into town to the doctor, bleeding the whole way, rather than let Cheyenne get near him with a needle." Wyatt managed a smile.

Win sounded rather faint when she added, "I'd've ridden to town if it was that or Cheyenne. Bear Claw Pass's doctor is overly fond of the bottle, but if his hands aren't shaking from drink, and you're lucky enough to get him when he's only seeing one of everything, he does a passable job with stitches, at least compared to Cheyenne. Show them your arm, Wyatt."

"No, not on an empty stomach."

"Probably better on an empty stomach." Cheyenne reached for a chair.

Wyatt laughed, and Win joined in. Even Cheyenne cracked a smile.

With slightly less neck-snapping tension in the room, they all sat down to the table.

Kevin said, "Let's ask God to bless our food and protect us all."

He saw the confirmation on each face that asking for protection suited everyone there. Kevin began a sincere prayer.

Partway through, Wyatt broke in as if he'd just had something leap into his brain and straight out of his mouth. "Where's Falcon?"

Kevin's eyes snapped up.

Wyatt met his gaze. They were both shoving back from the table.

Kevin had told them how Falcon had arrived at the scene and gone after the man shooting at them.

"He should've been back by now." Win sounded scared.

"Maybe he's tracking them," Wyatt said.

"Let's go find him." Kevin grabbed two biscuits and stuffed them in his pocket. He wasn't going to be able to swallow a bite of them.

Wyatt waved a hand as Andy stood, then Molly, last Cheyenne. "The rest of you eat."

"Be careful." Cheyenne's eyes were grim, her jaw tight with tension. "If Falcon's as good as you say he is, and they got him, then we're all in terrible danger."

Kevin's stomach twisted. *"And they got him."* Cheyenne's words hit him hard. He cared nothing for Falcon Hunt. Didn't know him worth a lick. He was part of this mess that Kevin wished had never happened. But if it was about the land, then it stood to reason that whoever was after Kevin was after Falcon, too.

Cheyenne rushed for the sideboard, snatched two canteens off a hook, and filled them with water.

Wyatt grabbed a couple of biscuits of his own, then both canteens as he rushed past Cheyenne.

Kevin was out the door a pace ahead of Wyatt. They saddled fresh horses and were on the trail in minutes.

It was only after he'd ridden long enough to stop being a headlong fool that it occurred to him that Cheyenne seemed to have let go of avoiding all of them out of concern for Win. And now she was going to get serious about the danger because she realized she might be in danger, too.

"We're all in terrible danger."

Well, welcome, Cheyenne, Kevin thought. Glad to see you joining in with the folks who were worried about losing their lives along with their land.

Wyatt didn't look back. Didn't check to see if Kevin was with him. Instead, he rode as fast as the conditions allowed, heading down the trail Kevin had come home on. They galloped along until the trail got narrow enough they had to walk—too many outstretched branches trying to grab them and drag them to the ground. With Wyatt leading, they were traveling this trail a whole lot faster than Kevin had while carrying Win in his arms.

Finally, Wyatt stopped, lashed his horse to a tree, and plunged into the woods. Kevin recognized the spot by the faint trail the doe and fawn had stepped out of. But he'd've never seen it if Wyatt hadn't. And then Kevin changed his mind. He saw blood.

This was where Kevin had grabbed Win and dodged down the trail. The blood trail got heavier. There was a heavy splatter of it where he'd stopped and set Win on the ground, hoping whoever had shot at them would pass. Then Falcon was beside him, and the pursuer hurried away.

Without saying a word, Wyatt studied the ground, then turned back toward their horses.

"The man chasing must've realized he could be walking into blazing gunfire, just like he'd dealt out to us," Kevin explained. "Falcon found our horses down the trail a piece and tied them up. He said I should make sure Win was able to travel and, if I could, get her to your house. I didn't even ask him if he should go after a gunman in these woods alone. He just vanished."

Kevin pointed at the ground. "There are twigs everywhere. Years and years of gathered, fallen leaves. Dried grass that's still standing after a long winter and a hot summer. It should have been impossible to move as silently as Falcon did. I'm pretty good, and he snuck up on me."

Wyatt nodded. "Let's go along the trail, try and see if we can find him."

As Wyatt led the way back to their horses, Kevin noticed Wyatt moved mighty quiet. But he wasn't a patch on Falcon Hunt.

SIXTEEN

*T*here was no trail left by Falcon to follow, but Kevin could see the tracks of another man.

This man wore boots, while Falcon had handmade moccasins. The tracks were long and stretched out—a man running away. Kevin had heard him running away. Had the man heard Falcon coming after him? Or had whatever sent him running been supplied by the dint of his being a woman-shooting coward?

They emerged into the rich, grassy meadow, and Wyatt went right along the trail left by the running man. Until he stopped and crouched by more blood.

"Falcon . . . he went into the stream." Wyatt sounded grim.

Kevin's stomach twisted at Wyatt's tone, but going into a stream was survivable. "So we'll walk along the stream until we find where he washed out. You said there was a waterfall just yonder past those trees, so he might be hurt. He might not be able to get back if he's got busted ribs, or maybe he knocked himself out."

"This is an ugly stretch of water." Wyatt's voice could chill blood. "There's no sense trailing him. This goes hard for miles.

It eventually drains into the Colorado River, which flows all the way to Mexico."

Wyatt turned to his horse. You'd think the man might be excited to be rid of one of the heirs to land he considered his, but there was nothing to show such thoughts in his expression or his words.

"We can't just go home." Kevin studied the stream, tumbling and gushing between rocks, the banks steep. The fall alone might kill a man.

"Follow me for a bit." Wyatt rode downstream along the banks. The horses walked until the stream was hidden by a stand of trees. As they went into the trees, Kevin heard a distant rumble he couldn't identify—but he suspected it was the falls. He'd never seen a waterfall before in his life.

Wyatt turned away from the water's edge, and Kevin followed him. The man oughta know his own land.

As they rode, Kevin tried to encourage himself not to give up hope. He was struck suddenly by having a brother—two brothers—he'd never known.

And if Wyatt was right, they'd never know Falcon.

"Having a father in common," Kevin said, "doesn't make us friends, doesn't mean we like each other or know each other. But if Falcon died today, I've lost the chance to know my own brother. I think we need to find a way to get along."

Wyatt reined his horse around to face Kevin. "So you want us to be family, then?"

There was nothing brotherly in his question.

"I don't *want* us to be family, Wyatt. We *are* family. Two different things. And without knowing a whit about Falcon, I'm struck with regret that we might never get to know him. We're brothers. Nothing changes that."

The rumble of water broke the silence between the two angry men. A hawk screamed overhead. A gentle breeze shivered the trees Win had called aspens. Pines soared above them and scented the air all around. The day was wearing down, the sun lowering in the sky, the temperature of the hot summer day dropping.

The horses started munching the grass beneath their noses, and Kevin rested one hand on his horse's neck, glad the strong critter was filling his belly.

Wyatt seemed to be considering an answer. Kevin probably didn't want to hear it.

With a shake of his head and a scowl, Wyatt got his horse going again, following that growing rumble until it turned into a roar.

When the roar took over so no other sound could be heard in the dense woods, Wyatt stepped out into a clearing. They'd been riding in deep shadows. Now the sun burnished Wyatt and his horse. When Kevin reached the clearing, he gasped.

The stream plunged over a cliff. The water moved with a speed Kevin could only think of as deadly.

He dismounted and walked close to the edge of the stream, then dropped to his hands and knees and stretched out, peering over the edge of the falls to see how far it dropped. Twenty feet maybe, into a large pool about a hundred feet across. At the far end, it narrowed into another stream rushing out of the south side of it.

"It's not that far. He could have survived it."

"Do you see him down there?"

Kevin looked around the edges of the water. There were jumbles of stone and bushes here and there, but they weren't heavy enough to hide a body. "No."

"That's because he'd've been swept on through that pool and out the other end. From here the pool looks quiet, but it's got a current that just tears along. On past it, there's what we call white water. Fast moving water that, instead of going over a cliff, twists and turns downward through a field of jagged rocks. It foams white, and it's said that if you fall in, getting out is almost impossible once the current takes you. If he survived the fall, he wouldn't survive the white water."

Kevin backed away from the edge. He didn't think Wyatt was a killer. Kevin couldn't quite look at this man who'd worked hard all his life at his family's side, building this ranch, asking for nothing they couldn't provide for themselves, and see a man who'd turn back-shooting killer.

Still, Kevin got well away from the edge before he stood, then went to his horse and mounted up. "Is there a way down?"

"You mean a way that's not quite so exciting as the water route?"

"Yep."

Wyatt nodded. "I'll go with you. We can check the shore until we lose the light."

"And you're sure he went into this stream?"

"You read the same signs I did."

"I just wish I were reading them wrong and you could convince me I'm stupid."

"You're not stupid," Wyatt said. "You're a pain in the neck, but I reckon you're smart enough."

Kevin sat silently, looking at Wyatt with eyes that matched his. Eyes that matched Falcon's.

With a sigh, Wyatt said, "Yes, I'm sure he went in the stream and didn't climb back out. And he was bleeding, so he may have been shot or maybe clubbed over the head to knock him into the water. Yes, I'm sure he, or maybe his body, went over the falls."

They both turned to look at the rushing water.

"I will say this," Wyatt added quietly. "Whether I like either of you or not, *no one* is gonna kill *my* brother on *my* land and have one more day of peace in his life. He's not gonna get away with it."

Hazel eyes locked with hazel eyes. "Finding Falcon's body, or giving up on finding it, doesn't change the fact that we've got a problem, big brother. Someone tried to kill you, Molly, and Andy. A real good chance the same varmint shot Win trying for a second time to kill you. And it's got to be the same one who killed Falcon. I won't stop until someone hangs for it. Let's go."

Wyatt guided his horse away from the stream and found a steep but rideable trail down. In grim silence, they headed out to find their missing brother's body.

SEVENTEEN

Win finished a meal that felt like it would choke her.

But Molly's gentle prodding got her to eat a good portion, then drink a lot of water. It steadied her and helped her feel returning strength . . . not counting the pain in her back.

Cheyenne ate with little talk beyond "pass the salt." Win knew Cheyenne was upset almost to the point of madness that her grandfather's ranch had been stolen from her. Win didn't blame her, but Molly and Andy had done nothing wrong.

"Cheyenne"—Win's gaze included the others—"Kevin told me today he wants one hundred and sixty acres. He says that open meadow along the west stream is close enough. That's all. He said he'll not make any use of the rest of the land Clovis left him, nor profit from it. And you can consider it restored to you, even if no law allows it."

Molly nodded. "We don't even have to stay long on that stretch of land. Kevin can't homestead because he's already done it, and once is all that's allowed. But I'll be twenty this winter. As soon as I'm twenty-one, we'll move on. Maybe go on to Oregon. No matter what's written on some piece of paper, you're the owner of half this ranch. We won't accept any of it, except a few acres for a few years to give us the means to live."

"That's not a home for Kevin, that'll be for you. And you'll want to marry, and the land will belong to your husband. Kevin's not going anywhere." Cheyenne said the words with such bitterness Win had to force herself to stay in her seat when she wanted to go to Cheyenne and pull her into her arms.

She wanted to try to ease the hurt done by the Sidewinder. Having a gunshot to contend with helped keep her still.

"I'll never marry." Molly rose and picked up the empty stew bowl.

"Of course you will. All women end up married, in fact—"

"No, I won't." Molly talked over her. "My ma did a poor job of picking husbands twice. No reason to believe I'd do any better." She got very busy clearing the table.

Andy jumped up and started helping her. "I'll wash." He rolled up his sleeves and ladled steaming water out of the hot water wells on the big rectangular cast-iron stove.

His actions struck Win as a mite strange. There wasn't a hardworking attitude in his movements. There was fear. Where had Andy learned to be afraid not to help? Molly's solemn expression held no threat Win could see.

"Was her second husband as bad as the Sidewinder?" Win asked. Kevin had said as much, and she knew there were secrets here. Molly had stopped Andy from talking about their father earlier. No one ever wanted to speak ill of their upbringing, but here they all were in the glaring facts of the Sidewinder. It seemed like an act of kindness on their part not to act as if everything had been all joy and plenty in their home.

Molly worked all the harder. She acted as if she hadn't heard the question.

Andy said, "My pa died a long time ago. I barely remember him. Ma died too. We were in the middle of what turned into the Civil War in Kansas. Bleeding Kansas, they called it. It was almost like the Civil War was going on, neighbor against neighbor. No law. Kansas got to vote on whether we'd come into the Union as a slave or free state. Hotheads who were proslavery came flooding in from the South. Antislavery people came in from the North."

He told the story as if he'd heard it a thousand times, and no doubt he had. "They all brought their guns ready to fight to the death for their side. In the end, it was a small version of the Civil War, even to the point we had two governments. The slaveholders' side won with a whole lot of illegal votes. The free side declared the election unlawful and claimed victory. Two governors, two sets of senators. Lots of shooting."

"But this was when you were really young," Win said. "You'd have been only five when the Civil War started."

"When it *started*, but things didn't calm down in Kansas even after the rest of the country settled down. The fighting went on through the war and after, all along the border states. We had Quantrill's Raiders and Bloody Bill Anderson, the James gang and the Younger brothers. And those were just the ones that made the news. All sorts of unhappy folks were running wild in Kansas and Missouri after the war was long over. Ma and Pa got mixed up in all that early on and died along with a whole lot of other folks at the start of the war. Uh . . ." He gave Molly an uncertain look. "You said I was five when they died. But I don't remember it, I've just heard the stories."

After his tidy little story about Bleeding Kansas, Win was surprised to see him not sure of the rest of it.

"It was such an ugly time, Andy. Bad things happened over

and over. Pa was one of the men riding with a group that thought of itself as raiders same as Quantrill. It was a bad business, and we got in the habit of not telling anyone because there were plenty who had free-state sympathies. I've never wanted to speak of it. Better to face forward and put the past behind."

Andy looked fretful, like he had questions, but he nodded and went back to washing dishes.

Win wanted to prod, but Andy's confusion stopped her. Maybe she'd be able to talk to Molly alone sometime.

Cheyenne was sitting at the table, her fists clenched together. She'd been like that since Molly had told her she could have her land back, and she had grown cold and silent as she listened to Andy talk of his parents' death.

Win thought of Wyatt and Kevin off hunting for Falcon. "You two need to sleep in here tonight. Wyatt will be in here, but we should get Kevin in here, too. There is safety in numbers."

Cheyenne's head came up at Win's invitation. She slammed her fists on the table. Her face flushed a furious red.

Win jumped and gasped in pain from the sudden movement.

Cheyenne shoved her chair back so hard it skidded across the floor.

"I told your brother, and I'll tell you—that land is mine. You've stolen it from me. To give me a chunk of it back as if it's a kindness? Well, that makes me want to pull a gun and start firing."

Win knew Cheyenne had been devastated by the reading of the will, but right now she seemed beyond that. She seemed killing mad. And she stood there with a gun on her hip. Molly moved quickly and stood between Cheyenne and her brother. Which was ridiculous because Andy was as big as her.

Win gathered herself to dive at Cheyenne if she drew her gun. Her old friend seemed near to over the edge.

It was gonna hurt, but Win would do it.

Cheyenne gave a harsh laugh. "I'm not going to shoot you. Hanging would be the result, and that would probably just make things easier for everyone."

Win was nearing the end of her sympathy for Cheyenne. She needed to get ahold of herself before she said or did something that couldn't be undone.

"You may have sworn off marriage, but I haven't. I've had an offer. It'll get me out of here, and I'm taking it," Cheyenne said through gritted teeth. She turned and charged through the kitchen door toward the stairs to her bedroom.

"Cheyenne, stop!" Win rapped out the order in her school-marm voice, and Cheyenne whirled to glare at her, hands on her hips, breathing hard.

"What offer? Who proposed?"

The harsh laugh came again, louder, longer. "I'm surprised you don't know. I thought he'd've told you."

"Told me? Who do I ever talk to? One of the cowhands here? Some friend of Wyatt's?"

The silence stretched until Win thought it might twang like a tight banjo string.

"Your pa proposed to me, Win. After he heard I'd lost everything."

"Pa?" Win's mind reeled. No. No. No. A thousand things tried to crowd to get out of her mouth. The first to escape was "he's too old for you."

"My pa was a few years older than my ma. The years aren't enough to stop me. Your pa knew I'd had the ranch stolen, and he still wanted to marry me. He's spoken of us stepping out together before, but I never took it seriously. But now, knowing there's no wealth in it for him, that means a lot to me." Her eyes swept over Molly and Andy. "And I won't share a home with thieves. I'm leaving first thing in the morning. Tomorrow I'll accept your pa's proposal."

Molly said quietly and with admirable sarcasm, "Calling him 'your pa' instead of by his name seems like a real bad sign."

Win thought that was an excellent point.

Cheyenne could have incinerated Molly with her eyes. "We'll be married as soon as it can be arranged."

"Cheyenne, no," Win sputtered. She could not allow this to happen. Her throat had gone bone-dry, and it was all she could do to force the words from her mouth. "You can't. You know Pa won't—"

But Cheyenne wasn't around to listen. She was charging up the stairs with thundering feet. Escaping to her room for now. And soon escaping for good. Or better to say, for ill.

EIGHTEEN

There's his hat." Wyatt kicked his horse into a trot.

Kevin's stomach squeezed. He was glad he hadn't eaten much dinner. "A hat and no man to go under it."

Wyatt rode up to the rugged bank of the pond. He sat atop his horse just staring, but Kevin swung down and grabbed the wide-brimmed hat. It looked homemade out of buckskin, or— he ran his hands over the brim—maybe something softer. A pelt of some kind. Feathers stuck out of the bright red hatband that looked as if it'd been woven in some intricate way out of thin leather strips. A very distinctive hat that definitely belonged to Falcon.

Kevin carried the sodden hat with him as he swung back up to ride, thinking this might be all there was to bury. "Where to now?"

Wyatt didn't speak. He just guided his horse on around the pond. It poured into a tight little channel that vanished into a heavy stand of trees. They wove through the woods, staying within hearing distance of the water, and suddenly the sound of it got louder. A thinner stand of trees gave him a view of the stream, foaming like it was full of soap.

White water for a fact.

The ground sloped downhill, though it certainly wasn't a cliff. Beside the trail, the water tumbled down a steep slide, over and around jagged rocks. He saw how impossible it would be for a man to survive this. What's more, there were stones enough that if a man had managed to come down this spate of water alive, he could've grabbed onto a rock and pulled himself to shore.

But there was no sign of Falcon anywhere.

The trees fell completely away, and a pasture opened before them. Kevin could see signs that a cattle herd had grazed here not that long ago. But the pasture, pretty with that stream coursing through it, stood empty. He watched a tree branch come blasting down that stony stretch of water. It broke up as it went, and Kevin could imagine what that harsh passage would do to a man.

"My grandpa used to talk of an old codger who followed this stream until it spilled into the Colorado River." Wyatt adjusted his hat, watching that same busted-up branch that had caught Kevin's eye until it vanished at the far end of the meadow, where the trees again swallowed up the stream. "That was clear back in the day before Grandpa settled into ranching. Before the river had a name. Before Colorado had a name. The old man knew his way around the West. He helped Jim Beckwourth find and widen a trail that turned into the lowest pass in the Sierra Nevada Mountains. He taught Grandpa a lot, including that the river goes all the way south to Mexico, through the Grand Canyon and some of the ruggedest land known to man. If Falcon went over those falls—and the hat is proof that he did—then he's dead and gone."

Wyatt looked over at Kevin, and the question was there in

Wyatt's eyes. The same one that Kevin knew had to be in his: Should they go on?

"It's wrong not to search for his body." Kevin looked at the deadly water.

"It's a greater wrong to leave your sister and mine behind when there's a killer wandering the area." Wyatt adjusted his Stetson with one gloved hand. "We have to go back."

Kevin studied Falcon's hat. "A brother we never knew and now never will. I'd go on. I would. Maybe his—his b-body snagged somewhere. . . ." There was a stretch of silence, and Kevin saw no reason to break it.

Wyatt sighed loud. "Yes, if that happened, we could find him and bring him back to a decent burial. But Falcon looked like a rugged man, used to untamed places. He might see this as more decent than being planted in a hole in the ground."

Kevin looked at the lowering sun. His sister was a teacher, and he'd seen the maps. He didn't know exactly how far Mexico was, but he knew it was very, very far. If he planned to go on, then he needed supplies, and he'd have to abandon his sister and brother to strangers who were unlikely to be kind to them. In fact, they had no standing here without Kevin.

"We have to go back." Kevin gripped Falcon's hat. Guilt goaded him to go on and search. But he couldn't. He knew it.

They turned and made their way back up the side of the trail that ran alongside the white water.

Then the more treacherous trail up the side of that waterfall. Then the long trail home.

"We'll be done with branding in a week. We'll get you a cabin set up. One that'll withstand gunfire."

Kevin didn't know what to say to that. Finally, all he could think of was "I don't see why Cheyenne couldn't have Falcon's third of the land. Then you two split my third except for the stretch I'm taking. You'll both be real close to half."

"Maybe that'll calm her down. She's mainly mad at Clovis, but he's beyond her reach, so she's been spreading that anger over everyone. Maybe this'll help her aim it at that grave I dug."

"I suppose we should do something about Falcon." Kevin lifted the hat to eye level. "We could bury this."

"Let's hang it up in the ramrod's cabin. Put it on a peg. It'll stay there until we . . . I don't know, uh . . . get your cabin built. Then we can . . . put it in your cabin or my house permanently. That hat can be a memorial to him."

"I hope you didn't buy a fancy memorial for Pa, like a marble headstone with a Bible verse carved in it. Or maybe the words *Beloved Husband and Father*."

"I buried him deep because it satisfied me to do that. I suppose somewhere inside I was thinking of him somehow escaping the grave."

Kevin shuddered at the thought.

"But it's not like I put him in a place of honor. I stuck him well away from my ma and grandpa, outside the edges of the family cemetery. I'm already driving a wagon over the hole I dug. It's my wish to someday not be able to remember where he's planted. And for sure the next generation won't find him."

"I think I'd be satisfied to never have the grave pointed out to me. Ma put flowers on a gravestone back home for as long as she lived, then I took it up and did it for twenty years. That's more than Pa deserved."

They rode the rest of the way to the ranch house in silence.

Then they got home to find Cheyenne gone.

"She's going to marry your pa?" Wyatt just plain screeched. Win didn't blame him, but it was hurting her ears.

"That's what she said, but she can't possibly mean it. She knows Pa isn't a good match for her." In Win's opinion, Pa wasn't a good match for anyone. He'd convinced her ma to marry him, but that was when he was young. She'd probably figured he'd mature. Grow into a fine man. She hadn't lived long enough to give up on that. Or maybe she had given up, but there was no escape.

"And she's gone? Where did she go?" Wyatt asked for the fourth time . . . or tenth.

"We never heard her leave. She went charging up the stairs. I waited down here awhile, hoping she'd calm down some. You know how she is, Wyatt."

"She usually calms down, given enough time."

Win had been giving her "enough time" for a month now.

"I'm afraid," Molly said quietly, "giving her enough time is going to be too late."

"I went up to try and talk to her, and she was gone," Win said. "She must've gone out the window because she never came back downstairs."

"We came and went through the bedroom windows a lot when we were kids, trying to get past Ma and Grandpa," Wyatt said.

"Well, she showed a fine skill." Win needed to go to bed, but once she'd found Cheyenne gone, she'd settled back downstairs on her backward kitchen chair to wait for Wyatt to return.

"Maybe she went to your pa's house tonight?" Andy suggested.

"No." Molly shook her head.

"A respectable woman wouldn't do that," Kevin added.

Wyatt scowled at the stairs as if he could make Cheyenne appear through the power of his eyeballs.

Win felt sure Cheyenne hadn't gone to Pa. "She'd never do something as outrageous as go to a man's home late at night alone. Much less go there with plans to stay."

"Is there a boardinghouse in town she could stay in?" Kevin asked.

"There is." Win crossed her arms on the back of the chair and rested her chin on her wrists. The bent posture was the least painful way to sit. Not to say there wasn't still plenty of pain, but this was the least. "And she knows who owns it, and they'd have room for her. But word would be all over town that she's left the RHR. She'd hate that."

"I'd bet she goes into the woods and camps out." Wyatt quit staring at the stairway. "Maybe she'll calm down out there."

"What should we do?" Win looked from Wyatt to Kevin and back. "Do we go hunt for her, try to track her?"

"In the dark?" Wyatt's brows shot up. "She's too savvy. We'd walk right past her. I probably can't find her in full daylight unless she wants to be found."

"Win." Kevin sounded like he was taking charge. It'd be interesting to see what he came up with.

"If you're able tomorrow, ride over to your pa's and watch for her. If you can't talk her out of marrying your pa, knock her over the head and toss her over her horse and bring her back."

Win nodded with a frown, doing her best not to let them see how terribly her back hurt. "I'm able." Barely. "I'll need to move carefully, but I can ride home."

She hoped.

"And whacking her is probably the best idea anyone's had.

Has the best chance of success." And Win could catch her unsuspecting.

Cheyenne trusted her lifelong friend, foolish woman. Oh yes, normally trust would be warranted. But in this case, the only thing Cheyenne had a right to trust was that Win intended to stop any wedding between Cheyenne and her pa, and if it came to whacking her, it'd be better than what she'd get as the wife of Oliver Hawkins.

"Wyatt, you can trail her," Kevin continued in his big-brother-taking-charge manner. "Set out after her in the morning, and if she goes into rough country, follow her. She might be good at hiding her trail, but she rode out of here pure mad. She's not stopping to cover hoofprints right now. Maybe after she's gone a ways she'll think of it, but chances are we can get a notion of where she's headed. I'll ride to town, figure out if she's at the boardinghouse. Town, Win's place, and the woods. We'll cover all three."

"That'll help us to know what she's planning." Wyatt jerked off his gloves and tossed them on the floor under the pegs that held Stetsons and coats.

"If I find tracks that say she's headed to the Hawkins ranch, I'll get there fast. Help you corral her, Win."

Kevin jabbed a finger at Molly. "You stay here with Andy. If she comes back, the two of you convince her to stay. Tell her . . . tell her . . ."

Win wondered what he was having so much trouble saying. He'd been doing a fair job of issuing orders up till now.

Something in his expression told her it was bad. She had to fight the urge to go to him, comfort him. Though she didn't even know what had upset him.

"Tell her what, Kevin?" Molly asked.

Kevin seemed to notice what he held in his hand.

Win saw it for the first time, too. "Why do you have Falcon's hat?"

Kevin shared a look with Wyatt. Silence stretched for too long. "Falcon went over the banks of that stream today. We think he must've been in a fight with whoever shot you, Win."

Wyatt quietly added, "We found his hat over the falls and nothing else."

Win shook her head. "Nothing else? What do you mean? Just say it straight out."

"He means Falcon is dead," Kevin stated.

Win gasped and shook her head. Molly covered her mouth with her hand.

"You didn't bring him back?" Andy's voice echoed with anger.

"We didn't find a body."

"Then you can't know he's dead." Win didn't even know the man and, honestly, wasn't inclined to like him, but this was shocking.

Wyatt rubbed a hand over his face. "You don't know that water like I do, Win. Falcon went over those falls and was swept downstream. Where we found his hat proves he went through a deadly stretch. He couldn't have survived."

"You have to go back. You have to search until you find him," Win insisted.

"We felt the same way, but that stream moves fast enough we might have to ride all the way to Mexico. We can't ride off and leave all of you here alone when gunmen are riding the range."

"And now we have to search for Cheyenne, too." Kevin spoke through clenched teeth. "She's out with those same gunmen."

Wyatt whipped around to face the back door. "I'm going to see if I can figure where she's headed."

He ran out the door and slammed it hard.

Kevin started after him.

"No, don't go after him." Win's voice cracked like a whip. "There's no sense both of you running around like headless chickens."

Kevin stopped. He ran one hand into his brown hair, then he turned to Win. "Why are you so upset about Cheyenne marrying your pa? He's pretty old, and it's a strange business having your friend married to your father, but you seem overly upset."

Win shrugged one shoulder. "Pa's a . . . difficult man."

"Difficult?" Kevin arched a brow at her and waited.

"He was best friends with Clovis."

Kevin winced.

"He was Clovis's only friend. My pa is a successful man but he's . . . he's n-not a . . . *normal* rancher, doesn't fit in well out here. He didn't build up a ranch like Cheyenne's family did. He came into the area with money and bought a big spread. Hired hands to run it, and he isn't very involved in it."

"Isn't involved?" Kevin tilted his head. "Is that another way of saying he doesn't do any of the work?"

"Yep, that's exactly what it means. He'd be the worst possible husband for Cheyenne. It'd be like she'd be marrying Clovis without his main problem."

"Clovis had a main problem?" Molly asked.

"Yes, and it was also the thing we all liked best about him." Kevin's brow furrowed.

"Clovis wandered off all the time. It was way better when he was gone. Pa stays right at home. Cheyenne will be signing on for a life of misery."

"Then why is she doing it?" Kevin asked.

"She's so upset she's not thinking clearly. I'm afraid she'll go through with the wedding before she calms down."

"We just have to find her and . . . and lock her up somewhere until she calms down." Molly crossed her arms, her jaw tight with determination. "Have they got a root cellar around here? That'd make a fine prison."

"Not so easy to do with a tough woman like Cheyenne," said Win.

"We can take her, can't we, Molly?" Andy looked eager to take on the fight.

Before his little brother and sister could start in kidnapping anyone, Kevin said, "We might not have to lock her up. If we can just talk to her, I'll tell her she can have Falcon's third of the ranch. Not sure about the will in the event of one of the owner's deaths, but Cheyenne could just take over quietly. With him gone, that sounds fair to me."

He gave Falcon's hat a glum look. "And with my few acres for farming taken out, Cheyenne can split a goodly chunk of my third with Wyatt. She'll come close to having her half back. Or maybe my acres can come out of Wyatt's half. It seems like, since he's the son of the man who helped create this mess, he's the one who oughta lose out a few acres."

"She might accept that." Win felt hope blaze through her. "I'll tell her all of that tomorrow. If I can find her. Molly, if she comes here, you and Andy do the same."

Kevin gave the hat a sad look, then hung it on a peg. "If we can't find her it might mean she's just taken off for a while to cool down. That'd be better than if she goes straight to your pa and tells him she wants to get married right away."

"Yes, she could live off the land forever," Win assured them. "Cheyenne is good in the woods."

"If there weren't killers roaming around," Molly said wryly.

They heard hoofbeats pounding out of the yard. Kevin looked in the direction Wyatt had gone. "Do I try and stop him?"

Win shrugged with both arms raised in the air, instantly regretting the pain.

"You probably couldn't even if you tried," Molly said.

"If they both run off," Andy said, looking around, "we might get this house to ourselves and not need to build a new one."

Nineteen

yatt came riding back in shortly after dawn. "I found her trail this morning. Followed it to the main road to town."

"She's not going to Pa's, then?" Win sat around the corner from Wyatt as Molly set breakfast on the table.

"She's going in the exact wrong direction. It heads toward Bear Claw Pass, but she could avoid town and ride into a heavy forest that rises all the way up the mountain. I can take the forest route, and Win, instead of riding to your place, you could go into town." He reached over and rested a hand on her wrist. "If you're able. How are you?"

"I'm moving mighty slow, but the stitches held overnight. Molly rebandaged them this morning, and there's been no more bleeding."

"What do you want Win to do in town, Wyatt?" Kevin began forking eggs into his mouth.

"I want her to see if Cheyenne stayed in the boardinghouse or anywhere else in town. It oughta be easy to find her in that little town." Wyatt rubbed his hands over his face as if he could wipe away exhaustion. Then he squared his shoulders and began shoveling eggs into his mouth.

"I'll go as soon as we're done with breakfast," Win said.

"I'll ride in with you," Kevin said. "With gunmen roaming around, I don't think you should be out alone." As if Kevin's being with her had helped yesterday.

Wyatt looked at Kevin. Their eyes locked. Kevin saw a union forming between them. Protect their family and friends.

Wyatt drank deep from his coffee, then finished up his eggs and bacon. He grabbed a biscuit, broke it open, and spread butter and a deep purple jelly on it. He ate it and a second one while he downed his coffee.

Then he rose from the table. Filled a canteen hanging by the back door and strode out of the house, leaving them all in a worried silence.

The rest of them finished eating, and Kevin watched Win stand slowly from her chair. He didn't like the idea of her riding anywhere today.

"You're sure you can do this?" He came around the side of the table and offered her an arm to lean on.

"I'll get my bonnet." She headed up the stairs.

"Should we come with you?" Andy asked. He looked eager to saddle up. The boy had asked earlier if he could go out and help with branding. Kevin didn't think that was wise.

"Someone needs to stay here in case Cheyenne comes back." Win came back into the room. "Someone needs to tell her she can have a good share of the ranch back."

Kevin nodded as he reached for his hat, hanging on a peg by the door. "Maybe she won't feel so bad if someone is here to tell her."

"If she does come back," Win added, "she'll go straight out to help with branding."

"I'm gonna ask if I can learn how to brand." Andy's eyes flashed with excitement.

Kevin was glad someone was having fun.

TWENTY

Kevin picked up the pace to a trot as they left the ranch yard.

"I'm not going to be riding with any speed, Kevin," Win called after him. Honestly, she was tempted to just let him go.

Her back was in agony. She'd done her very best to hide that from everyone, but trotting? For heaven's sake, it was out of the question.

Kevin pulled back, and she caught up to him.

He frowned. "I'm sorry. I shouldn't be making you come along." He sounded so concerned, so kind.

"I can get to town, but we won't be making good time. I need to move carefully, at least at first. See how I hold up."

Kevin studied her as if he got to make this decision.

"Kevin, you can decide what I am supposed to do all day long, but I'm not paying it any mind. I'm riding to Bear Claw Pass to find Cheyenne. If you find her and try to talk to her alone, it'll only make things worse."

"I know you're right about me talking to Cheyenne. But if you pass out in the saddle and fall off your horse, Cheyenne and Wyatt will have my head. And I wouldn't even put up one moment's fight about it."

They were heading mostly west to get to Bear Claw Pass. Facing forward, the land they rode through was like a hollow between rising land on the north and south. Here in the hollow, there was grass and rolling hills studded with cattle all around them, grazing quietly, the picture of a civilized country.

Kevin looked over his shoulder at the rugged land rising up to his right. "What mountains are those?"

Win didn't turn around because she knew it would hurt. She didn't need to look, she knew this land. "Casper Mountain. It's the northern end of the Laramie Mountains."

"Laramie like the fort?"

"Yes, and the town and the river."

"But not Wyatt's grandpa Jacques LaRemy."

A small grin touched Win's lips. "He was real proud of how deep his roots were sunk out here. I don't know as he could actually track down his connection to the man they named all the Laramies after, but he knew there had to be one, and I suppose there was."

Moving her hand gingerly, she pointed north. "On to the north are the Bighorn Mountains. I'm told up there it all looks like endless mountain peaks. If you get to the top of some of the highlands around here, you can see them. Plenty of trails heading west go through this gap between the Laramie range and the Bighorns."

"There are no mountains in Kansas." Kevin caught himself looking back for long stretches. "These are majestic beyond anything I've ever imagined."

"Yes, they look like a throne God built for himself right here on earth. They say there's a waterfall hidden in the mountains somewhere around here that few have seen. It's hidden in the rugged mountains rising up alongside a river with water pouring out of the stone. Cheyenne has never seen it, nor did her ma, but her pa and grandpa talked of it. They said it was a place of uncommon peace and beauty. A man could find that place and let every care in the world lift off his shoulders." Win smiled at the thought.

"Cheyenne's pa died before she was old enough to remember much about him," Win continued. "And her grandpa was getting older and found that exploring didn't suit him any longer. Her ma used to promise she'd take Cheyenne and Wyatt and ride over there someday and explore until they found those hidden falls." Win's shoulders lifted, and she breathed deep. "That place—those mountains, all of it—well, there may be things *as* beautiful, but nothing could ever best them."

"I've been here only a day. I've barely had time to talk to anyone out here or do much beyond dealing with whatever's come my way." Kevin paused, thinking of Falcon—found and lost in a single day. The bullet crease in Win's back. The sight of bullets blasting into the bedding where he and his brother and sister slept. "I sure hope and pray the worst is behind us. I want to—"

Win turned to face him when he quit talking. "You want to what?"

"I just wondered if the thing I almost *said* is the thing my pa *did*. I can feel a longing in me to just ride out into those mountains and look around, find those hidden falls, stay awhile, let all that beauty surround me."

"You're only like your pa if you leave a wife and child here, then never come back and marry another woman and have more children somewhere else, then do that again. That's a big difference from wandering in the mountains for a spell."

Nodding, Kevin said, "I reckon it is." After a bit, he added, "Do you suppose Pa married more women? You said he was gone from here."

"Probably not. He'd've listed them in the will if he had."

"Unless any other women never had a child. Maybe he wasn't interested in providing for a herd of *wives*."

"You make him sound like an old bull elk."

"I've heard most animals stay around the same area where they were born. They may have a *herd* like my pa did, but they stick with them and watch over them. That means your average bull elk is a more decent critter than my pa."

~

Thinking of the Sidewinder riding off and finding a new family made Win say out loud what was on her mind. When she'd rather not speak of it ever.

"We need to talk about something, Kevin." She might've dozed off a few times during the night, but the pain had mostly kept her awake, giving her plenty of time to think.

He quit looking over at the mountain peaks and rode closer, setting his pace to match hers. "About what?"

His eyes flashed with something warm, and she thought he knew what.

"We've had a couple of moments of . . . closeness."

Kevin watched her, intent on every expression on her face. He seemed to be looking for signs of pain and any meaning he could glean from her words.

When she didn't say more, stubbornly waiting for him to take part in this talk, he finally said, "Go on."

Not all that much help.

"And it's not going to happen again. I'm a single woman

of marrying age who happens to be the sole heiress to a vast Wyoming cattle ranch."

Kevin jerked back as if she'd slapped him.

Win was determined to finish before he started defending himself. "I've seen how that brings the men running. It happened to Cheyenne's ma, it has happened to Cheyenne, and it's happened to me."

"You think I—I am pretending an interest in you to get your ranch?"

Win didn't respond. She didn't know what to think.

"You did hear me tell Wyatt I wasn't going to claim but a few acres of the RHR, didn't you? And I suggested we give Falcon's third of the ranch to Cheyenne."

"I heard."

"Well, I've already got a ranch gained through thievery. If I'm the kind of low-down varmint who'd marry a woman to get her land, why wouldn't I just hold on to the land I already have?"

Why not indeed?

"I'm just telling you"—she reached across from her horse to his and clamped a hand on his wrist. Stretching hurt, but she wanted him to understand her point—"we don't know each other. We met yesterday for heaven's sake. You almost . . . we almost . . . well . . ." She cleared her throat to give herself time to think before she went on. "As I said, we shared a close . . . moment or two. Two strangers."

"I've been feeling like we're getting to know each other, Win." Kevin pulled his arm away, and she realized she was sinking her nails through his sleeve into his skin. He got loose and tilted his hat back to scratch his head, looking forward down the trail instead of at her. She missed his gaze.

"But you're right. My life is in an upheaval. I've got a family to think of. I'm too late this year to plant any crops, so I've got to figure out how to feed my family for the winter."

He turned toward her, and she saw the weight he took on his shoulders. He accepted it and didn't shirk. "But Win," he said, "you're the most likeable person I've met out here."

"Most everybody hates you. I don't have to be all that nice to be the most likeable," she teased.

"True. But here I am surrounded on all sides by people who hate the very thought of me. And yet for some reason you don't. Is that just because you're an uncommonly sensible, good-hearted woman? Or is there something more? You have to admit we're drawn to each other."

Win intended to admit absolutely nothing. Instead, she said, "How will you feed your family this winter?"

Kevin got a mulish look on his face as if he didn't want to change the subject. Then with a shake of his head, he said, "We have some cash. Not much but enough, I think. We sold everything we could, including Ma's homestead and mine. But they didn't bring much. I hope I can afford to buy food in town, plus hunting. How long does winter last up here so near the mountains?"

"Four solid months of mean, bitter cold, two more before and after of chilly weather. You go up in those mountains and it can snow on the fourth of July. And the snow comes in feet, not inches."

Kevin winced. "I've heard the winters are longer up here than they are in Kansas. And come spring, I'll need to buy a plow and seed, so I can't spend every penny I have. I don't need six horses though. We only had three back home. I bought three extras as packhorses for our trip out, so those can be sold. Maybe Wyatt will want them, otherwise I can see if there's interest in town.

I'm no rancher, or I'd ask Wyatt if he was hiring. But maybe there are folks in town who need help." He flashed a grin at her. "But I'd better not steal the schoolmarm job from you."

Horrified to think she might lose her job and end up living at home with her pa, she said, "You'd better not. You're a practical man, aren't you, Kevin?"

"I've had to be. I was a father almost before I was an adult man."

"You've got children?" She squeaked more than talked.

Kevin laughed. "No, good heavens, no. I had the raising of Molly and Andy. They were youngsters when Ma and Pa died. Molly helped a lot. She just had to. I couldn't manage alone. And Andy, he was five. Old enough to have some sense and help out, but for the most part, I was in charge. Managing everything for the family."

He scowled. "No, I don't have children I abandoned like my pa did. I know we just met. I reckon you can't begin to know what kind of man I am. But what my pa did, surely that's not a usual way for a man to act. And he was gone from my life almost from the first. I'm not like him."

"I'm sorry," Win said. "I didn't mean to imply that. You seem like a fine man, Kevin. I suppose your ma raised you hating the way Clovis ran off. Just like Katherine hated Clovis out here."

They walked along quietly for so long Win didn't think he'd have a response to that. And maybe that was all right. Maybe it was time to quit talking and concentrate on how much she hurt.

"Ma raised me to almost revere my pa." Kevin sounded young and confused, even though he was a full-grown man. "Clovis, that is. She'd take me with her out to visit his grave—"

He quit talking for a second. "That is, the memorial stone we put up because we thought he was dead—and she talked of him as this great explorer. A mountain man, a pathfinder. Wh-when I saw Falcon stepping off that train . . . Pa left when I was mighty young. I have few memories of him and even those . . . Ma had a picture of the two of them together. She wasn't overly fond of her second husband, Molly and Andy's pa, and she tended to speak to me of my pa like he'd been the great love of her life."

"What were you saying about Falcon getting off the train?"

"Except for that one photograph, I'd've thought I didn't remember Pa much at all. But when I saw Falcon, it was like seeing Pa again. Everything about him was the same as Pa—the deep voice, the drawl, the height, the overlong hair. No, my ma never talked bad about Pa. She said he was a charmer. Could talk the bees into giving up their honey."

He looked over at Win and smiled. "Not much like Falcon after all."

They were silent again for a while thinking about Falcon. A man who'd come and gone from their lives as quick as a candle being lit, then snuffed out.

"Nope, Falcon wasn't like Clovis, and I liked him better for it." Not that Win really liked him, but more than Clovis.

"Clovis Hunt didn't just ride off for good from this place, not like he did to you and Falcon," Win said. "He'd go, then he'd come wandering through. He'd stay awhile, then he'd go again. Jacques hated him, and Katherine would show him no wifely attentions—she made that very clear. Still, he'd come, sit up to the table, warm his feet by the fire, then he'd get itchy. . . ."

"Or get run off?" Kevin asked.

"It's true Jacques had no use for him and made it difficult for him to stay around. But he'd've gone off regardless. He was here enough that he was well-known to me. Your ma said it right, when she said he was a charmer with a fine way about him. But if he stayed around long at all, you could see he expected to get everything given to him by using that charm. Katherine and everyone else on the RHR were well and truly tired to death of him. I have no mistaken illusions about him. And I've seen none of his behavior in you."

"I don't know my own pa well enough to see what I do that's like or unlike him."

"Can I . . . ask you a question?"

Kevin got a wary look in his eyes, probably from her hesitant tone. "I reckon getting to know each other is a sensible idea."

"Yesterday, when I asked Molly how she learned to handle an injured person so well, she said she set stitches on your ma, and the way she said it upset Andy. He didn't remember your ma needing stitches or being otherwise injured. Andy thought Molly had learned doctoring from trouble during the war. And I could tell Molly had spoken without thinking and regretted it. What happened to your ma?"

Kevin's jaw tightened, and he turned to look straight forward. He tugged the front of his broadbrimmed hat low over his eyes as if the sun were shining right into them, except they were riding west in the morning sun.

Win suspected he didn't want her to see his face.

His reaction reminded her a lot of Molly's. "Was your ma hurt in all that went on in Kansas before the war?"

Silence was his only response, and in a way, that *was* an answer. Why wouldn't he just say yes if that was it? "So she was hurt some other way? Some way you find . . . hard to talk about?"

Win wanted to know. "I've been shot. Now I'm riding to town with the man who probably got me shot. It seems to me . . . you owe me some honesty."

He whirled his head to glare at her. Then the glare melted away to regret. "I think it's probably right that whoever was shooting wanted me dead, and you got in the way. I'm sorry for that."

"It's none of your doing."

"No." He tugged on his hat brim again. "No, it's not. But you got crosswise of someone who's gunning for me."

He looked left and right, then behind them. This trail was wide, grass stretched on both sides of them.

"We're safe enough on this trail to town." But Win glanced around too.

"Probably. We're even out of rifle range. And so far, they seem to come at us from cover with pistols. That night by our campfire they unloaded pistols, and that was a six-gun firing yesterday."

More quietly, Kevin said, "I almost got you killed, and I did get Falcon killed. He got pulled into yesterday's trouble because of me."

"Is there any chance you're wrong about him? You didn't find a body after all."

"What Wyatt said about that river . . . He had no chance." Kevin reached out and rested his hand on the neck of the brown gelding he'd been riding when he came into the area.

Win saw the horse toss its head a bit, in a gentle way that said it knew its master and liked him.

"I wanted to go after him. Wyatt did too." Kevin looked away from the horse to meet her eyes. Those strange hazel eyes were the image of Clovis Hunt's. The image of Wyatt's eyes. And

Falcon's. The one thing that, to Win, proved more than anything else these men were truly brothers.

"It's strange to grieve for a person I didn't know. I feel like we're doing wrong by Falcon not to have a funeral." He gave his chin a firm jerk. "When things calm down around here, I'm going to set a headstone in the family cemetery. It's right he be remembered someplace on this earth."

"I'm sure once things calm down, once you get settled here and Cheyenne isn't in such a fury, and you figure out where you're going to live and what land will be yours, and people quit trying to kill you, there'll be time for a memorial service and a marker."

"That sounds like a long time."

"About your ma, Kevin. You didn't—" Win quit talking when she saw a buggy rolling toward the trail from the north, pulled by a slightly swaybacked mare. The man driving was wearing a black suit, not usual Western clothing.

"That's Parson Brownley," Win said. "He's probably been out to visit some of his flock. He wasn't here when I was sent away to school, but I'm told he's been a good parson to this area for a long time. I mentioned yesterday that I live with his family when school is in session. I'll introduce you."

They were a bit behind where the parson had converged on the trail, but he saw them, waved, and pulled his single horse to a halt to wait for them.

Win said, "I'd as soon he not know I've been shot. He's so kindhearted he'll be very upset and his wife along with him. It's possible he'll speak of it, then the whole town will know. And then my pa will know. And he might make me move home."

"If Cheyenne marries him, you'll probably want to move

home anyway. She'll need a friend when she tangles herself up in a marriage you seem overly opposed to."

"I can't move home."

"You may not have a choice."

Win was silent for so long Kevin probably thought she was finished with the topic. At last she said, "Until Cheyenne makes that decision—and I'm sure I can talk her out of it given a chance—I'd as soon Pa didn't know there was a lot of gunplay at the RHR."

"Neither the parson nor your pa, no one for that matter, will hear it from me." Kevin eased his hat back farther on his head. A friendlier expression settled on his face. In fact, it was so friendly it struck a false note. It reminded Win again that this was a man who'd faced plenty of trouble in his life. A war fought almost over his head. Neighbor against neighbor. Never knowing who to trust. And Kevin had survived it. Probably not without a fair amount of sneaking and lying. There was a good chance he could make anyone believe anything he wanted. She had to wonder if that included her.

When they reached the parson, the kindly man greeted them, then started up his horse so he could ride alongside them. As the group continued on, Win remembered that Kevin never told her about his ma and Molly's doctoring. He'd made it plain he didn't want to talk about it, and he'd done a skillful job of changing the subject by speaking of whoever had shot at him twice and hit her.

Kevin struck her as a smart man. A wily man. Those were two different things. And he probably didn't say much he didn't want to. The only way to really get to know him was to get past the barriers he'd built up tall as a fortress around himself. His family on the inside of those walls, and the rest of the world on the outside.

Considering he'd come mighty close to kissing her, and considering she was hoping he'd come a lot closer, she needed to set out to get to know him a lot better. And whatever he was hiding about his ma was the key to him. She knew it at the same time she admitted to herself that she didn't know anything.

TWENTY-ONE

*C*heyenne wasn't in town.

It had been a wasted ride, and one that was too much for Win.

Kevin had taken a little time to stop at the land office and study the property lines for the RHR. He wanted to ride around and find a place he could have on the border. It'd make it easier to expand from his land and eventually give back to Cheyenne what had been taken from her.

A piece of paper with a quickly drawn map of the ranch was tucked in his pocket. He should have gone to the sheriff to tell him what had been going on, but Win was past the limit of her strength. She never should have made this ride.

Kevin had kept a nervous eye on her, ready to catch her if she started to topple, but she was a tough Western woman, being educated back east notwithstanding. She held up . . . barely.

As Kevin rode his horse up to the hitching post at the kitchen door of the ranch house, he saw the last of the color drain from Win's face.

He swung down fast and rushed to her side to help her down before she fell off her horse. "Let me walk you in."

"I can make it on my own, Kevin. You go on and tend the horses."

He slid his arm along her back, careful to stay low, far from her stitches. She didn't protest further and leaned heavily on him. He had gotten her inside, determined to get her straight up to bed—carrying her if he had to—when Molly came into the kitchen. She took one look at Win and shouted, "Andy, get in here!"

Win jumped, and Kevin felt her knees wobble, but she steadied herself.

"You go on, Kev." Molly rushed to Win's opposite side. "I can see you left the horses at the hitching post. Andy and I are going to make sure Win rests awhile."

"No, she needs to lie down, and I want to make sure she gets up the steps."

"Keeeviiin, I'm—I'm fine." The faint, high-pitched tone to her voice was nothing like her usual sass.

"Wiiiin." He matched her whiny protest and kept moving. He'd get her to her room while she fussed for him to stop. "I'm coming up with you."

He had her halfway up the stairs when her knees buckled. He caught her in his arms. She gasped with pain. He wasn't touching her stitches, but with one arm behind her back and the other under her knees, he knew it was hurting her badly enough. He rushed up the stairs, moving as fast as he could without shaking her up too much. He just wanted to quit hurting her, and the only way he could do it was to put her down. And he had to get to her room to do that.

"Which room is yours?"

Win pointed to a door at the end of the hall on the left. "I stay there when school is out of session, it used to be Katherine's room. Cheyenne is next to me."

172

Kevin glanced at the closed door as they passed it. He wondered where Cheyenne had gotten to.

"Wyatt was always across the hall from Cheyenne, and Molly is staying in the empty room where Jacques used to sleep. That was where Clovis stayed after Jacques died."

"Bet it made you sick to see him in there."

"I wasn't here much. I work and live in town mostly. But I know Cheyenne and Wyatt just gritted their teeth and put up with it."

Kevin paused at her bedroom door. Looking down at Win, he said, "I'm sorry this hurts you. I'm sorry so much has hurt you that has to do with me."

She lifted one hand up and touched a pretty, feminine finger to his chin. "You've got a dimple here."

"It's a nuisance to shave, but I don't spend much time looking in a mirror."

That coaxed a smile from her. "I like it."

He felt himself flush and was glad Molly was behind him so she couldn't see. He reached Win's room. "Can you get the door?"

She was already twisting the knob. He entered a pretty room. Large by his standards back in Kansas. Molly had slept in the single bedroom, and he and Andy had slept on cots in the only other room, where they also cooked, ate, and rocked in front of the fire.

Win's room had windows on two walls, one facing east and the other south. The bed had a quilt in shades of blue. Kevin's ma had made what she called a crazy quilt out of scraps of whatever clothes had worn out. But this was a pattern, with cloth obviously purchased deliberately to make it match the colors in here. There was a chest of drawers to his left, on the wall dividing this room from Cheyenne's. On top of the chest was a lace doily underneath a blue-and-white flowered china basin holding a matching pitcher.

Win had a bedside table with a lantern on it. The oversized glass globe on the lantern was white and had flowers on it to match the colors of the basin, pitcher, and quilt.

Beside the lantern, there was a heavy black Bible with a neatly placed bookmark.

On the far side of the bed was a row of hooks that held several dresses, a nightgown, and a few other things.

He walked across a braided blue rug and wondered how anyone had time to fix a room up to be so pretty.

"It's nice in here." He stood her up, letting go slowly to make sure she stayed up.

Then Molly was at his side. "You can go on now, Kevin. I need to check her bandage. I hope she'll rest in bed for a while afterward." Molly gave Win a pleading look. "Won't you?"

Win nodded as if it took every ounce of her strength to move her head. She looked at Kevin. "Thank you for your help. I needed it. I'm glad you insisted on it."

"You're welcome." Kevin tugged on the brim of his hat— that's when he noticed he still wore it. A man normally took off his hat inside, but his hands had been full.

"Rest, Win. This morning was a long ride. I thank you for coming along." Kevin turned to leave, and Molly closed the door behind him.

He joined Andy downstairs, and barely a moment later, Wyatt came rushing in, waving something.

"I found—"

"Hush." Kevin cut him off with a slash of his hand and said under his breath, "Molly's trying to get Win settled into bed.

She's almost asleep on her feet after the ride to Bear Claw Pass this morning. I never should have let her come."

"Well then, why did you?" Wyatt sounded disgusted—conveniently forgetting it was his idea—but he kept his voice low.

Kevin rolled his eyes. "As if you've had any luck getting a woman to do as you say. That's why we're all tearing around searching for your sister."

Wyatt gave his head a sideways tilt as if to concede the point. Then he held up the paper. It had a hole in the middle of it. Looked like the paper had been stabbed.

Wyatt,
    Leave me alone. I'll come back when I'm ready.

Cheyenne

Kevin felt a scowl on his face to match Wyatt's. "What direction was she going?"

"I found plenty of signs to the north."

"She's not headed to Win's pa?"

"No, I tracked her long enough to be sure of that. She's heading into rough country. I decided to just let her have her way. I'd probably have to hog-tie her to get her back here. Then keep her hog-tied, or she'd just run off again." Wyatt tucked the note into the front pocket of his shirt. "One good thing—"

"There is not a single good thing in this mess." Kevin thought of Win's back and absolutely believed what he'd said.

"— is she wrote this note on a sheet of paper." Wyatt ignored Kevin's interruption. "She had to take the paper along. She even used a knife from the kitchen to stab the note into a tree. I brought the knife back with me as I'm sure she meant me to. She knew when she left here that she was heading into the high up country—not for Win's pa. She'll come back when she calms down."

"Since she's cranky as a rabid badger, I'd say she won't be back for a spell."

Wyatt shrugged one shoulder.

"I wish I'd had a chance to tell her she can have most of the land she had coming."

"You did tell her once. She called it charity and threw your offer back in your face."

"I should have told her harder. And if I have another chance, I will."

"And now," Wyatt said quietly, "she can have Falcon's land."

Wyatt and Kevin were silent as they thought of Falcon.

Andy didn't pay the solemn moment much mind. "Can you teach me to brand a calf, Wyatt? I want to be a cowpoke."

Kevin almost smiled. It was the most normal thing anyone had said for a while. He expected Wyatt to refuse. He hoped Wyatt was at least a little bit kind when he shoved the kid's dreams back in his face.

"Sure, you can come along."

That surprised Kevin, but Wyatt didn't act like he begrudged Andy the wish. And he didn't act like he was dismissing the idea at all.

"I was roping and branding by your age. You'll catch on fast, and there's plenty to do with Cheyenne gone. She's next thing to ramrod around here."

Once again, Kevin wondered what a ramrod was.

"Kevin, I'd teach you, too, but I think someone needs to stay around the place until we find whoever is after you."

"Do you think Cheyenne is safe out there alone?" asked Kevin.

"Probably. Especially since she's nowhere near you."

Kevin gritted his teeth but didn't respond to that unfortunately true statement.

"She has her horse, and her saddlebags are gone along with her pistols and rifle and one of the gun belts full of bullets. With that rifle, she can feed herself forever if she wants. And she knows a hundred hidey-holes out in the mountains."

"She might be the smartest of us all, not staying close around here," Kevin said.

"The trouble sure does seem to be close at hand," Wyatt agreed.

"You're sure she'll keep an eye out for trouble? She'll hide if she can or fight if she has to?"

"Not sure about the hiding part. She's been looking for a fight since the day we read that will. But, yep, she's good out there. Wary as a doe in full flight and mean as a grizzly with a sore paw. She'll take care." Wyatt swung the door wide. "Let's go, Andy. Kevin, stay in here and watch over Win and Molly. There's chickens with eggs to gather and cows to milk and other chores that, if you can do them, will make it easier on everyone when we quit for the night."

Andy rushed out the door, and Wyatt went right behind him, quietly closing the door.

Kevin might've gotten the very important job of guarding the womenfolk, but somehow he felt like he'd been left to putter around the house while the men went to work. Maybe he could stitch up a quilt.

TWENTY-TWO

*F*or the first time in six days, when Win woke up in the morning, her back didn't hurt like she was wearing a Sioux tomahawk in her shoulder. It was more like she'd been slammed with a sledgehammer, but she noticed the improvement.

Her eyes fluttered open to see Molly coming in with the pretty blue-and-white pitcher, most assuredly filled with hot water, since steam rose and curled from it.

"I think I'm ready to get up today and go downstairs."

"You've said that every day since you got back from town."

"This time I mean it."

Molly lifted the pitcher and poured a stream of water into the china basin.

"Today I'm inclined to believe you. I'm about ready to take those stitches out. I'll leave them two more days to be sure, but they looked well healed last night, and what redness and swelling there was is gone."

"Can I use that water to wash up, instead of you just using it to bathe my wound?"

"Let me check you over first. Then yes, you can get up, wash, dress, and come down to eat if you've got the gumption. You do as much or as little as you feel up to."

Win swung her legs slowly over the edge of the bed, shoved herself into a sitting position, and almost toppled face-first off the bed. But she was ready for that and held herself upright.

She didn't leap right to her feet. She'd learned that from sitting up for a spell every day. Buzzing rose in her ears, then slowly faded. She let her head finish the odd spinning thing her brain seemed to be doing and waited for her vision to clear.

"Has there been any more trouble?"

Molly gave one shoulder a little shrug, and one corner of her mouth curled up in an expression more dismayed than amused.

"Not unless you count Andy setting Mr. Walsh on fire."

Wincing, Win guessed the RHR foreman gave Andy a wide berth after that. She wondered how Andy was doing learning to rope and brand a calf. She'd heard Molly's exasperated version of new mayhem most every day.

"Did you go out and watch?"

"No, Kevin and I are more or less prisoners here. We don't feel right leaving you alone at such a dangerous time."

"And there's been no word from Cheyenne?"

"Still nothing. Wyatt rode over to your pa's house on a pretext, and while he was there, he snooped around, checking for her. But she seems to be serious about having time alone."

Cheyenne had always been better in the woods than Wyatt—though he was very good. And they were both far better than Win, who could at least follow an animal's tracks under normal circumstances. If Cheyenne wanted to vanish, few could find her. And if Wyatt was giving her the time she asked for, then he wasn't even trying to find her anyway.

A bit weakly, not even really wanting to hear, Win asked, "He really set Rubin on fire?"

"There was trouble with a branding iron and a kicking calf. No flames actually shot up. But his pants were smoldering, and by all reports he was required to jump out of them really fast. It was the first time anyone out there was glad Cheyenne was gone. His hair is singed, too, and that nice big moustache he wore is gone."

Win let her head drop, partly to hide a smile. She knew the hands here at the RHR quite well, and she knew Rubin Walsh loved his moustache more than he loved most people.

"Is he injured? Was he badly burned?"

"Nope. Needs new pants though. I'm planning to sew him a pair when I get a chance to do handwork."

Win heard the door to the kitchen open downstairs.

"That'll be Kevin bringing in milk or eggs or water or firewood or something else. He's been running things outside while I do it inside," Molly explained. "We do most things together, but I've got a few skills he doesn't. Sewing a pair of pants is one of them. I should make him learn, but I don't have the patience."

Win had been confined to this room and was shocked at how easy it was to do nothing. She still couldn't believe she could now say the words *I've been shot*. The very thought made her dizzy.

Between being shot and that ride to town, she'd been wrung out like an old dishrag. She'd spent the last five days sleeping, healing, and sitting.

But she *had* been sitting. Molly had moved the bedside table to the window and brought up a chair. Win had been sitting in that chair to eat and for a stretch each day.

From the window, she'd seen Kevin working around the ranch, tending horses, chickens, the milk cows. Wyatt even had

a few pigs. He bought piglets every year to raise up his own
side pork and hams.

Kevin tended them all. He weeded the garden, watered it,
and harvested whatever was ripe. He seemed content, happy
in his work. Steady.

She hadn't had much *steady* in her life.

Win felt ready to get out of the room. Like every day, she was
careful. She reached for the wooden post on the headboard to rise.

"Don't get up yet," Molly said. "Let me put a clean bandage
on first. Are you up to getting dressed?"

"I've been in this nightgown day and night for five days. Putting on clothes sounds like all the excitement I can stand, but
yes, I want to get dressed."

~

"You're up." Kevin stood at the kitchen table peeling potatoes with a paring knife. His brows slammed down, and he
glared at Molly. "You should have come for me so I could help
you get down here safely."

Win walked over to the table straight across from Kevin and
sank into the chair. She didn't even flip it around backward,
though she didn't lean back, either. "I'll try and remember to
obey your every order—including reading your mind and obeying orders you haven't given—from this moment on."

He didn't see how sarcasm was called for. "I shouldn't have
to give you orders that involve common sense. You could have
fallen."

"And yet somehow I survived."

"We were real careful, Kev." Molly hurried toward the kitchen
cookstove. "She was on her feet for a good bit of time before we
got brave on the stairs."

Kevin didn't like it, but Win was down here, alive. She'd managed fine, and Molly knew what she was about with doctoring, so Kevin held back the lecture that he burned to give them both.

"I got a plate ready for her." He went back to paring potatoes. He didn't need many. There were only the three of them for the noon meal. The cowboys, including Wyatt and Andy, ate food cooked at the campfire they used to heat the branding iron.

"Thanks, Kev." Molly smiled over her shoulder at Win. "He's got eggs, some fried potatoes, and a slice of ham warming on the back of the stove. I asked him to get it ready while I changed your bandage, so it's real fresh."

"That sounds wonderful. Thank you."

Molly hurried to get it while Kevin continued peeling.

"How are things going outside my room?"

Kevin smiled at her. "You have been shut away awhile, haven't you?"

Molly had taken food up, of course, and tended her wound. But Win had been like a ghost haunting the upstairs. Kevin hadn't been allowed back in her room. It wasn't proper, and he knew that. Carrying her in there couldn't've been avoided, but after that one visit, he'd been banished.

He missed her.

"I have indeed. Molly has kept me up to date with Andy's adventures."

"Enough to turn the hair gray on every person on this ranch. Molly's lucky to have light hair, and you're lucky not to have to witness any of it. Though I reckon I haven't, either. Haven't budged from the ranch yard." Kevin paused to yank on his short curls. "Even so, just from the hearing of it, I've got dozens of strands of white—maybe hundreds."

Smiling, Win said, "The stories are harrowing enough without me seeing a thing."

Molly set the plate of food in front of Win, and Kevin fetched a pot of water to boil the potatoes while he said, "Wyatt thinks they have one maybe two days left of branding. He said he's got men combing the hills for maverick calves, and those will be the last. Things will settle down then."

"Not for long. In a couple of weeks, they'll be sorting the three-year-old steers out and culling the older cows. Then they'll be on a cattle drive."

"Wyatt told me he'd planned to head for Denver this year to get a top price, but he's leery of riding off at such an unsettled time."

"He usually drives them to Laramie. They get buyers in there, but he's right that the market is stronger in Denver. No chance of leaving for Denver with Cheyenne missing and a gunman roaming the range."

"Maybe things will get cleared up, and she'll be back before it's time to head out with the herd."

"There's been no more trouble?"

"None. I'm the one they seem to be after. I'm careful about going around the ranch yard. I haven't heard nor seen any sign of danger, but I'll be glad when there are more men around the place. Right now, I wouldn't want either of you going outside."

"When are you going to build a house?"

"I don't know when, I only know, not yet. I need to do some scouting first. I haven't talked much about it with Wyatt. I've told him I don't like being so close to that dangerously fast creek, and he agrees after what happened to Falcon."

Kevin thought grimly that the creek wasn't at the root of Falcon's disappearance. "I'm going to ride the edges of the property and try to find land I can work that won't take a big chunk right out of the middle of the ranch."

"Oh, that's right, I remember you getting the map in town."

"Yep, we talked about it some, but you weren't feeling well, so I didn't go over—"

The front door slammed open. "Winona?" Her name was a roar. "Winona, are you all right?"

"Pa's here." Win's eyes met Kevin's for just a moment, then she closed them.

Kevin thought she looked as if the pain in her back had just shifted higher. She now had a pain in the neck.

Footsteps thundered nearby. "Winona?"

"In the kitchen, Pa." She called out loud enough to be heard over his headlong rush.

"He must've heard you were shot." Kevin spoke quietly. "You can't blame him for worrying."

Win's eyes narrowed as if to declare Kevin dead wrong.

Oliver Hawkins barreled in. He came at Win from behind, his arms flung wide.

"No, stop." Kevin's knife and a potato clattered to the table. He rushed around and rammed into Hawkins hard enough to stop him from grabbing at Win.

"Her back is still sore. You have to be careful where you touch her."

"But I'm all right, Pa." Win turned slowly. Stood carefully. She stepped to her father and gave him a solid hug, trying to prove she was all right.

Kevin firmly removed her from her father's arms. And her pa must've been shocked enough by Kevin running into him that he was careful not to hang on too tight.

"She needs to eat, Mr. Hawkins. Come and sit down. You'll

see for yourself she's fine. But don't touch her. Be gentle. Other than that, she's fine." Kevin hoped old Oliver here didn't notice those two things didn't match.

"Why did I have to hear about this in town?" Hawkins sat at the head of the table, around the corner from Win. "Someone in town heard it from a cowhand on the Rolling Hills. Why didn't you tell me?"

"I didn't want to worry you over such a trifle." A calm wave of her hand seemed to brush aside all her pa's fears. "I'm sure the story got blown all out of proportion. A stray shot. I got scratched by it. A frightening experience, and I needed a couple of stitches."

Kevin figured about thirty. But not a straight-out lie—much. He didn't correct her. He remembered how firmly she refused to let anyone go for her pa when she'd been shot.

"I'm taking it easy, and Molly did a lot of nursing back in Kansas, so she set the stitches and said she'll be taking them out soon."

More reassurance. And not exactly a lie.

Hawkins fretted and fussed at her. Win went back to her breakfast. Kevin got the man coffee. Molly gave him a serving of apple cobbler, and then they all settled at the table.

Hawkins let himself be calmed by Win and distracted by the dessert and coffee. By the time Win had eaten her breakfast, the man had finished with his dessert and set his fork down on the table with a firm click.

"You have to move home, Winona. We've discussed this before, and I've allowed you to have your way. But I've wanted you back home since you came out here. You have no need to work as a schoolmarm or as a cook and housekeeper over here on school breaks."

Win appeared calm, sipping her coffee and murmuring words meant to reassure her pa—when she could slip them in between Hawkins's pronouncements about what she must do.

Kevin remembered the first day he'd gotten here and met Oliver Hawkins. He had gotten the sense that Win endured him. Kevin sure as certain didn't know what that meant, but his impression today was deeper.

Love beareth all things.

The Bible verse about love popped into Kevin's thoughts.

Was this the kind of love a daughter had for a father she'd been separated from for most of her life? Was Win so deeply hurt by being sent away that now she could only just bear to be near him?

He knew whatever complicated relationship Win had with her father, her polite calm was deceptive. Kevin saw the grip she had on her china cup. Her knuckles were near white.

Kevin didn't know why she couldn't bear to live at her father's house, he only knew she couldn't. Which is why words came pouring out of his mouth, cutting Hawkins off. "She can't go yet, Mr. Hawkins."

"Call me Oliver, Kevin. We're neighbors and friends now."

Kevin didn't make friends all that easy. A hard-learned lesson. But he didn't discuss the state of his friendship, or the lack thereof, with Hawkins.

"Oliver, the ride home would be tiring for her. It might even open that wound up again." Kevin winced internally.

She's fine. Her wound might open. Her wound's almost healed. She can't ride.

"It's only a few more days until she gets the stitches out," Kevin said. "And there's been no sign of danger here around the ranch yard. In fact, it's possible that was a hunter's bullet.

A stray shot. I'm sure she's safe. If you think it's best she comes home, you'd be well advised to wait until her stitches come out."

He hoped Hawkins hadn't heard about Win riding to town the day after she'd been shot. Of course, that'd been stupid. And she'd've never done it if she wasn't half-crazed worrying about Cheyenne. Worse, she was worried about Cheyenne ending up married to Oliver Hawkins.

That struck a deep chord in Kevin because marrying poorly was a mistake his ma had made twice.

Hawkins frowned at his daughter in a way that was almost as phony as Win's calm. Kevin kept quiet. It felt like Hawkins was teetering about his decision, and Kevin was afraid the smallest word would bump things the wrong way.

A tiny nod, a furrowed brow, little signs of concern from a loving father. Kevin watched Win closely and realized she was holding her breath.

"I'm sure it's only good sense to stay until you're healed." Hawkins folded his arms and scowled at his daughter. "When you're up to it though, I want you home. I'm not agreeable to you being the town schoolmarm anymore, Winona. You're my daughter, and your place is with me, out at our ranch. I'll ride to town before I head home and tell the school board you're done working. When you're up and about, you're coming home and that's final."

He rose from the table. Win matched the move, maybe to appear strong. Hawkins touched her cheek with a gentle kiss, resting his hands on her shoulders. Her smile was frozen until it might've been carved from a block of ice.

Kevin found himself standing, too. Molly got to her feet next. Kevin rounded the table to be closer to Win.

Hawkins straightened and looked around the room. "Thank you all for taking care of my Winona."

His eyes went to Molly in a way that reminded Kevin that Oliver Hawkins had proposed to Cheyenne in secret. No one even knew about it until she'd announced she was accepting his proposal. What kind of strange courtship was done in secret?

And why was a man who'd proposed to one woman looking at another one in a way that struck Kevin as overly familiar. Both of them too young for him.

Kevin felt his hands fist, but kept them at his side.

For now.

"I'd better get on. The branding is all but done. Still, I need to be on hand." He kissed Win again, then turned and left almost as quickly as he'd come in. When the front door clicked shut, Kevin turned to study Win's face.

"Sit down before you fall down." He spoke softly. The words weren't just for her, though he wished they were, but Molly was close enough to hear them, too, so he couldn't say half of what he wanted to.

Win sank down so suddenly that Kevin had to move quickly to get the chair under her backside. She might've kept sinking all the way to the floor otherwise.

"It seems there's considerable trouble between you and your pa," Kevin stated.

With a prim move that shouted finishing school, Win pushed her plate away and set her coffee cup to the side, and only when everything was tidy did she fold her arms on the table and bury her face on them.

Speaking directly into the table, she said, "Trouble is a fair way to describe it."

Molly removed the mostly eaten breakfast plate.

Kevin leaned down over her left shoulder. "What can I do to help?"

"What can *we* do to help," Molly corrected.

Win lifted her head as if it weighed fifty pounds and stared straight forward. Kevin wanted to rush around the table so she'd be staring at him and he could glean information from her expression, because she wasn't telling them much.

"I can't go home. I *won't* go home." She slammed a closed fist on the table. Her words sounded like an oath sworn straight to God.

"Can you tell us why?" Kevin did move then. He needed to see her face.

"I won't go home. If I have to do something desperate, then I'll do it. Get on a stagecoach heading for San Francisco. Go find a fort that needs a cook. Something, anything."

And Kevin saw it. The resolve in her blue eyes. They blazed until he felt like he was looking straight into a lightning bolt.

"Can you leave me in here for a time? I need to pray."

"Molly and I can find a quiet place and pray for you. Call us back in when you need us." Kevin leaned across the table and touched Win on the cheek. She stopped looking through him and focused those bright eyes on his.

"And we will help you, Win. There's no need to run. No need for some desperate act. You're an adult woman who supports herself. Your pa can't make you do anything." Kevin knew the power a man had over a woman. A wife, a daughter. His bold words probably weren't true. "Wherever God leads you in your prayers, we'll stand by you."

"Thank you, Kevin. I'll pray, and then I may ask for help."

TWENTY-THREE

*Y*ou want me to what?" Kevin stumbled backward and slammed into a wall.

Probably a good thing, Win decided, or he might've fallen all the way to the floor.

"Shhh—"

Kevin's nerves had seemed steadier than this.

Steady. Hadn't that been the word she'd come up with while she'd watched him out her window this last week?

Now he had a look of horror on his face, and he was having trouble staying upright, as unsteady as any man she'd ever seen, the big idiot.

Her cheeks burned with embarrassment. The heaviness in her heart echoed as if she stood shouting on the edge of a cliff, only to have her worst fears repeated back at her. Suddenly cooking at a fort didn't sound so bad. "Don't talk so loud. I don't want Molly to hear."

Molly had gone upstairs when Win had asked Kevin if she could speak to him alone. But she wasn't that far off. "I'm sorry I asked. I can see it was a foolish idea. You said you'd help, but now I know you only meant if it was easy."

Her quiet voice snapped with anger but that wasn't fair. That must not have been God's still small voice speaking during her prayers. Instead, this notion had sprung from pure reckless desperation.

"It's just that, while I was praying this—this—*solution* to my problem jumped into my head. But you're right, of course. That isn't possible." Win turned to march out of the room.

Kevin's hand closed over her upper arm and whirled her right back around to face him. "You're not going anywhere."

She felt the sting of unshed tears. How could she have—

"You're coming with me and telling me what this is about." He dragged her out of the kitchen, down the outside steps. After looking all around, as he had been all week, he must have decided they were safe because he kept moving into the yard.

It was nearing sunset. Wyatt should be back in the next hour or so. He always came in nearly staggering with exhaustion and hunger. He was filthy, but he seemed to want to put off bathing until the branding was over. He shoveled food down, spoke in single syllable words, stumbled up to bed, and collapsed until he woke up before dawn and did it all again.

Win would ask him to ride with her into town. She could stay in the boardinghouse until the stagecoach came through. She couldn't wait for the train. She had money in the bank. Plenty to get a ticket and ride off down the trail.

Next to Cheyenne, Wyatt was Win's oldest friend. He'd ride with her to town if she asked—definitely if she begged. She hoped she didn't have to threaten, but she would, if she had to, to get out of here.

She didn't quite have the nerve to ride off alone.

Kevin towed Win along like he was leading a horse. A stubborn one. Win wanted to dig in her heels and refuse to accompany him. She wanted to go to her room and lie down with the covers over her head and pretend she had never asked. Then Wyatt would come, and she'd pack a few things and ride to town. First thing in the morning, she'd get her money, buy a ticket on the next stagecoach, and ride it to wherever it went.

And then she'd find a fort that needed a cook or a laundress. Oh, what did it matter? Maybe they'd let her enlist in the cavalry. She was in the mood to shoot someone.

Kevin dragged her up some steps and only then did she even notice where he was taking her. Before she could protest, he had her inside the ramrod's house, where he and Andy had been sleeping.

It certainly wasn't proper for her to be alone with him in here. But that seemed like a minor problem all things considered.

Kevin turned her to face him. "What is going on with your father that you would even think of something so—so—"

"There really are no words to describe it, are there?"

Silence stretched between them. He gave her a gentle shake. "Tell me."

"No. Maybe if you'd gone along with my idea, maybe then. But otherwise, no. It's a reason that belongs to no one but me. A s-secret that I won't—can't—share."

"But it's a secret that explains why you're next thing to living over here? You've never told Wyatt this secret?"

"No." She shook her head hard. Such a thing was impossible.

"Nor Cheyenne? Your lifelong best friend?"

"No."

"Your best friend who's announced she's marrying your pa and will go live in the house you can't bear to live in?"

And that made her sound like the worst kind of evil coward. "I would tell her before I'd stand by and see her married

193

to my father. You have to remember, when she told us Pa had proposed, that was the first I'd ever heard of it. Then she ran off, and I haven't had a chance to speak to her since. Yes, of course I'd tell her. I'd stop the wedding."

One corner of Kevin's mouth turned up as he watched her. Win had never had anyone watch her this closely, and Kevin had done it before. It was odd to have a man so focused on her.

"I respect that the idea came to you during prayer time." Kevin let go of her arms and put one hand over his mouth, rubbing as if he were trying to keep words inside.

Maybe he was praying right now, just as she had earlier. And that sparked a bit of common sense, and she started praying, too.

~

Kevin quit rubbing his mouth and ran both hands into his hair, then held his skull to keep his mind from exploding.

He tried to see beyond the stubborn refusal to share a secret. The fear. The embarrassment that had turned her face pink all the way to the roots of her hair. Why had she said such a thing?

But then, he'd known she didn't want to go home. The *why* didn't change the fact that she didn't want to.

She'd about knocked him over, but that wasn't the same as him not finding her idea appealing.

He reached out one hand, caught her upper arm, and reeled her in, until she bumped up against him. She stood before him, her cheeks pink, her dark hair in a tidy bun made of a long twisted braid at the nape of her neck.

She wore a red shirtwaist and a tidy black skirt. She always looked nice. No, *nice* was too mild. She was the most beautiful woman he'd ever seen. And her spirit and sass made her every word and gesture come alive. It was fascinating.

194

He lost hold of every ounce of his ability to think. He looked down into her flashing blue eyes and lowered his head slowly, giving her time to slap his face or run or shout.

Instead, she stood on her tiptoes and kissed him.

Kevin had known this was between them right from the start. And from the generous kiss, he knew Win had felt it, too.

He slid both arms around her waist, careful of her stitches, and tilted his head to deepen the kiss. Her arms had come around his neck so hard and fast he felt it almost like a blow. The nicest blow imaginable.

Time meant little as Kevin explored what it meant to kiss a woman. He'd never done such a thing before.

The world opened up before him so differently from what he'd imagined. Full of color and joy and . . . and . . . and a woman who had terrible secrets.

Just like he did.

He tore himself away from the kiss. Broke her hold on him. It wasn't easy with as firm a grip as she had.

Breathing hard, he looked down at her. Her lips were swollen from his kiss. Her hair mussed. He could still feel the silky weight of it. He'd pulled it free of the tidy braid she'd worn it in.

Searching her face, dreaming, fearing, he asked, "Will you tell me why you don't want to go home if we're . . . f-family?"

Her eyes dimmed. All the passion, the spark, replaced by fear. "You mean, will I tell you if you accept my proposal?"

She'd asked him to marry her.

When he thought of it rationally—and honestly, after that kiss, he couldn't claim anything about his thoughts were rational— at the very base of her request was her implying that marrying him would be an answer to prayer. It struck Kevin as about the nicest thing a person had ever thought about him.

"Yes, that's what I mean. I'd like there to be honesty between us."

"Then you'll tell me where Molly learned her doctoring skills? You'll tell me why both of you get tense as a banjo string when I ask about it? You'll tell me the truth about why she had to stitch up your ma?"

Kevin admitted to himself that he didn't have much room to accuse others of keeping secrets.

"My secrets are old and dark and dangerous." He watched her to see how she'd react.

With a tiny shrug of one shoulder she said, "My secrets are old and dark and dangerous."

Kevin imagined saying out loud what he had hidden inside him. He and Molly had decided they'd never speak of it. They'd take the secret to their graves. That was a heavy promise Molly had made when she was far too young.

"To tell you, I'd have to betray a vow I made to Molly. To share such a secret with a w-wife . . . that would be reasonable. A husband and a wife should share such a thing. I'm . . . That is, I'd be . . . I suppose, w-willing to speak of it." He swallowed hard. "But you'd have to agree she'd never know."

He looked hard in her eyes, trying to convince himself he should refuse her proposal and keep to himself. Keep his secrets. Hold faith with what he'd promised Molly. "I'd prefer to ask her permission to tell you, but I don't think she'd grant it."

"So it's her secret more than yours?"

Kevin had already said too much. "I reckon it's both of ours. It's not fair to insist you open up to me, and then I don't do the same. But if I tell you, I'm not sure you'll be able to act as if you don't know in front of Molly. And do that for the rest of your

196

life. That's a heavy burden for you to carry. I know because I carry it and have for long years."

Win's eyes seemed to look deep into him. Her expression solemn. She understood the importance of what he was willing to share. "I'll tell you my secret once our vows are spoken. And yes, I want to know yours. Believe me when I say I can keep a secret, hide it from the whole world, and do it well for years."

Kevin had to admit just from the way she hesitated to tell her own, the way she'd only broken from her years of silence out of desperation, that she would lock his secrets away like a vault.

He should talk it over with Molly and Andy. The wedding. Talk with Molly about the secret. He should figure out where in the world they were going to live, for heaven's sake.

He should get things settled with Wyatt. Get to know Win better.

He should pray. And he did, silently, fervently, but, he admitted, too briefly.

The look in her eyes. The wanting. The fear. The hope. He found it absolutely irresistible. Add in how much he liked kissing her and how much he wanted to do it again and forever. And just maybe he heard the still small voice of God giving him the idea as He'd given it to Win.

Kevin just could not deny her.

"Yes, I'll marry you." He opened his mouth to discuss details. When, where. Who to tell, invite, whether to tell her father, if they should—

Win threw her arms around his neck and kissed him into silence. And that answered all his questions and none of them. But what it did tell him was that the answers didn't matter.

When the kiss ended, she said, "We'll ride into town tomorrow and get married. We'll tell everyone about it when it's done."

That had to be wrong. Maybe at least Molly—

She kissed him again, and he decided they'd do everything however she wanted them done. If she kept kissing him like this, he'd be thrilled to do things her way forever.

～

"What did she want?" Molly had picked her moment.

Kevin almost made it out. Win had stayed in the kitchen. She'd helped with the evening meal and did more than she had for days. She'd stayed downstairs and eaten the apple cobbler for dessert. Finally, exhaustion won out, and she headed up for bed. Kevin walked beside her to make sure she didn't collapse on the stairs. Then he tried to go fast through the kitchen and get to the ramrod's house without talking to Molly. He didn't want to lie, and he didn't want to tell the truth. That made silence about his only choice.

Molly cornered him before he could get out.

Kevin couldn't talk to her, so he told the only truth he had. "I'll tell you later. Not now."

Whispering, she said, "I'll come with you out to the ramrod's cabin."

"No, please, Molly." He leaned close so there was no chance of Win overhearing. "Win wants to go into town tomorrow. There's more to it, but I promised not to talk about it."

"Not even with me?" Molly's eyes were wide with hurt.

Kevin realized how close he'd been to his little sister. He'd always loved her, since the moment Ma had first presented him with that tiny soft bundle. Ma was barely able to care for the child, so Kevin had stepped in. Been a parent to her in many ways. And Andy even more so simply because Kevin was older and more capable, and Ma was more downtrodden and incapable.

But along with being Molly's parent, he'd been her friend, her loyal protector. They'd held each other's confidences in a bond that was stronger than their blood ties.

And now he couldn't tell her about the most important decision of his life . . . until after she had no chance of stopping him from making it.

"When Win and I get home tomorrow, then we'll talk."

Molly held his gaze. She couldn't guess about the wedding, but he could see she felt the weight of whatever it was. See the hurt, the betrayal.

He couldn't stand to see all that in her eyes, and he couldn't say the words he needed to say to fix things. So he ran.

He turned away from her and rushed out of the house, feeling like a slug. Like a slug stomped on by a hobnail boot. Like a slug stomped on by a hobnail boot, then knocked off on a boot scraper.

Yep, he felt mighty low-down.

But he would tell her tomorrow. And he'd tell Win their old, dark, and dangerous secrets, and let Molly know he had. He probably shouldn't tell Win. Their secrets were like an unexploded bomb left buried after the Civil War. As long as it lay there undisturbed, it would never hurt anyone.

But uncover it—expose it even a little bit to the world—and who knew what harm could be done? The lives that could be torn apart.

He stomped up to the ramrod's house and shoved inside, knowing he was going to tell Win. Because he wanted to marry her and felt that God would bless the marriage. And because it was fair. Their secrets would bind them together forever as surely as their wedding vows.

And he most certainly did want to be bound together with Win.

They'd marry. Then they'd find a place to build a cabin for Kevin, Win, Molly, and Andy. Wyatt could have his ranch back. Cheyenne would get Falcon's third and most of Kevin's. Or she'd split what Kevin didn't lay claim to with Wyatt.

He might be unable to sell it to her, but he could step back, make no claim on it, and let them go on as they had before.

Cheyenne would come home, and she and Wyatt would calm down and get back to owning their ranch together.

And with what land Kevin got, maybe he'd run a few more cattle on it than he had in Kansas. Andy would be a cowboy on his own family's land.

Maybe by now he knew enough to teach Kevin a few things.

TWENTY-FOUR

*D*early beloved." Parson Brownley smiled as he spoke the vows. He'd been delighted to be called from the parsonage behind the church to perform a wedding ceremony.

His wife was here as a witness. He'd offered to wait if they wanted to send for Win's father. Or Kevin's sister and brother.

Win had no idea what she'd looked like, but it must have not been pure panic because the parson never quit smiling while they told him they wanted to go ahead. He'd said something about an elopement, as if he could hardly contain his excitement at this runaway marriage.

He'd commented on Win's age. Kevin's too. He'd said it was high time they both settled down. Time to start a family.

Kevin was holding her hand tight, or she'd've collapsed at the notion of starting a family. She really hadn't thought of that.

And what that entailed.

And yet, without hesitation, here she stood taking vows to do many things. Starting a family most assuredly included.

"Do you, Winona Hawkins, take Kevin Hunt to be your lawfully wedded husband? To have and to hold . . ."

She'd been daydreaming. Or panicking. Or contemplating the enormity of what she was doing. Whatever it was called, she hadn't been listening while she stood here before the parson, his sweet-faced wife, Kevin, and God himself, making vows that were to last a lifetime.

Considering she'd yet to have the stitches removed from her back from being shot, a lifetime might not be all that long. So maybe it wasn't that big a vow.

"I do." She said it quick. She made the vow, but she thought of loving, honoring, and obeying as more of goals than true promises. She'd certainly try to do all three. Given enough time, she might even succeed.

"And do you, Kevin Hunt, take Winona Hawkins to be your lawfully wedded wife? To have and to hold . . ."

Have, certainly. Hold . . . well, she and Kevin would have to talk about that. Oh, they had to talk about so many things, they might not get around to much holding for months.

She hoped.

Except she'd thoroughly enjoyed kissing him, and there'd been plenty of holding then, and she wouldn't mind more of that, and—

"I now pronounce you man and wife."

Win flinched because she'd missed most of what the parson said, though she'd said "I do" at the proper time. Since the wedding proceeded onward, she assumed Kevin had, too.

Kevin drew her around to face him.

"I ask God's blessing upon this holy union. You may kiss the bride." The parson smiled and raised his arms, a Bible in one hand. His wife just behind him clasped her hands together at her neck and stifled a giggle.

Winona knew about this part. She wasn't afraid of kissing.

She was surprised by that and not really proud of it, but it was the truth.

The parson smiled so big it struck Winona. He had always been a good parson and a nice man, but maybe his extra-large smile was covering up how he really felt. This might be a wedding he had serious doubts about.

He was from Bear Claw Pass, and he knew Kevin was a newcomer. But the parson always found the joy in the life God unfolded before him.

Win decided then and there she'd be more like that. She was a worrier, mostly only where her father was concerned. Although she'd done plenty of worrying about Cheyenne here lately.

And she'd been all set to start in worrying about her new husband. But instead she'd find what joy her new life held and try to let go of her worst fear, her dark secret.

Maybe speaking of it would ease the weight from her shoulders. She could hope. But whether it did or not, she was redeemed. A believer. She'd find a way to be joyful.

Smiling at Parson and Mrs. Brownley, she took Kevin's arm, and they left the church. Win kept a smile on her face and felt at least some of the happiness.

~

"Now we go home and face Molly." Kevin led her to the horses, hitched right outside the church.

He reached for Win's waist to lift her onto the horse. Then he stopped midlift and set her back on the ground.

"Unless you want to ride out to your father's place."

Win blinked up at him. "I have no wish to tell my father what I've done."

Kevin pondered that for a very few seconds. His hands tightened on her slender waist. She felt so soft and strong and sweet he almost forgot what they were talking about.

He raised one hand from her waist and touched the silky softness of her hair. She'd worn it in a special way today. No braid, just a soft bun on the back of her head with tendrils of curls loose here and there. She always had a tidy, efficient way of dressing. It reminded him that she was a schoolmarm—though he couldn't ever remember having such a pretty teacher when he was a kid. But today she'd taken pains with her appearance. For their wedding.

His heart lifted.

She had on a split skirt for riding, so that wasn't overly dressy, though it fit her like a glove. Her shirtwaist today was white with lace at the collar and cuffs, and it buttoned down the front. It was her wedding dress. But a dress a woman could manage while riding a horse. He found he liked that practical side of her.

And then he realized what she'd said and found it stung. "He won't like that you've chosen me for a husband? He'll think the daughter of a prosperous rancher shouldn't marry a Kansas farmer who doesn't even have a roof to put over your head. He'll think—"

Win rested her fingertips on his lips as her mouth formed a little circle, and she shook her head. "Oh no, that's not what I meant. I just . . . he'll just . . ." She let one finger caress his lips before she quit touching him.

"Now that you mention it, he won't like it that I married you. He won't like it that I didn't tell him, or rather ask him. He won't like it that I eloped. He won't like it that—"

It was Kevin's turn to rest his fingertips on her lips. "It doesn't sound as if he'll like hearing you got married no matter who you picked."

"That's exactly right." Her brow furrowed. "It's time we talked. Can we ride toward home, that is, toward the RHR? I know I probably wasn't fair to you by not telling you—well, my secret."

Kevin was enjoying these stolen moments with his new bride. Before all the deep troubles from both their pasts came out. They stood between their hitched horses, and he felt like they were alone in the world. Considering they were going home to a ranch where Kevin lived in a cabin with his brother, these might be a few of the only moments they had alone.

He was in no hurry to ride home, but she wanted to talk, and he found in himself a desire to do whatever she wanted. He boosted her onto the horse, then swung up on his own, and they rode out of town. As soon as the town fell away, and they could be assured of privacy, Win looked nervously at him and opened her mouth but didn't speak.

To break the silence, Kevin said, "You know he's going to hear you got married. Unless you want to go back in and swear the parson and his wife to secrecy. Even that would only put it off. Usually facing trouble right square is better." Kevin clamped his mouth shut as he thought of the trouble he hadn't faced right square.

"Then we'll just wait for him to find out and come to see us."

"That seems—seems—honestly, it seems like the easiest thing. But will he show up raging? I can see you don't care much whether he holds you in affection, or even high regard, but what is the way to handle this without him making the most trouble?"

Win stared at Kevin for long moments. Finally, in a very quiet voice, she said, "I don't want to go out there. I don't want to see him. Please, can we just go home?"

What she meant was go to Wyatt's house. Neither of them had a home. A man ought to have a home for his bride.

Kevin let the silence stretch as the horses clopped along on the wide dirt trail. They were headed east, and the mountains rose up in front of them. All that wilderness. Wyatt said some of it was suitable for grazing cattle, but a lot was rugged wasteland. Somewhere in that vast wilderness, Falcon Hunt's body was borne along on the rushing waters of the Colorado River.

It made Kevin sick to think they hadn't searched until they'd found him. It wasn't fitting or decent to have left him, but the women needed protection. The pure truth was they'd turned away from their brother to take care of what had to be taken care of. There'd been no choice.

"My father killed my mother."

Kevin's dour thoughts were whipped back to the present. He turned to see Win's head hanging down. She stared straight down at the saddle horn as if her neck had lost the strength to hold her head up.

A hundred questions flooded through Kevin's mind. They seemed to clog in his throat, and none of them could escape.

And then he decided none of them *should* escape. He should let her tell her story her way.

"Tell me more." There, that seemed safe enough.

"I told you my ma died bringing a new baby." Win's hands trembled until she quit guiding the horse and just clung to the saddle horn, the reins tangled in her hands.

"Yes, and soon after you came to live with Wyatt's family. You stayed with them most of the time until you were sent to boarding school."

"That's the story I've always told. My father tells it that way." Win's head lifted, her gaze locked on Kevin's. "I have long-ago memories of my parents fighting. Sometimes ugly fights. I didn't really understand why Ma was bruised up, sometimes bleeding."

Kevin gasped. "No, it can't be true. Not you too."

Her head jerked back. "Me too? What does that mean?"

"My father killed my mother, too."

"That's your old, dark, dangerous secret?"

"No. Mine's worse." Kevin's jaw tightened, and his teeth clenched. He couldn't force the words out. They'd been packed down deep inside for too long. And anyway, it was Win's turn to talk. "Go on with your story. Did you—did you witness it? See your pa?"

A firm shake of her head gave him the tiniest bit of relief. It was all bad enough, but at least she hadn't seen it.

"My mother was a wealthy woman. I didn't know that. I didn't understand how well off we were. A child just accepts circumstances as they are."

Kevin remembered all he'd come to accept. And a few things he couldn't accept.

"I've pieced things together over the years. From the time she died, I had a bad feeling about what had happened to Ma, but I was a little girl, heartbroken over losing her mother. I was scared all the time. I was happier at Cheyenne's house. Then I was glad to be sent away.

"After I got to St. Louis, I learned my mother's family name. I have only the faintest memory of my grandmother dying. Mainly I just remember Ma crying. That was frightening because she was the most important person in the world to me.

"I remember a picture of my grandparents with my mother when she was a mostly grown girl, but I don't know where I saw that picture. My memories are a jumble. I think mostly I just remember that picture.

"I'm not sure what is a true memory. The fighting. Ma bleeding. I'm sure that happened. But I found out some things while I was living in St. Louis and asked some questions about my grandparents. They were from Chicago, but a certain elite group in St. Louis knew of my grandfather. He was a powerful man and very rich. He died before I was born, but my grandma lived until I was three. I found folks who knew Grandma and knew of her only child marrying and, after my grandmother died and all her wealth turned to cash, heading west with the entire fortune."

"Do you remember the trip out?" Kevin asked.

Win nodded. "Some. We came out here in such a different way than Wyatt's grandpa. He tore civilization out of a wild land. He faced wild animals that had no fear of man and lived on land with no trail save that left by elk. In the wilderness, Jacques carved out a ranch, built up a herd, wrested money out of the dirt and rocks. His business partner and later son-in-law, Nate Brewster, worked alongside him. Both of them strong, bold men.

"My father simply bought a huge spread and thousands of cattle and hired hands to tend all of it. And then there was a lot of excitement because another baby was on the way. Then Ma was dead. And when she died, my father finally had complete control of Ma's money. I was sent first to live with Cheyenne's family, then I was off to St. Louis. Even that made sense later. You'd think, coming from Chicago, Pa would've sent me there, but he chose a place no one knew him, so I'd never hear about my mother's family—or so he believed."

Kevin didn't want to ask a lot of questions. He wanted her

to unfold this story in her own way. But she fell silent, and he wanted the whole tale.

"When did you decide he killed your ma?"

"When I talked with old friends of my grandparents and heard the stories of how scared my grandparents were for my mother. How Ma was a woman of grace and beauty and charm, a popular socialite. And how she became a recluse. How she was known to be in failing health. That she was frail and unsteady on her feet, which explained her bruises on the few occasions she was seen by someone."

Kevin shuddered deep inside. He knew what those bruises would look like. He knew what a closed fist did to the delicate skin of a woman's face.

"In St. Louis, a wise old woman who knew Grandmother and heard that my ma was lost bearing a child asked me sharp questions that drew out old memories. I began to wonder if Ma had even been carrying a child."

"You think—" Thundering hoofbeats cut Kevin off. He and Win both saw a man rounding a curve in the trail, coming from the direction of the ranch. He was riding flat out, bent low over the saddle.

Kevin's hand went to his gun.

"No." Win reached over and grabbed his arm. "It's all right. I know him. He's Bern Tuttle, the foreman from Pa's ranch."

"Being suspicious of everyone's a reasonable way to go on out here, considering someone's tried to kill me twice now," said Kevin.

Another man came around the curve, only a few yards behind the first.

"That's Ross Baker. He's the RHR ramrod."

"I've been meaning to ask, What in tarnation is a ramrod?"

209

His pretty wife took her gaze off the approaching riders, still a hundred yards away on the wide trail. She smiled. "Fair question. A ramrod is second in charge after the foreman. The foreman tells everyone what to do, along with Wyatt of course, and the ramrod makes sure they do it."

"It's a bossy-sounding word, so I guess that makes sense."

"It's really just a man who steps in and takes charge if the foreman and the ranch owner can't do something. For example, if they've got to split up and do work in different areas. Maybe three groups of riders go out to check the cattle, and the owner, foreman, and ramrod will head the different groups."

"And we're living in his house, right?" Kevin glanced at her. A woman he very much wanted to share a house with. "So where do we go now that he's back?"

A shiver of nerves rushed down his spine as he thought of sharing a room with Win. Wherever it was, the idea scared him, and excited him. He had no idea what to do with a wife, and he couldn't wait to do it.

And now it seemed the house he had planned to stay in with his wife—already overcrowded with a little brother—was closed to him.

"I have no idea where we go." Win blinked at him as if she was just now realizing wherever they were to go, they'd go to-gether.

"I'm surprised you even know your pa's foreman with the little time that you spend over there." Kevin changed the subject before she decided she'd move back into her room in Wyatt's house and he could sleep in the barn.

"I've met him, that's about all I know about him. Pa hired him this spring. Our old foreman took off, didn't even tell Pa he was quitting. I only found that out in passing when I met

Bern Tuttle. He happened to ride into town with Pa once. It was just a few days before the school break for branding. Pa stopped to see me at the school building right after the children left, and Bern was with him."

Tuttle drew near. He wasn't a young man. Broad shouldered, with neat blond hair with a little silver at the temples, wearing a black Stetson. He had an overlong nose, in Kevin's opinion, and he looked intent on finding Win.

Baker, the second rider, was even older than Tuttle. He had black hair shot through with gray, and a square jaw. He wore a black Stetson with a small tufted circle of feathers on a silver band.

Tuttle came up and pulled his horse back hard. It was rough handling, and Kevin didn't like it. Tuttle looked at Win with eyes black as coal.

"You have to get home, Miss Win." Tuttle tugged the brim of his hat. "Your pa sent me to fetch you from the RHR, but we found out you'd ridden to town."

"What's happened?" Win's voice was sharp with alarm. Her horse tossed its head, and Kevin saw the tight grip she had on the reins. "Has something happened to Pa?"

Shaking his head, Tuttle said, "He just sent me riding, miss. I don't know what he wants, but he was very upset and insisted I bring you home."

Kevin looked at Win. They were both thinking of her pa yesterday, demanding she come home after hearing she'd been shot. Was this his way of bringing her back to the Hawkins Ranch? Or was something really wrong?

Win looked back at the two men, then at Kevin again.

Kevin said, "Let's go. We'll see what's the matter, then go on over to the RHR."

He saw her bleak expression and expected her to refuse to go. He'd back her if that was her choice, but there was a look in Tuttle's eyes that said he wasn't going to take no for an answer, not without a lot of protest. And why would he? He worked for Oliver Hawkins and was following urgent orders.

Reining her horse around, Win changed directions. "There's a trail right this way that's a shorter way to Pa's."

"Miss Hawkins, your pa made it clear he wanted you to come alone." Tuttle's voice had something menacing in it. Kevin wouldn't have let Win ride off alone with him and Baker on a bet. Not even if they'd offered him a ranch the size of the whole territory of Wyoming.

Win gave Tuttle a smile so cold Kevin felt another shiver. "I won't come if I'm not allowed to bring my husband."

Both men froze.

Tuttle's jaw sagged.

"H-husband?" Baker said.

Win sounded stiff, annoyed as if making this announcement was the last thing she wanted to do. Her pa was going to find out anyway, but Kevin didn't blame her for being upset at being ordered to go by these men.

He didn't blame her, mainly because he found in himself an intense loyalty to his new wife, and she couldn't do much wrong in his eyes.

"Wh-when did you get married?" Baker stumbled over the words in surprise.

"I haven't heard of any wedding." Tuttle's eyes shifted between Kevin and Win. "Your pa would've told me. He was clear that he wanted only you to come home."

Since he'd met her, Kevin had known Win as the cook and housekeeper at the RHR. A servant who did whatever was needed because she wanted to stay away from home, but also because she loved being part of her friends' family.

Now Win changed before Kevin's eyes. She sat up straight until her spine nearly snapped. Her eyes focused in cool disdain. She looked down her nose at these two men. She was reminding everyone she was the daughter of one of the richest men in the territory. She was a graduate from an elite finishing school. She was a woman who moved among the wealthy in St. Louis due to the connections she had there through her grandparents.

She lifted her chin in a way that Kevin suspected could match any princess. This was a woman who was finished.

"Your questions and comments are overly familiar. And it wouldn't be proper for me to ride off with two men I know only slightly, so Kevin would come with me to my father's house regardless of our wedding."

Kevin almost flinched at her cold response.

"You can be sure, Mr. Tuttle, that I'll mention your rude treatment to my father. And Mr. Baker, Wyatt Hunt will hear about how you've acted toward me." Win reined her horse around and went toward a wooded area to the southwest.

Kevin rode up beside her. The two men dropped back to ride behind. Having them bring up the rear made Kevin's back itch. The woods ahead made Kevin think of the last time he'd ridden through heavy woods with Win. She still had stitches in her back, and she'd had a very lucky escape from something much worse. There was nothing about this he liked.

He nudged his horse closer to her as they reached the trail that cut into the forest. Whispering, he said, "I don't like feeling closed in."

Win shot him a surprised look.

"Someone could be watching for us."

Riding on Kevin's left, she studied the woods on her side while he studied them on his. A quick glance back showed the two men with their heads together. Talking quietly just as he and Win were. Tuttle said something that made Baker jerk back and shoot Kevin a hard look.

Facing forward, Kevin felt that itch between his shoulder blades grow. It reminded him of how things had been back in Kansas. And how he'd learned to be suspicious of everyone. How he didn't like someone he didn't trust—which was almost everyone—riding at his back.

Kevin heard the sound of rushing water somewhere. He thought of his brother, swept away down a rushing stream, and suddenly he wondered what this water was. Could it be the same stream? The fast-moving creek that went over waterfalls and coursed through jagged stones, kicking up deadly white water?

A stone wall rose up to border the trail on their left. Win rode closest to the wall. The trees were suddenly gone. The solid stone reached higher than their heads. The water still wasn't visible, but its roar grew louder. They left the dappled light in the woods behind, and now the sun shone brightly. Kevin saw that he and Win and their horses cast a solid shadow on the light gray stone. He wondered briefly if they should turn back and refuse to accompany these men. Then he and Win were past the rock, and a deep gully cut alongside the road.

Kevin looked down at the water, and then behind him, he saw the shadows of the two men—and the shadow of an extended arm and an aimed gun.

He dove at Win and hurtled them both over the backs of their horses just as the gun fired. A tearing pain nearly drove him into darkness. Then he hit the water, and it helped him stay awake.

They were blasting along on the same twisting river that killed his brother.

A loud shout of rage sounded from behind them, and gunfire echoed as the water plunged down a twisting drop, then flung them over a short waterfall. Something sliced Kevin's arm, but he wasn't sure if it was a bullet, or if he'd been scraped by a jutting stone.

They soared into the air over another fall and slammed into water so hard it felt like hitting rock. He realized he was still holding on to Win. His hands still wrapped tight around her from when he'd tackled her off the horse.

They surfaced, and Win said, "Let me go. You need your arms to swim."

"I don't know how to swim!"

He let her go so his lack of swimming skill didn't drag her down to her death. They raced along faster than a galloping horse. He didn't have time to drown. Tumbling, careening around curves, crashing into rocks, grating against sand when the water was shallow. Minutes stretched, the beating went on and on.

He'd sink under, then the water would toss him back to the surface, where he could grab a chestful of air. He felt as if the water played with him, taunted him, mocked him, throwing him high, then dragging him down, tipping him over, and spinning him around.

When he could look around, he saw Win being tossed around same as him, but at least she was staying within sight.

Time sped by as quickly as the wooded banks. With no idea how long they'd been riding the river, they finally rounded a tight curve, and the water spread into a wide, slower-moving stretch. Win caught him by the arm and dragged him to shore. He lay on his belly on the gravel, gasping for breath, barely conscious. He must be half-drowned. That would explain his inability to clear his thoughts.

"Kevin, you've been shot!"

Or maybe drowning wasn't his biggest problem.

TWENTY-FIVE

his wasn't how Win had envisioned her wedding day.

A wave hit the bank, and it looked like Kevin was going to be pulled back into the water. Panting hard—partly from the lack of air, partly from panic—she scrambled to catch hold of his shirt. Coughing until she had no strength, she waited for another bit of high water, then clawed her way farther up the sandy shore, dragging Kevin along on his belly until the water was too shallow to drag him away—she hoped.

She couldn't get him all the way out. He was just too heavy. His face was out though, so he should be able to breathe. He was awake but groggy. And she figured that bullet crease had plenty to do with it.

As she lay in the sand, she thought of when Kevin had tackled her off her horse. She'd thought he'd gone mad, but then she'd heard the crack of the gun as they'd fallen over the steep bank. Those men had planned to kill them.

Had her father even wanted her to come home? Was this all a lie to somehow kill her and Kevin both?

Kevin moaned, drawing her out of her rabbiting thoughts.

He turned his head and rested his face left side down, and she was satisfied that he wouldn't be swept downstream if she let go.

"Sh-shot?" He lifted his head, then let it drop back to the ground.

It was no wonder the man was confused. "You've got what looks like a bullet crease over your right ear."

His arm was bleeding, too. She decided not to mention that yet.

Now that the water wasn't washing it clean as fast as it could bleed, it was easy to see the furrow left by the bullet. With a sickening twist to her stomach, she suspected her back looked much the same, although the pain there wasn't bad. She hoped that meant her stitches had held.

Kevin's wound bled heavily. Stopping the bleeding was her first priority. It had been barely a week since Kevin had been staunching a bullet wound on her. And what were the chances this was someone new doing the shooting?

If she made what seemed like a logical guess, that meant her own father's foreman had a part in whatever was going on. The attempt on Kevin's life, along with his family on their way out here. The bullet that had hit her. And it stood to reason that these same men killed Falcon Hunt.

And for what?

The ranch probably, but she didn't own either ranch, and Kevin only had a third. How did Wyatt's ramrod and her father's foreman plan to profit from this day's villainy?

Her brain was too waterlogged to reason it out, and Kevin's head needed attention. She pulled up the hem of her riding skirt and ripped at the bottom. Soaking wet, the fabric was too tough to get a strip loose. She studied Kevin and figured him for the type to carry a pocket knife.

"Kevin, do you have a knife?"

He started coughing, which set off her coughing again. Sympathy coughing? She'd never heard of such a thing. She waited until she could breathe again, then jabbed him in the shoulder until he drew a steady breath.

"Kevin!" She shouted to penetrate his confusion. "I need a knife."

More coughing from him. More poking from her. "Kevin, listen to me. Have you got a knife?"

The whole side of his head was bloody. It probably wasn't enough to kill him, but the longer he bled, the weaker he'd be, and the slower he'd heal. She had no idea where they were. They'd come who-could-say how far on that raging river. The sun was at high noon, and it had been morning when they'd gone into the stream. And they had no supplies to help them survive in the wilderness. She wasn't skilled enough to live off the land, and Kevin wasn't going to be much help if she didn't get his wounds bandaged.

"B-boot. Right boot."

She'd have been a while searching before she'd've hunted there. She crawled, her sodden split skirt tangling up around her legs. She took a moment to be grateful it was a riding skirt. A dress with the petticoats that went under it would have weighed her down in the water and probably killed her.

She got to his feet, still in the water, found the knife, scooted back to dry land, and cut a strip of cloth for a bandage. This is what Kevin had used when she'd been shot. She had a riding skirt with one leg knee high. Now she'd have another.

She folded the cloth into a pad, then as she prayed for him—including for him to forgive her—she pressed it against the wound.

"Ouch!"

She knew he wasn't fully conscious, or he'd've never admitted to any pain. That was the kind of toughness she'd seen in Wyatt many times, and Kevin had similar grit. If they'd inherited it from their father, Clovis, he'd kept any toughness well hidden.

Surprised by the burn of tears behind her eyes, she decided she might be more upset by this whole thing than she'd realized.

It seemed like she had a right to some upset, so she ignored the tears that trickled down her cheeks. Just more water.

Kevin lifted his head so his chin rested in the sand, and his hazel eyes glared at her. "Why are you doing that?"

He was groggy all right, but the pain seemed to be helping clear his thoughts.

"You're bleeding. I'm trying to stop it. You've been shot."

"Oh, that's right." With visible effort, he pulled his hands up to rest his head on them, then turned his head to the right again and let her do her rough doctoring.

She smelled the blood, water, and wild of the place. She had no idea how far they were from any kind of help. Well, they'd just have to help themselves.

She left the folded bandage balancing on the wound and cut another long strip, spiraling up her skirt leg. As she wound the strip around his head to hold the bandage in place, she saw that the left side of his face was coated in sand.

Win clenched her teeth to keep from apologizing for hurting him. Tears came faster, but she ignored them. She didn't have the strength to control herself, but she managed to be silent about the crying. Kevin was being brave, she could do no less.

When she was finished, she tied another bandage around his right arm. That might not have been caused by a bullet but rather a slashing rock. Near as she could tell he didn't have a bullet lodged inside him, so it didn't matter what had caused the bleeding. She bathed the worst of the blood away, then let him rest for a few minutes while she staggered to her feet, wrung the water out of what was left of her skirt, and looked around. The stream was quiet here, but it roared from upstream, and she thought she could hear more rushing water downstream. If they'd failed to reach shore right here, who knew what kind of danger they might have faced?

This sandy beach was at the bottom of a steep bluff, and she could well imagine that in spring the flood waters might reach to the top of the banks. She could see no obvious trail, but it was by no means a sheer cliff. They could climb it.

She'd've liked to let Kevin rest a good long while. Maybe sleep. Maybe she could get a fire going. She knew how to manage that without matches. But they didn't dare to stay here and rest. They had no food. Worse yet, those men might come after them. Maybe there was an easily followed trail right alongside this stream, and they were coming fast.

"Can you get the rest of the way out of the water?" Win hated to ask him to so much as move, but he had to help. There was no shelter here. Not even tall grass to hide in. If those men came, she and Kevin would be easy prey.

A groan escaped him.

"I'm sorry." She promised herself she'd stop saying that. "But we may still be in danger. If those men follow the stream, and it seems to me that they will if it's at all possible, they can't fail to find us as long as we stay here."

For a few moments, a long deep breath was Kevin's only response, then she saw him gather his strength. He shoved himself to his hands and knees, then looked around. A jumble of stones off to the side drew his attention. He crawled to the boulders on all fours. She hovered near in case she could help.

Or catch him when he collapsed. He used the stones to lurch unsteadily to his feet.

Standing on trembling legs and leaning hard against the largest of the boulders, he said, "I'm ready."

Win thought he looked about as far from ready as a man could be, but he was standing. That was him doing more than his part, considering the bullet wound in his head.

She had to do the thinking for both of them, and a little help would have been appreciated. And this was her home—they might even be on her pa's land by now—so she was in charge until Kevin showed the gumption to take over.

She was hoping that came very soon.

Slipping her arm around his waist, she took his left hand, sparing his injured right arm, and lifted it around her neck. "Let's go. We take one step at a time. We'll get to the top of this bank, and maybe then we can see where we are and figure out where we need to go."

And so they began. Prayer for each step, for God's mercy and protection, kept her moving as she bore as much of his weight as she could. The bank was a curve that created the wide sandy beach. There were stones studding the climb, and clumps of grass and scrub brush growing all over, which would give them something to hang on to. Studying the bank as she neared it, she saw what looked like the least difficult stretch and guided Kevin toward it.

"We won't be able to walk up. We'll have to crawl."

"Crawling is probably more of what I'm up to doing."

That was the longest sentence he'd said so far. Maybe he was coming around.

The climb was probably forty or fifty feet. Not a long distance under good conditions. These weren't even close to good.

They staggered up about ten feet before the bank made walking impossible. Dropping to her knees, Win began the laborious crawl.

Despite being split for riding and with one leg cut off to the knee, her sodden skirt wrapped around her legs, making the going difficult. The dirt stuck to the wet fabric, turned the water to mud, and added weight to what was already a hard effort.

Win glanced back to make sure Kevin was still coming. The trek looked to be taking every ounce of Kevin's battered strength. Win kept moving. She'd go back if she had to, but Kevin looked like he was climbing with more pride than true strength, so she did nothing to make him believe she didn't think he could make it.

Win, exhausted herself, reached the top and looked carefully around them. With no armed gunmen in sight, she rolled over the edge and lay flat on her belly.

She didn't have time to catch her breath.

She pivoted to look down and almost bumped noses with Kevin. Drawing back, she saw the clump of wall he clung to crumble under his hand.

Diving for him, she caught his wrist, heaved forward until his scrambling fingers could get ahold of something solid, then watched as he inched over the top of the bank.

He was slower about it than she had been. She'd be proud of herself except for his being shot. She thought that made him the strongest. She hated to admit it, but truth was truth.

He flopped like a landed trout and lay there gasping. Win let him lie because she needed a break, too. But she didn't dare take a long one. She still didn't know where their enemies were.

Shoving herself to her feet, she staggered forward to an oak sapling, one of dozens that lined the top of the bank. She clung to the tree and held herself steady while she looked around, still catching her breath.

The afternoon was upon them. The sun past its peak in the sky. They'd hoped to be back to the RHR for the noon meal. They hadn't made it. Thankfully, they had long hours of sunlight left on this warm summer day.

Win studied the rugged mountains that rose up around them. The stream had discarded them far from where they'd fallen in. Her father's ranch was to the west of Wyatt's land. She couldn't be sure if this was part of his holding. It didn't matter if it was. She dared not go to him for help.

A terrible thing for a daughter to admit. But she'd realized it before now. She'd just married a man to escape from being under her father's thumb, after all.

She didn't want to believe he'd be a party to killing her—but if she was right about her ma, then her father was capable of anything.

No, the people she could trust were Kevin's family and Wyatt. And Cheyenne, wherever she was. No one else.

With that in mind, Win said, "We need to go east. This stream has carried us a long way west. If we head east, we'll cut the trail we were on . . . eventually."

After nodding silently and for too long, Kevin finally managed to say, "My vision is blurred. I've taken a blow like this to the head before, and I know it's a bad sign. But I'll keep up with you as long as I can."

"The sun's past its peak. We'll put it to our backs and walk along that line of trees." She pointed to the downward slope ahead of them. There was an open stretch followed by more trees, thicker than these.

"It may take all day. It may take a week. We'll watch for those men, hide if we need to, but we'll get back to the RHR. We have to report to Wyatt that his hired man is part of this. Baker must have lied about his need to go home to Texas. He's probably been roaming the area since he left. He and our foreman, Tuttle, may be plotting together to somehow take control of both ranches. They must have—"

She shouldn't say it. She took Wyatt's arm, and they started down a slope, not as bad as the stream bank they'd climbed, but steep enough that Win held on tight to keep Kevin on his feet.

"They must have, what?"

She'd hoped Kevin wouldn't notice she broke off her little string of advice. She hadn't started out with the same notion in her head that she'd ended up with.

"I have no idea if there's a lick of truth in this, but it did cross my mind that—that Tuttle might see marrying me as a way to get his hands on Pa's ranch. And if he's teamed up with Baker from the RHR, then their plan may extend to somehow gaining control of Wyatt's ranch."

Kevin kept moving. She felt his arm tremble, heard his heavy breathing, but he kept on. Held up by his determination and strength of purpose when he was barely able to stand.

"Killing Falcon and me would clear up a lot of things."

They walked downhill. There were scattered trees, and Kevin leaned heavily every time one came within clutching distance. But he never stopped. "Y-your pa, if he married Cheyenne, would be in a good position to gain some control of the RHR. If he conspired with his foreman to kill me and Falcon, and then your pa married Cheyenne . . . it's possible your pa's foreman took your pa's scheme and twisted it around to benefit himself."

Or Pa is in on it. But Win didn't say that out loud. It seemed like saying it made it more possible. "I'd've never married Tuttle. Never."

They reached the bottom of the bluff they were descending and walked across a wide clearing.

This was the most dangerous part of Win's plan. They were out in the open. There was no sign of a trail. In fact, she had to wonder if they were the only human beings to ever walk on this land. But the valley looked passable by a rider. If those men came riding along following that stream and found Win and Kevin out here, they'd be helpless. Kevin had a rifle in the boot of his saddle, and he'd had a pistol in a holster on his hip. The rifle stayed with the horse, and his holster was empty. The gun had been dropped somewhere in their turbulent water ride.

"Win, you know there are circumstances where a man could . . . could ruin a woman. Make off with her and hide her in some wilderness refuge for many days. He could do it in such a way that it seemed she went willingly. When they returned to civilization, a wedding would be unavoidable. Short of the woman simply leaving the whole territory. People have very long memories."

Kevin's lips curved down in a harsh frown. "They can change overnight. They can believe you're decent and a good friend and neighbor. Then some new—" Kevin gestured recklessly with his right arm, as if searching for a word, then flinched in pain and let his arm fall to his side—"some new *detail* about your past comes out, and you're nothing. Your whole life, everything you've said and done, means nothing. Everyone . . ."

He fell silent.

Win wanted him to talk about it. She'd told him her old, dark, dangerous secret. But he hadn't kept his side of their bargain. But then, he'd been too busy, and now too battered, to do much talking. He'd keep his word. She was struck by how completely she trusted him to do that.

But now wasn't the time.

"Kevin, we have to move fast. We're in the open. If those men come—"

"Yes. I know. Let's get across."

The talking stopped. They emerged from the trees on the north side of the broad, grassy valley and walked across it as quickly as Kevin could manage.

Win felt like she was nearly dragging him. It was a forced march to humble a cavalry soldier. And she wished fervently for a bunch of cavalry soldiers right about now.

They needed to reach the trees lining the valley's southern side. On that side, instead of the sparse trees they'd walked through down the bluff, the trees were thick and filled in with underbrush. It was a solid forest that reached up the next hill and stretched to the left and right. Once in there, they could move without being seen.

Kevin staggered once, and she had to hold him up with brute force. Not easy with a man as big as Kevin.

They reached the far side of the valley and ducked into trees so dense it was hard to take each step. By the time they were twenty paces in, she felt safe, or at least safer.

Once they were in far enough that she couldn't see the valley and no one in that valley could see her, she guided Kevin to a broken tree lying on its side. It was an ancient tree, large enough that resting flat on the ground, it made a decent chair.

They sank down, breathing hard. For a minute, she thought Kevin might go on over backward, but he caught himself before he tumbled, and they sat, gathering their strength.

"I'm sorry that happened to you back in Kansas." Win turned

to Kevin, and he looked back. She smiled, and considering the day they'd had, she thought that was pretty good.

And while she smiled at him, she remembered they'd gotten married.

Touching the dark bandage on his head, she said, "I'm sorry you were driven out of your home and for all this mess with Clovis, but I'm glad you're here."

He studied her eyes as if he could see what was behind them, see her thoughts and her feelings. "I'm glad too. I'm glad we're married."

He leaned down slowly. She stretched up.

Their lips met.

The kiss, as it had been last night, was wonderful. His arms came around her, and the kiss deepened. She rested the palms of her hands on his chest, felt his heart speed up in a way that couldn't be explained by their hike. And it matched the racing of her own heart.

Smiling against his lips, Win felt the kiss bless her wounded, frightened, lonely heart. She slid her hands higher until her arms were wrapped around his neck. Time stretched until she considered just staying here on this fallen tree, maybe forever, in her husband's strong arms.

At last the kiss ended. He lifted his head to gaze into her eyes. "We probably can't get back to the RHR tonight. But we should make a start. We have no food unless we find some kind of berries or nuts. We don't dare start a fire for fear those men might see it, so there's no sense trying to rig a snare to catch a bird or sharpening a stick to spear a fish."

"I expect we'll face a cold night." She gave him one more quick kiss. "But maybe if we hold each other tight, we can ward off the cold."

He kissed her forehead. Laid his lips there and kept them there a long time.

At last Kevin said, "Let's make a start. We'll miss a meal or two, but we can survive that. I've heard tell of folks taking a trip after their wedding called a honeymoon. Maybe we can call this night in the woods a honeymoon."

"Maybe." A small chuckle escaped her lips.

They stood and walked along in the trees, far enough back no rider would spot them. They crossed game trails several times, but they all seemed to head north and south. The woods were hard to move through, but to Win, the scented pines and the coarse bark of the oaks she used to steady herself were a fortress. Stumbling along, they kept on their way east. Broken trees and thick scrub brush made the going hard. Kevin needed to stop and rest every once in a while.

The afternoon passed, and Win had no real notion of how long it had been. In the woods like this, they couldn't see the sun in the sky or notice shadows lengthening.

"Ah!" Kevin bit back a shout as he tumbled forward.

Win grabbed for him, but her fingers slipped, and he went down hard, scraping his hands as he tried to break the fall.

She dropped to her knees and saw what he wouldn't admit. Kevin was done for the day. The woods were in such deep shadows they could call it night.

She shifted him around as best she could until he was lying down without any fallen branches jabbing him in the belly. Then she said, "I'm going to look around to find a sheltered place for us to sleep. I see a broken tree ahead with the trunk sticking up like it landed on another downed tree or maybe some rocks. I think we can crawl under it, and I hope that will shield us from any night winds."

"It's August. We'll be fine."

She saw the sheen of sweat on his brow. He was too new to this country to realize how cold it could get in the mountains at night. She'd wandered in high country with Cheyenne enough to have seen it snow in August.

She rose, and he caught her wrist and dragged her back down so they were nose to nose. "Don't lose sight of me. I don't want us to get separated."

The notion sent a chill of terror down her spine. Somehow, out here with Kevin, she had only thought of making progress, heading home. She kept up her strength to encourage him. She suspected he was doing the same to encourage her.

But alone.

What would she do if she were out here alone? Search for him for the rest of her life? What other choice would she have?

"I won't go far. I won't lose sight of you, I promise. If I can't find shelter under that tree"—she pointed her finger at the tree only a few yards away—"then I'll come and get you, and we'll have to move on until we do find a place. But we'll do it together."

He held her gaze for a long time, then finally nodded and let her go.

He was done in. If she couldn't find shelter, she'd just lie down here beside him. It would be very uncomfortable, but they'd make it through the night, and they'd make it back home.

TWENTY-SIX

*W*hat do you mean they didn't make it back home?"

Molly wanted to slap Wyatt, but she knew she was being irrational, so she didn't do anything she felt inclined to do.

"Kevin and Win went to town this morning and never came back. Win told me they would probably be home in time for the noon meal but not to wait for them." Molly flung her arms wide. "I'm here alone. What meal am I making that needs to be done perfectly on time anyway?"

"You should have come and got me."

"I didn't know where you were. And you"—she stormed right up to his face and jabbed him in the chest—"told me not to go out alone."

He swatted her hand aside. Since he was likely as scared as she was, she didn't hold it against him.

Much.

"And even so I stepped outside and listened, trying to hear any sound coming from your cattle that might lead me to you."

"I told you not to go outside!" He fisted his hands and leaned down until their noses almost touched.

This time she came even closer to slapping him.

"There are gunmen running around. You need to stay inside, and they shouldn't have gone anywhere, either."

"I told them that. In fact, I was yelling that very thing when they rode away."

Wyatt slammed one fist into the other hand. Despite Molly's fierce interest in slapping him, she didn't for one second worry he'd use that fist on her.

That was a nice way to feel about a man. It's how she felt about Kevin and Andy. She'd sure as certain never felt that way about her pa.

Wyatt pivoted toward the door. Andy was on his heels.

Wyatt glanced back, then held up the flat of his hand in Andy's face. "No, you stay here. Molly shouldn't have been left home alone all day. Kevin and Win should've never done that. What is *wrong* with them?"

He pointed at Andy. "She needs a man to stay here with her."

"I'll be on guard." Andy jerked his head, and his chest swelled with what could only be pride.

Molly watched Andy stand up straighter. Wyatt calling him a man seemed to make him taller and stronger. Probably better than when she treated him like a kid brother all the time.

"You're on duty until I get back, and lock this door behind me."

"I thought your ramrod was going to find them, but he never came back, either."

Wyatt stopped so suddenly he skidded. He turned to look at Molly. "Ross Baker was here?"

"Yes."

"Today?"

Molly rolled her eyes. "Of course today. Didn't I just tell

you he went to find them?" Molly was yelling and acting like a lunatic, and this wasn't like her. Worrying all day about Kevin and Win had clearly driven her mad.

"How did you know it was my ramrod?"

Molly faltered for a moment. "H-he told me. He said that was who he was, Ross Baker, and that he worked at the RHR as the ramrod. He came up to the back door of the house—this was shortly before noon—and he asked where you were working. I had no real idea. I thought he probably wanted to find you and get to work. I mentioned that I was worried about Win and Kevin, and he asked who Kevin was and who I was. I told him enough of it that he seemed to decide I had a right to be here in the house. Then he said he'd ride into town to meet them and ride shotgun while they came home."

"What did he look like?"

"You don't know what your own cowhands look like?" Molly's voice rose until the sharpness could have cut Wyatt's ears off.

"Just tell me!"

"Um . . . uh . . . black hair with a lot of gray in it. Dark eyes. Older. Forty or even fifty years old. He had a heavy forehead, and it seemed like he only had one eyebrow. He wore a black Stetson with a strange circle of feathers on a silver hatband."

"That's him. That's Ross Baker."

"So then that's a good thing. He's out there hunting."

"No, that's not a good thing." Wyatt's jaw formed a tight line. "Baker took off three weeks ago to ride to Texas. He was supposed to go see how his pa was doing. But he couldn't have gotten to Texas and back in three weeks."

"So he changed his mind." Molly shook her head, not understanding.

"Or he went into hiding and waited until you and your family got close enough he could attack you. The time he left was mighty convenient to the time I found out about Pa's will."

"He must be the one behind all of this," Andy said. "He's already tried to kill Kevin twice, and he might've waylaid Kevin now. My brother would have been back. Did Baker do it out of loyalty to you and Cheyenne?"

"No one shoots innocent people in my name. No one who's known me for a week would ever believe I'd think such a thing was right."

Wyatt's eyes narrowed at Molly. "Except your family would believe it of course."

"Quit fussing at me and get going," Molly said.

"Before I go, I'll tell you flat out, no, I don't think he did it out of some twisted notion of loyalty. I think he's got his own plans. I can't think what they might be, but I don't plan on turning my back on him for a single second."

Wyatt grabbed his hat, which he'd hung up on a peg as he'd entered the kitchen. He slammed the door and headed for the hitching post. Within seconds, he could be heard galloping out of the yard. There was still some daylight, so just maybe he could find Kevin before nightfall.

Or his body.

Molly turned to look at Andy, and his scowl had to be a match for hers. Then the long day of fretting caught up to her, and she launched herself into her little brother's arms.

He caught her with a strength that told her Wyatt was right to give him a man's responsibility. She had to stop thinking of him as a kid. Her brother had grown up.

He held her tight as they shared the fear for their big brother.

At last, she said, "So far Wyoming is measuring up to be a mighty poor excuse for a place to live."

~

Kevin woke slowly to the sound of soft rain and the pounding of aches and pains everywhere. He was dry, tucked deep into the shelter of a fallen tree, but he was so hungry his belly button was rubbing his backbone.

The more he woke up, the more miserable he was. His head felt like someone was trying to chisel their way out. His shoulders were on fire. One arm managed to be numb and ache like mad at the same time. He tried to swallow, but his mouth was as dry as dust.

His whole life was pure misery. Then he moved. The pain ratcheted up, and the reason for his misery roared through him.

He'd been shot.

And shot by men that would very likely be coming to make sure he was dead, maybe Win, too.

Win.

That's when he remembered something else. Something with no misery involved.

He was married.

And he was holding his wife in his arms.

He felt her move and realized he had, not just a wife, but a *beautiful* wife who was strong and had good sense. Everything in the world wasn't cold and pain. He had a warm wife who had gone beyond the strength of many to keep him alive.

But those men tried to kill her. . . . Though Kevin thought they might want to take her as a prisoner. Or had they really meant to take her back to her father? Their actual plan was muddled—or maybe his head was.

A lot of yesterday was muddled. But he remembered Win helping him, bearing so much of his weight because he was too wounded and addled to be of much use. Holding Win outweighed all his troubles by a long shot. And if they could just get home and put a stop to this madness of people trying to kill him, he could live himself a fine life.

"Kevin."

He'd been lost in thought, lost in the pleasure of holding her. Lost in the pain.

He shifted his gaze without moving his head and saw the prettiest blue eyes in the world. They were a bit puffy from sleep, and seeing her eyes first thing in the morning while he held her stirred something deep inside him. A sense that to wake up with her each morning would be a precious gift from a gracious God. He'd be delighted to begin every day like this.

He prayed they'd survive so they could.

"Good morning, wife." He smiled, and she managed a wobbly smile back. To encourage her, since she'd spent all day yesterday encouraging him, he said, "We'll head out for Wyatt's as soon as the rain ends. This rain should wipe out any tracks we left on the banks of that stream climbing out. They shouldn't be able to find us."

He looked out of their shelter and saw a fog so dense he wasn't sure he could find himself.

"Wyatt, Molly, and Andy will be sick with worry."

"And there'll be no tracks for Wyatt to follow, either." Kevin's spirits drooped. "Wyatt is a fine tracker, and you know he'll be looking. He might not mind overly if I vanished, but he'd object to you disappearing. Not to mention he'd want me to take Molly and Andy with me." He sighed. "I wonder if we've got a long day's walk, or if we'll be hiking for a week."

She shook her head. "Do we just stay in here, then, while it rains?"

A fine shiver went through her. She was as cold as he was. Should they head out into the rain and fog, or should they stay safe and warm and hungry while worrying their families to death?

Kevin tugged gently until some of her weight was flat on top of him and she faced him. "We haven't talked much about our faith."

"We haven't known each other long enough to talk about anything."

"But if we are decent people, who try to live by the vows we took yesterday, we can have a good marriage. I believe that."

"As do I. It's true you were the only man around when it became obvious that I had to do something to avoid being forced home to live with my father, but I am glad it was you."

That got a smile out of him. "You could have proposed to Wyatt."

"I couldn't propose to *Wyatt!*"

He had a firm grip on her shoulders and felt a delicate shudder go through her—this one not caused by the cold. "Why not? He's a good man."

She snorted. "He's like a little brother to me. Ick."

Kevin couldn't stop a chuckle. "Ick? I don't think Wyatt deserves that."

"Well, try and imagine yourself asking Molly to marry you."

Kevin felt the scowl wrinkle his face. "Molly's not *like* a sister to me. She *is* a sister to me."

"You're making my point. Because Wyatt is like a brother to me. A pestering, bad-smelling, loud-mouthed, prank-pulling, hair-yanking little brother. If I married him and he irritated me, I'd be tempted to wash his mouth out with soap or send him to sit in the corner."

Kevin left off his scowling and laughed loudly.

"What kind of foundation is that for a marriage?" A smile crept over Win's face, too. "I know he's not my brother, but it would just be very weird. I never considered it for a second. Actually, I've never considered anyone but you. We have had a few . . . uh . . . moments together. I think if I'd had more time, and I wasn't forced into this, I'd have hoped you . . . that is . . . we . . . I mean . . ."

Her cheeks turned pink, and she shrugged as if she wasn't quite able to finish her thought.

"You hoped we might get to a wedding after a bit more time had passed?"

She nodded. The pink deepened. She was admitting to the attraction between them. Admitting it had been there before she'd proposed. After she proposed, that kiss . . . well, there'd been no denying it.

"You're right. I felt it, too." He eased his grip on her shoulders and rubbed his hands up and down her arms.

Feeling foolish and weak, he said, "Can you help me sit up?"

"Oh, Kevin. I'm so sorry. I wasn't even thinking of your injuries. I shouldn't have put my weight on you."

"I hurt. There's no denying that. But a little thing like you doesn't make it much worse." He brushed his thumb along the line of her jaw. "And holding you made it a lot better. But now I'd like some help. I'm afraid I'm going to need it."

Win got her weight off him. He missed it, while at the same time wondered if he might have a cracked rib. Her slight weight hadn't been helping, though in his overall agony, he only noticed the pain being just slightly less when she moved.

She slid an arm behind his shoulders. Kevin, his teeth clenched to keep from groaning, sat up an inch at a time. Every muscle and joint protested. He shoved at the forest floor with his left arm. His right one was useless. He was glad the ground was soft. Win helped him turn a bit so he could rest his back against some stones that made up the far wall in their crude shelter.

"Sit there just a moment." Win crawled to the edge of the overhead tree and tugged on a sheet of bark still sticking to the trunk. She got off a piece shaped like an irregular square about a foot across. She rubbed her hands over the bark, then held it out in the rain and rubbed some more.

Water. She was getting them a drink.

She curved the bark, and the water ran out one end. Then she rubbed on the bark some more. The inner part that had been against the tree crumbled, and the rain rinsed the bark thoroughly. The next time she curved it, she said, "I'm going to have a drink."

She looked over her shoulder at him, frowning. "Can you get over here? I don't think I'll be able to exactly collect it. I've just made the bark into a sort of trough. I can't bring it to you. Well, maybe I'd be able to bring a sip or two, but it would take a long time to get you a real drink."

She put her mouth to the edge of the curved bark, tilted it toward her, and drank steadily as the rain came down.

The desert dryness in his throat was enough to make him move. He did it by ignoring the pain as best he could and enduring what he couldn't ignore. He wanted water bad enough to do whatever he had to do.

By the time he'd crawled the few feet to her side, she lifted her mouth from the edge of the bark and grinned at him.

"It's the best water I've ever had."

He'd've laughed if he wasn't so thirsty.

"Your turn." She angled the bark in his direction, and he saw the precious flow of water being wasted.

He sipped at it, and the cool wetness seemed to fill the cracks in his mouth, tongue, and throat. He was a long time drinking enough to make his throat moist all the way down, then he moved away. With a smile he could finally manage, he said, "You're a mighty handy woman to have around, Mrs. Hunt. I declare if I wasn't married to you already, I'd haul you off to a parson right now."

Win finished another drink and turned the bark back to him.

While he drank, she said, "And I believe I'd go, Mr. Hunt. Even if I didn't have all the reasons I do to marry you, I'd do it anyway."

Taking turns, they at last had their fill. Kevin crawled deeper into their shelter and sat down, resting his aching bones. His arm was starting to come back to life, and with the end of the numbness came pain. Sighing, he leaned back, ready to do what needed doing no matter how puny he felt.

Win set the bark aside and sat next to him.

Yes, she had strength and good sense. Every time he saw another sign of that, he liked her more.

And he already liked her real well.

Side by side, they watched the fog shroud the whole world as if they had their own secret hiding place. The sound of the rain relaxed him and helped ease the stiffness out of his battered bones.

They sat there, just the two of them, and watched the world outside their shelter. Kevin felt a bond growing between them, connecting them in a way that belonged inside a marriage.

And that connection reminded him of his earlier question.

"When I asked about your faith . . . Yes, there's a lot we don't know about each other, but maybe nothing so important as that. And thinking about whether to strike out in the rain, or stay here cold and hungry, I thought we should pray. You prayed yesterday after your father left, so I know you're a praying woman."

"I am indeed."

"That's a comfort to me. I really don't know what's best to do. I don't know how far we have to hike or how long it'll take us to get back to the RHR. I don't know if walking out is safer now with the cover of rain. The fog is deep enough that I'm not sure I can even pick the right direction to walk. Who can tell north, south, east, or west in this fog? Those men might give up their pursuit because of the weather. Or they could have holed up somewhere just like we did. But if they picked a spot back near the trail from the RHR to Bear Claw Pass, they could be biding their time, watching for us. We should ask God for guidance, and see if we get a still small voice advising us of what to do next."

Win looked into his eyes, and their gazes caught and held. Then she leaned forward and kissed him. A gentle kiss that ended far too soon. "To answer your question, yes, my faith is important to me. I agree that there is nothing so important. Yes, let's pray."

Kevin kissed her back, far longer, more deeply. Then he ended the kiss and pulled her tight into his arms. And they prayed.

TWENTY-SEVEN

*W*in didn't hear the still small voice of God telling them to go out in the rain. Neither did she hear God telling her to stay put. Following the leading of God could be tricky.

"I suppose being told nothing means we stay here." Kevin sounded restless, like a man who thought he needed to *do* something.

Win could only agree with his fidgety decision to do nothing, so they sat wrapped in each other's arms.

The wind gusted and blew a bit of rain into their makeshift cave.

"Staying here isn't going to keep us from getting wet, I'm afraid," Kevin said into her ear.

The rain fell faster, and the day, which had been warming slightly, turned cooler.

Kevin tucked them into the deepest spot against the boulder. It did provide a bit of shelter as the wind gusted the rain toward them.

Turning her in his arms, Kevin kissed her. She wrapped her arms tight around his neck and let herself be drawn into the kiss.

A crash of thunder jolted them apart. She smiled at her husband. "You are doing an excellent job of distracting me from wanting to head for home."

"And I don't pay much mind to my aches when you're in my arms. We're helping each other get through this."

"By kissing?"

"Oh yes." He ran a hand deep into her hair. It had to be a terrible mess, but his eyes held only appreciation.

He lowered his head again just as a crash sounded that wasn't thunder. A sudden movement from the far end of the tree-trunk cave whirled them both around.

A man ducked under the tree trunk, saw them, and froze.

Win gasped.

~

Wyatt charged back into the ranch house. "Have they come back?"

"No." Molly sat, scared and pale, at the kitchen table clutching a coffee cup.

Wyatt, drenched, cold, and exhausted, took off his soaking wet coat and hung it up to drip. He kicked off his muddy boots and went for the coffee pot as he heard Andy's feet thundering down the stairs.

Andy, with his pants pulled on but not buttoned and gun in hand, charged into the kitchen, saw Wyatt, and lowered the gun to aim at the floor.

Wyatt thought it showed some good sense that the boy hadn't shot first and seen who he was shooting at later.

"You didn't find him?" Andy asked.

"Nope. But I rode all over last night until it was too dark to see, then I rode into town and ran around waking people up and asking questions like a fool. I finally got around to Parson Brownley. He told me . . . He told me . . ." Wyatt plucked a tin cup off a nail on the wall and slammed the cup on the stovetop. "He told me Win and your brother got hitched yesterday morning."

Andy's eyes popped wide. "They did what?"

Molly surged to her feet. "Kevin married Winona Hawkins?" Her voice was screeching like a trapped hen by the time she finished.

Nodding his sodden head, Wyatt poured the steaming, rich-scented brew. "I'll take your reactions to mean you didn't know."

"God have mercy, what brought this on?" Molly slapped herself in the face.

Wyatt drew in a long drink of steaming hot coffee, hoping it'd melt his deeply chilled innards . . . and his deeply chilled brain. He gripped the cup tight to warm his hands, trying to remember what sleep was like. Food. Warmth. Win and Kevin had taken a big risk to make a blamed fool decision. And now they were missing, and Wyatt had no idea how to find them.

Sickened, he admitted he also had no idea how to find their bodies. Two more people lost in the wilderness to join Falcon Hunt. And the killers, including, it seemed, Ross Baker, were still around. Maybe still with plans to kill.

"Why would he do that?" Andy asked.

"Go get a shirt on," Molly snapped.

Andy looked down at his long woolen underwear and a dull red blush bloomed on his cheeks. He darted out of the room, but the pounding feet on the stairs told Wyatt he'd be back soon.

Wyatt turned on Molly. "What went on around here this last week?"

"Nothing," she sputtered. "Win spent all of it in her room.

Kevin never went near her after he carried her up there that first day." Her eyes widened. "Well, almost nothing."

Wyatt felt his teeth clench until he thought they might crack. "What is 'almost nothing'?"

Molly shook her head and swallowed hard. "Yesterday her father came over. Well, no, I mean the day before yesterday." Molly rubbed her eyes with the heels of her hands. Wyatt could see she hadn't slept a wink and was on the brink of keeling over with exhaustion. He knew what that felt like.

"Mr. Hawkins came in acting mad enough to spit bullets. He'd found out Win had been shot and was furious because we hadn't sent word to him."

"That sounds like Win not to tell him, and spitting bullets sounds like Hawkins. He's always on about something. That's why I don't put much stock in his smiles and good-natured talking. When something gets him worked up, all that good nature shows itself to be nothing but skin deep. What did he do? What did he say to her?"

"H-he demanded she come home. He said he was riding to town to tell the school board she was quitting, and she was going to live at his ranch from now on. We managed to get him not to just haul her away by warning him her stitches weren't healed enough for it to be safe for her to ride. He said he'd give her until the stitches were out, no longer. Win tried to calm him down, but he wouldn't bend on it. He said she was coming home and that was that. I could tell Win was desperate not to go. And then . . ." Molly rested a fist against her brow and started slowly punching herself in the head.

"What is it?"

"She asked us to leave her alone to pray. We got out of the kitchen and didn't come back for a while. Later she asked to talk to Kevin alone. I left them down here. When I heard them go outside, I hurried to the window and saw them go into the ramrod's house. I was shocked that they'd close themselves together like that, but I trust Kevin's judgment and didn't go out and interrupt them as would be proper."

Wyatt growled. "Proper is the least of our worries."

"After Win went to bed, I finally cornered Kevin and asked him what was going on. What did Win have to say to him that needed such privacy?"

She looked up at Wyatt, and he saw the hurt in those pretty blue eyes.

"Kevin wouldn't tell me. Kevin and I talk about everything. We always have since Ma died. We've always trusted each other, so I was surprised he wouldn't tell me what she wanted. I admit it hurt my feelings. Instead of demanding to know, I let him go to bed. He did say Win wanted to go into town. I told him they shouldn't, not with gunmen roaming far and wide, but he said she had a really good reason, and he'd tell me about it when they got back."

Molly's cheeks flushed with sudden anger, and she pushed back against her chair. "I'll just *bet* he'd've told me then. It'd've been mighty hard to explain Win moving into the ramrod's house with him if they didn't say there'd been a wedding."

Wyatt added it all up fast. "She talked Kevin into marrying her to keep from having to move home."

"That is ridiculous," Molly sputtered. "Why would she not want to go home so badly that she'd marry a near stranger? Does this have to do with Cheyenne threatening to marry her pa?"

"I know Win has no use for her pa, but I've never seen how she'd react if he refused to let her stay here because he always has. But . . . I've always thought she just liked it over here. Maybe it wasn't staying here she wanted, maybe it was staying away from home. She lives in town while the school is running and out here the rest of the time. He seems agreeable to that. Why would he want her back so bad now?"

"Maybe he's truly scared for her after she was shot."

"Maybe." Wyatt was mighty doubtful, but it was possible.

"Have they done more than get married?" Molly asked.

"What's that supposed to mean?" Wyatt's mind raced as he thought of the things married people might do. It was mighty improper of Molly to ask such a thing.

"Did they run off? Not just get married, but . . . but . . . but get married and move to . . . to Topeka?"

"What's Topeka?"

"It's the capital of Kansas!" Molly roared.

Wyatt was stunned. Not to find out that Topeka was the capital of Kansas, but Molly shouting at him was mighty stunning. She wasn't a roaring kind of woman.

Win running off like that . . . Was it possible?

No, it wasn't. Kevin didn't believe it, and he almost wished he could because that would mean she was safe, missing but safe. "She'd know I'd worry. She wouldn't do that."

Molly's shoulders squared, and her chin came up. "Kevin would never just run off for good. He wouldn't abandon me and Andy."

Wyatt's mind was running around like a trapped rabbit fretting over Win. But one tiny part of that mind took notice that Molly's blue eyes flashed like the summer lightning that was sparking outside, and she was about the most beautiful woman he'd ever seen.

Her brother might've abandoned her to Wyatt's mercies.

And if he had, then Kevin had left his little sister to live here with Wyatt. For good.

A dart of anticipation cleared his thinking. Because anticipation was just pure stupid. "I don't know Kevin as well as you do, but nope, he wouldn't do that. And none of this even includes the return of Ross Baker and why he went off after Win and never came back."

Andy came running back down, still buttoning his shirt.

"And that means wherever they are, they're in trouble." Molly got up from the table and went to hug Andy.

Wyatt felt a little sorry for himself since no one ever hugged him. Thunder cracked outside. He turned to look out the window in the back door. The rain changed from a light patter to a downpour.

"I'll never find a trail, and I just have no notion of where to look."

"Somewhere between here and Bear Claw Pass," Andy said with a grim expression. "Let's get going."

Wyatt turned to look at the young man he'd started thinking of as a little brother. A smart kid, hardworking. A lot to learn, but Wyatt had had a lot to learn once, and his grandpa, Ma, and Cheyenne had helped him, like he was helping Andy.

Now that young man had the look of a grown-up. The look of a tough hombre who was going to search for his brother, and no rainstorm was going to stop him.

A crack of lightning flashed, followed by thunder so loud it seemed to shake the house.

"We'll wait until the lightning passes, then we'll go. And it has to be all three of us. We can't leave Molly here alone." He thought of his foreman and his other cowhands. They'd all be around the home place today. No calf was getting branded in this weather. But for the first time in his life he was stumped about whom to trust. Surely he could trust Rubin. Rubin Walsh had helped raise him.

But a day ago, he'd've put Baker on the list of men he'd trust with his life. Now he had to ask if Baker was on his third murder attempt.

Molly looked at the slashing rain. Another bolt of lightning lit up the murky outdoors. The thunder crack came right with the light.

"And this time, we'll keep searching until we find him," Molly said scornfully. "Unlike how you did it with your *other* brother."

TWENTY-EIGHT

alcon?" Kevin asked.

The man was drenched. He looked filthy and scruffy. Like a man who had been in the wilderness for a week.

His eyes locked on Kevin with suspicion and something feral. Something so untamed that Win slid her hands around Kevin's waist in a futile effort to support him or, God help her, protect him from his own brother. Falcon darted into the far end of the shelter, willing to share with them to get out of the rain. He subsided and watched them.

"Falcon, we thought you were dead." Kevin made a move toward Falcon.

A knife appeared like magic in Falcon's hand. Drawn fast and held in a way that was a pure threat. What Kevin's intent was, Win couldn't say. If he was planning to hug his brother, that was a real poor idea. Wisely, Kevin froze at the sight of the knife.

"What's the matter?" Kevin eased back.

Win felt like a bear had climbed in to share their meager space. A fierce, filthy, furry bear. With claws.

The man shook his head to try to end the water dripping in his face. "Can I . . ." His deep Southern accent reminded Win of how completely he resembled Clovis. Except right now it took a powerful imagination to picture the clean-shaven, expansive, smiling Clovis Hunt looking like this untamed man.

"Can you what?" Kevin waited. When Falcon didn't answer him, Kevin said, "We thought you were dead. You went over a waterfall, possibly shot."

Falcon's eyes locked on Kevin's as if Falcon found every word fascinating.

"Then we found your hat at the bottom of a stony, viciously fast-moving stream."

Falcon's lips moved.

Win was sure he murmured "my hat." Why would his hat be the first thing he'd comment on?

"Wyatt said you couldn't have survived going over those falls," Kevin continued. "We trailed you for a time, looking for your body."

Win remembered Kevin and Wyatt talking of it. They hadn't trailed him for long. Wyatt was so sure there was no point. She wanted to box Wyatt's ears. Another good reason she was wise not to marry the little half-wit.

"I'm so sorry. We should have kept hunting for you." Kevin moved forward again just a bit. Win wondered if he wanted to touch Falcon, to convince himself his brother was really here, alive and well. The brandished knife stopped him.

"Whoever shot you or—or knocked you over the falls, or whatever they did—is still around. We were afraid they might harm Win and the others back at the ranch house, so we quit hunting for you. We should have searched until we found you."

Falcon just stared. His eyes on Kevin as if nothing he said made sense. As if Falcon's brain was racing, and he couldn't figure out any of this.

Then Falcon lifted a hand to the back of his head, still staring.

"Is that where they shot you?" Kevin touched the bandage on his own head. "They shot me, too. We think—"

"Who are you?" It was only the second time Falcon had spoken. And his voice sounded like a hundred miles of graveled riverbed. That strong accent twanged through the three words, but otherwise he sounded like a man whose voice was near rusted shut from lack of use. A man who hadn't spoken to anyone for a long time.

His question shut Kevin up.

Win was speechless herself.

Something was very wrong with Falcon Hunt. Realizing that didn't make her a genius.

To break the silence, Win dropped a few words in, and they seemed to explode like a cannonball bursting into their little hideaway. "He's your brother."

Falcon looked from Win back to Kevin. "My brother?"

He hadn't put that knife away yet.

"Yes, your brother Kevin Hunt. And I'm his wife, Winona Hunt." Then she felt absolutely unable to stop herself from saying something outrageous. But she was sorely afraid it had to be said. "And you're Falcon Hunt. You've come from Tennessee to Wyoming to claim an inheritance from your father."

Slowly Falcon began shaking his head, not shedding water this time, just pure confusion and doubt.

Kevin leaned against the back of their shelter, worry etched on his face. Falcon's too. Win figured she probably looked the same.

Falcon lowered the knife very slowly. The steady beat of the rain was the only sound. Win decided giving everyone time to think was the best policy so she eased back, too.

Finally, Falcon said, "I've been wandering for days."

"You disappeared a week ago, Falcon." Kevin kept leaning away. Giving his brother a lot of room to consider it all. "You must have been out here alone all this time."

"First thing I remember is waking up on the banks of a stream and didn't know nothing. Not a dad-blasted thing."

"Not even your name?" Kevin asked.

Shaking his head, Falcon stared down at his hands as if they held his memory. "I didn't know where I was . . . I mean, sure, in the mountains, but they didn't look like anywhere I'd ever been, but then, I couldn't remember being anywhere ever. I knew I should've had a gun. Why would I remember I normally have a gun, when I didn't remember my own name?"

He rubbed the back of his head again. "I knew how to un-ravel the threads from my shirt and rig a snare to catch birds. I could start a fire using my knife and a flint I found in my pocket."

"All that but not who you are?" Kevin sounded bewildered.

Falcon gave a small shrug. "I didn't exactly *remember* how to do those things, I just knew how." His eyes flickered up to meet Kevin's. They shifted to Win, then he pulled his hands together in his lap and looked at them as if they confused him. "It was like the knowledge just came out of my fingertips without me thinkin' much about it."

"I've heard of someone losing their memory." Win drew both men's attention when she said that. "A sickness or a blow to the head can cause it. *Amnesia*—that's the word I learned."

"Amnesia?" Falcon said the word slowly as if he wanted to remember the thing that made him forget. He looked calmer. A man ready to settle in, rest, talk, and figure out what was wrong with him.

Win figured talk and a long rest might help the poor man.

A bullet blasted louder than thunder, and wood exploded from the log inches over Kevin's head.

Falcon dived out so fast, so silent, that Win wondered for a second if he'd even been there. Another bullet hit so close wood chips scratched her face. More bullets peppered the back of their shelter as she clawed her way out, slowed down by Kevin having a grip like a vise on her wrist.

They leapt toward the end of the tree, a massive root that stuck high enough in the air that Win couldn't see the top of it in the deep fog and driving rain.

Kevin dodged around the huge root, top stretching like skeletal fingers into the air. She caught one of the tendrils to swing herself around, and a bullet clipped the root off. She fell sideways when she lost her grip, landing on her shoulder. Then Kevin had her again, and they were behind the trunk.

"Shhh," Kevin whispered to her. "If we're quiet the fog will hide us."

Looking at the wrist he clung to, she saw that she still had that piece of root clasped in her fingers. And her hand was bleeding but not badly. She hadn't been shot, just scratched by flying bark and wood. Rainwater sent the blood washing away in rivulets.

Kevin moved on, quiet as he could be. It was impossible to be truly noiseless while walking through a hundred years of dried leaves and tight scrub brush with branches reaching out to scrape at them. She thought of how Falcon had vanished out of that shelter. Completely silent. Kevin had described Falcon as a ghost on the day he'd come to them in the woods after Win had been shot.

Kevin found another downed tree. An oak so long dead it

had only a few heavy branches left. Kevin jumped up on it and drew Win along. He shocked her with how quiet he was. He'd talked some about the war years and learning to sneak. She realized for the first time just how dangerous it had been. No farmer needed this kind of woodland skill, especially not a farmer who'd lived mostly on a prairie.

The fog wrapped around them, swirling as they stirred the air. They reached the end of the tree. Kevin paused until the sound of an oncoming thunderclap rolled across the sky toward them. In the racket, he stepped down, caught Win around the waist and lowered her, then walked a very few paces to another downed tree, his footsteps cloaked by the thunder and pounding rain.

These woods were full of the dead growing along with the living. It helped, too, that the leaves were soaking wet. They weren't as crunchy as they might've been.

They moved from one downed tree to the next, putting space between themselves and whoever was firing.

Win had to suspect it was Baker and Tuttle.

A bullet whizzed by, but not close. Their assailants were firing blind, wasting ammunition. Kevin lifted her to the top of another fallen tree, and they rushed the length of it. The roots on this tree were even bigger than the one that had sheltered them.

Kevin turned to Win. Touched his finger to her lips, then waited, slashed by rain, until the thunder came again.

In the noise of the storm, he stepped down off the tree. This time, instead of holding her by the waist, he scooped her up into his arms and moved around the outreaching expanse of roots and ducked up against the base of it. The roots formed another near cave. The rain came in, and Kevin crouched low, pressing both of them against the trunk. And there they waited.

He'd picked his hiding place. They were hiding more in the storm than in any good spot. Win could only hope the rain kept falling and the fog helped to conceal them.

~

Minutes ticked past. Kevin listened to every crackle of leaves and branches. But the gusting wind and the pouring rain, battered by the thunder and lightning, gave them a world full of noise. How to pick out a man among them?

Then he heard something that could be a footstep. He pressed Win behind him, pinned to the huge, splaying hand of the tree roots. He drew his pocket knife from his boot. A pathetic weapon but all he had.

Another rumble of thunder told him the storm was moving past. He'd be able to hear now, but those in pursuit would hear, too, and they might be able to see.

If the fog thinned, Kevin feared his hiding place would be worthless.

Branches broke as if someone snapped them off with impatient hands.

Win clutched the back of his sodden shirt. He nodded, hoping she'd see his response. Hoping she'd trust him to protect her. Hoping her trust wasn't misplaced.

"This way," said a rough, angry voice close on his left.

Kevin could no longer tell himself those men weren't closing in. He reached behind himself and tugged Win's hands loose from his shirt. He needed to be free to move.

More footsteps slopped through the wet leaves, coming closer, moving faster. As if the men saw something that drew them this way.

Bracing himself to leap at anyone who found them, Kevin

knew he was going to get shot. Men with knives didn't win battles against guns.

But he didn't have to win, he only had to stay alive long enough to take the gun away from the first man and use it on him and his partner. Though sickened to think his last act on this earth might be killing a man, Kevin knew he'd do it. To fail was to leave Win to these villains.

Praying for forgiveness, wisdom, strength, and eternal peace in the next life, he bunched his muscles to leap. A man took form out of the fog. He was looking straight ahead. It was Ross Baker. He had his gun out, and aimed forward while Kevin hid on his right.

Suddenly Baker pivoted, cocking his gun as he turned to aim straight at Kevin and Win. Kevin dove upward, blocking the gun's path to Win. He slammed into Baker, who went over backward, falling hard under Kevin's weight, his gun flying sideways. It fired harmlessly when it landed on a stone.

Kevin dropped his knife and swung a fist, then another, but Baker didn't struggle, didn't hit back. He lay limp and unresisting. Not sure how the man had failed to shoot him, Kevin jumped away from him to look down at the wide-open eyes and slack jaw of a dead man.

There was no time to try to figure out what had happened. He whirled to find Win right behind him with a fist-sized rock in her hand.

Kevin whispered, "Let's go."

A gun cocked somewhere in the fog. "Don't move."

Kevin recognized the chilling voice of Bern Tuttle from yesterday.

"Stand still, or I'll kill all of you."

Kevin froze. His eyes searched the white fog. All? That sounded like more than two.

A man stepped close enough to see.

Falcon.

For a second, Kevin thought Falcon had come to kill them. He'd heard Tuttle, but was Falcon in cahoots with him somehow?

And then he saw Falcon's hands were extended high. And another form came out of the fog, right behind Falcon. Bern Tuttle.

"Get your hands up." Bern gestured at Kevin with his six-shooter.

Kevin's hands rose to match Falcon's.

He noticed Falcon's knife was gone from the sheath on his belt. Then he noticed a trickle of blood pooling under Baker.

The way a man might bleed who'd had a knife stuck in his back.

Without being told, Kevin knew Falcon had saved them both, when a man with his woodland skill could have saved himself. For an instant—now they were plunged back into trouble. Baker's partner was here to settle things.

Falcon's piercing hazel eyes were locked on Kevin. The man was planning something and wanted to give Kevin plenty of warning. Warning of some desperate act most likely. Kevin readied himself to jump in and help wherever he could.

"Stand beside your brother."

The rain was slowing at last. The thunder fading as the storm raced on eastward. The fog was still thick but thinning a little.

"Why are you doing this?" Win sounded shrill and panicky. Not a voice he'd heard from her before, and he'd been with her when she was shot and when she was desperately trying to escape her father's control over her life.

Which meant she was faking her panic. Which meant Win was planning something, too.

Kevin tried hard to plan something himself; it seemed like everyone else was. But all he could do was be ready to jump whatever direction seemed called for.

"Did my father hire you to kill Kevin and Falcon? Does he want you to kill m-me?"

Win's voice broke. She was drawing the killer's attention to herself. If the man's aim lessened for even a moment, Kevin and Falcon both had a chance.

"Your pa's as big a fool as Wyatt Hunt. Ross and me saw how things were gonna be when Clovis split up the ranch. We saw a chance to make something of ourselves. Kill the heirs before they knew what they were inheriting."

The man gestured at Falcon. "We tried to kill you in Independence, Missouri."

Kevin looked at Falcon. "Someone tried to kill you, too?"

Falcon gave him a look of pure frustrated fury. Kevin understood then that Falcon couldn't remember, and he didn't want to reveal that weakness.

"Never figured it to have much to do with this," Falcon said dryly.

Tuttle gave a harsh laugh. "You're a hard man to kill, Falcon Hunt. You not only got past us, you stole our horses, guns, money, and supplies and headed on west. You're a thief."

Falcon drawled, "Sounds like justice to me."

"Then we hit Kevin on the trail and missed."

"You both had good jobs." Kevin couldn't keep the contempt out of his voice. "You didn't need to turn to thieving and murder."

He saw the rise of color in Tuttle's face at the insult.

"I aim to finish this. Then marry you, Win."

Win gasped. "I'd never marry you."

Tuttle smirked. "Sometimes a woman has to learn a lesson or two before she does as she's told. I'll enjoy teaching you that lesson."

Win sniffed. "But you're standing there with a gun aimed. You must intend to kill me."

A smiled crossed the man's face that spoke of pure evil. "Oh, I'll marry you, Miss Hawkins, then get you back to your pa's ranch. With your pa the kind of worthless man he is, I'll be running the place and running it right. When he dies—which might not take him long—it'll all be mine."

"You're a fool to think I'd agree to that."

"You might agree fast enough if I took you into a hideaway in the woods and kept you there awhile. I'd learn you to mind me with the back of my hand."

"What about Baker?" Win asked. "How was he going to profit from any of this?"

"His part was to marry up with Miss Cheyenne." A grim frown tightened Tuttle's face, and he glanced down at his partner in this crime.

"Despite your plotting and all the attacks, you haven't killed anyone yet, Tuttle. What you should do," Win said with crisp command, "is ride out of here. Just go. Find a new part of the country to live in. You won't have a murder charge hanging over your head. If you leave now, you'll have a good head start by the time we hike out of here, and I doubt anyone will look for you long."

"Or I can kill these two men and drag you off, get some

revenge for the death of a friend, and end up a rich man." Tuttle laughed, revealing blackened teeth.

Kevin shuddered to think of Win in this man's power. He'd braced himself to take a bullet, and he'd been spared. This time if he jumped, Falcon would be here to get Win back to safety. Kevin did have a plan.

He held back, wanting one chance, one distraction. Tuttle aimed right at Kevin's gut, and his hand tightened on the trigger.

A shot rang out. Win screamed. Kevin felt nothing. He looked down at his chest and saw no blood.

Then he looked up to see Tuttle standing, staring at his empty, bleeding gun hand. The gun lying on the ground. Tuttle fumbled with his left hand for a knife in a scabbard on his right.

Kevin jumped forward and slammed a fist in Tuttle's face. Kevin yanked the knife away and watched Tuttle collapse backward, cradling his damaged hand to his chest, mewling like a wounded kitten.

Kevin turned, noticing Falcon did the same, to see a rifle smoking in the hand of—

"Cheyenne!" Win rushed past Kevin and threw herself into the arms of Cheyenne Brewster. Kevin and Falcon's runaway sister.

Cheyenne looked at Falcon and said, "Who are you?"

Well, sort of sister.

She was covered from head to toe in a black slicker. A hood pulled low over her face, but not so far over they couldn't see her.

"That's Falcon Hunt." Win's voice was muffled against Cheyenne's hood.

Kevin felt Falcon come up behind him. Falcon whispered, "Who is she?"

"More family. She's a sister . . . sort of."

Cheyenne looked over Win's shoulder. Ice cold eyes, black as night, glared at Kevin. "I am in no way your sister."

There was a way, but Kevin decided not to try to explain it. Cheyenne wouldn't welcome it, Win wouldn't notice it, and Falcon wouldn't remember it.

Cheyenne took Win by the shoulders, thrust her back, and studied her face. Since Kevin couldn't see her face, he walked up to them and looked, too. Win had a smile that nearly pierced the gloomy fog.

"Falcon, huh?" Cheyenne said. "I've been following you for days."

Falcon ran one big hand into his drenched hair and said, "Yep, I saw you back there and didn't want to talk. Once I was close enough to you to tap you on the shoulder and say, 'Leave me alone,' but I let you sleep."

Cheyenne took it like the insult it was and narrowed her eyes, then she let go of Win and strode over to the man she'd shot. She knelt beside him. "He's dead."

Kevin caught Win by the hand and pulled her along to Tuttle's other side.

Cheyenne looked up, her eyes riveted on Win and Kevin's hands, then she went back to studying Tuttle. "I must've cut through the wrist and set it to bleeding."

"It's an artery." Win-the-know-it-all slid one arm across Kevin's back.

"You don't need to see this," Kevin said to Win.

"What is going on with you two?" Cheyenne stood. She didn't appear all that upset to find out she'd killed a man.

Win smiled at Kevin. "We're married."

"What?" Cheyenne shoved the hood off her head. That was when Kevin noticed the rain had stopped.

"Yep, well and truly married. Vows spoken before God and man." Kevin put his arm around Win, finding it a pleasure to annoy Cheyenne. And considering she'd just saved his life, that seemed petty and yet . . . true.

"You're married. Falcon has been wandering in the woods for days. Armed gunmen hunting everyone." Cheyenne flung her arms wide. "I can't leave any of you alone for a minute or trouble comes flooding."

"This one's dead, too." Falcon knelt by the man he'd killed.

Kevin wondered if Falcon would speak words over Ross Baker or bow his head in prayer. Instead, he lifted Baker up by one shoulder and flopped him over on his face. He yanked his knife out of the man's back, swiped it on the wet leaves to clean the blood off, and thrust it back into his scabbard.

"We were going to be kicked out of the ramrod's house with Baker coming home." Win winked at Kevin. "I guess we don't have to worry about that anymore."

TWENTY-NINE

*T*hey started the trek back to the RHR, and Win was grateful for Cheyenne's presence. She was the only one who knew where they were. And with Cheyenne leading them out of the woods, the going was easier.

When they reached an open stretch with a clear game trail, they shifted to walk four abreast through the grassy valley. Cheyenne said, "I knew someone was out there. I figured him for a troublemaker, so I tried to track him, but he always kept out of sight." She glanced in Falcon's direction. "Not many could've led me on such a chase. You're good."

Falcon grunted. "So are you. I heard, saw, and smelled you the whole time, and I done my best to slip away. Never fully managed it."

Cheyenne dragged her slicker off over her head, revealing a holster on her hip and a rifle strapped across her back. She carried a heavy haversack over her shoulder and under one arm. She folded up the slicker without missing a step and shoved it into her bag. Then she drew thick chunks of beef jerky out.

"That looks freshly smoked." Win rested one hand on her growling stomach.

Cheyenne studied her a minute and asked, "Are you hungry?"

"Yes, I haven't eaten since supper night before last."

Cheyenne handed over a strip of meat. "Now tell me why those men were trying to kill you."

"A lot has happened since you rode off," Kevin said. "When Falcon tracked the man who shot Win, he fell or was shoved into the creek that goes over a waterfall on your land. We thought he was dead. Wyatt said no one could survive those falls and the rocky white water beyond."

"I know those falls and that stretch of water. No one could survive it." Cheyenne turned to study Falcon.

He just kept walking. Whatever else he'd forgotten, he appeared to remember he was a man of few words.

Kevin reached out and took the jerky from Cheyenne when it was offered. Falcon shook his head when Cheyenne made the same offer to him. Miraculously, his small fur bag had stayed strapped around him during his trip over the falls, and after scavenging in the woods for days, he had his own supply of food.

Kevin took up his story again. "Yesterday on our way home from town—"

"Where you got married?" Cheyenne arched a brow.

Win nodded, and Kevin took her hand. "Yes," she said, "where we got married. Baker and Tuttle met us on the trail back to the RHR."

"Baker said he had to go to Texas and see his pa once more before he died," Cheyenne said. "That was two weeks ago. No, it was maybe three weeks. But not long enough that he could've gotten back."

"He could have gotten back if he didn't really go to Texas," Win said. "Rather, if he heard about Clovis's will and took off to try and kill Kevin and Falcon."

"If he can get to Missouri and back to attack Falcon, then he could get to Texas and back, couldn't he?" Kevin asked.

Cheyenne shrugged. "He set out on his horse to ride to Texas. That's a long ride. But he could get to Missouri by train mighty fast."

Kevin told her about being shot, going downstream, and getting this far hiking back toward the RHR before they slept.

"And that's why we haven't eaten," Win added quietly. "Can I have some more of your jerky?"

Cheyenne handed both Win and Kevin a good-sized chunk of bread, a couple of strips of jerky, and an apple.

"How'd you get all this food out here?" Kevin asked through a mouthful of bread.

"I was headed into the wilderness." Cheyenne's voice echoed with scorn. "I packed food, bullets, supplies. I even included a slicker in case it rained."

Win chewed on the salty jerky. Nothing had ever tasted so good. "You don't have to say it like we should have packed. Falcon was knocked into a rushing stream, and we were attacked by two gunmen."

"Ross Baker and Bern Tuttle . . ." Cheyenne thought it over. "I listened to him while I angled around to get a clean shot. And they thought to marry us, kill Falcon and Kevin before they got here, and then what? Kill Wyatt too? Or did they plan on letting him stay on and own half? Tuttle might've been able to run your ranch, Win, with your pa's way of hiring the work done, but Baker could never have taken over the RHR. Wyatt and I wouldn't have allowed that."

"Maybe he saw himself as another Clovis Hunt," Win suggested. "Maybe he planned to lie about in the house and spend money."

Cheyenne chomped into an apple while she heard more details about their time in the woods. Then they got to Falcon not remembering his name. "Amnesia? You really have that?"

"Win called it such," Falcon said. "Strange word."

"New word for me." Cheyenne crunched into the apple again.

"Me too," Kevin said.

Win shrugged one shoulder. "I'm not even sure I'm saying it right. It's just something I heard of years ago in school."

"What do you want to know?" Cheyenne asked Falcon.

Falcon seemed to relax a little with that question. "I'm not sure. I had no notion of having such a big family. If you're my brother's sister, then you're my sister, too."

"Not in any way. I'm not even *close* to being a sister to either of you." Cheyenne crunched on the apple as if it were Falcon's head.

Falcon's brow furrowed in confusion. He turned to Kevin. "And two brothers. It doesn't sound right. It just doesn't seem like it fits who I am. But that makes no sense. I—I guess when you said Tennessee that sounded like something I've heard before. Maybe."

"You lived there your whole life," Kevin said. "Until news reached you that a pa you thought was dead for years turned up truly dead just a few weeks ago. He left you a share of his ranch, and you rode out here from Tennessee to claim it."

"What use do I have for a ranch?"

Cheyenne shook her head as if Falcon was hopeless . . . or she was.

Kevin decided it might help Falcon to hear familiar things. That's when it struck him how little he knew about Falcon. Were there brothers or sisters back east? There couldn't be more of Clovis's get, because the old scoundrel probably would've left them a share of the ranch. But Falcon's ma could've had other children. What had Falcon's growing-up years been like? Had he been caught in the Civil War? He was a little older than Kevin, but was he old enough to be fighting age? Whether he fought or not, the war would have been all around him.

"Cheyenne, there's a lot more you need to know, too," Win said. "But first, I'm so glad we found you."

"Admit it, Win. I found you." Cheyenne tossed her apple core away. "How did you end up married to the man who stole part of my ranch?" She glared at Kevin, and it was all he could do not to hunt for cover.

Win kept Cheyenne walking and talking, and they gradually pulled ahead of the men. Kevin wondered if she'd tell Cheyenne about her ma's death and her suspicions about her pa.

Falcon fell into step beside Kevin.

"So do you . . ." Kevin wasn't really sure what to ask Falcon. Questions flooded his mind.

Do you believe the things I've told you?

Do you want to hear more?

Are you coming back with us to stay?

Are you sure you got all the blood off that knife before you put it in your sheath?

Instead, he said, "Those two women don't seem real interested in whether we're coming along or not." Kevin frowned at Win's back.

"Yep, and it sounds like one of 'em's your wife."

Kevin was almost as likely not to remember that as Falcon.

The women didn't even look back. In fact, they were leaving the men behind.

"They oughta have more sense." Kevin wanted Falcon to

come in out of the rain. Come back to the family. But he didn't think taking him against his will would be easy. It was a relief when Falcon kept coming.

"And the one with the gun and the mean mouth?"

"Her name is Cheyenne Brewster. She's not your blood sister, but she's your brother's half sister."

Falcon rubbed the back of his head. "Well, maybe it's us that oughta have more sense than to let her get too far ahead. We might need her to shoot someone for us."

It was a good point. Kevin picked up the pace, which reminded him he'd been shot and battered.

"Tell me more about this ranch."

"You know what a ranch is?" Kevin didn't know how amnesia worked.

Falcon walked along silently for a long stretch. Then, still moving, he raised one hand. "I know this is my hand. I know I'm wearing moccasins, and I know I could make another pair if need be. I know trees, rocks, and streams. I can even name some of the birds and plants, and I understand the ones I can't name are because I'm not familiar with them—it's got nuthin' to do with forgetting. But I don't know anything about myself."

He looked at Kevin, who shrugged and said, "It makes no sense to me."

"Well, tell me more about the ranch."

Kevin took that to mean Falcon wanted to hear more talking but not do much himself. Kevin set out to do plenty of it. After a time, he said, "I'm a newcomer here, too. I inherited land just like you did. We've both only been out here a week."

Falcon arched a shaggy brow, or maybe his brows weren't shaggy. Maybe his hair and scruffy beard were so shaggy Kevin just added the brows in.

"You've been out here a week, and you're married already?" Falcon furrowed his brow. "Am I forgetting that a week is not a normal length of time to know a woman before you marry her?"

Kevin just kept talking. He found plenty to tell. Nothing about Win's father because that was a secret, but he hoped she was telling Cheyenne about her suspicions of how her mother died. Cheyenne hadn't done any more shouting, but the woman seemed to be mostly capable of self-control.

They were hours hiking in the direction set by Cheyenne before they reached the trail Kevin recognized as the one that connected the RHR to Bear Claw Pass. Finally, he knew exactly where he was. By now the fog was long gone, the rain was over, and the sun had come out, but they stayed to the side of the trail to avoid the mud.

The weather warmed up enough to make his soggy clothing less miserable, which reminded him again of his headache and all the bruises he'd earned in that chaotic river ride.

They turned toward home and had walked a fair distance when they met Wyatt riding down the trail, Molly and Andy along with him.

Wyatt's shout stopped them all in their tracks.

THIRTY

Wyatt swung down and charged at them. Win was afraid he was going to punch someone, but he went straight for Cheyenne, grabbed her around the waist, and swung her in a big circle. "You're all right!"

Cheyenne slapped his shoulders, but she was grinning at him. "I'm the only one of this sorry group who was never anywhere I didn't want to be."

Wyatt set her lightly on her feet, then his eyes swung to Win and Kevin, a frown on his face. "And you're married?"

He sounded a little horrified, which Win could hardly fault him for. She wondered when he'd found that out. She saw Molly rush to give Kevin a hug. Andy slapped his big brother on the back. Then Molly gave Win a worried look and started speaking in quiet earnest to Kevin.

Wyatt had looked them all over and finally got to Falcon. He glanced away, then his head almost snapped when he looked back. "You're alive!"

Falcon rubbed the hair on his face. Almost like he was trying to remember what he looked like by touch. "I heard you didn't even bother hunting for my body. If you had, you'd have found me alive a week ago."

"Falcon, you survived those falls and those rocky rapids." Wyatt turned to Cheyenne, who stood beside him. "Have you ever heard of anyone going through that stretch and living?"

Cheyenne shrugged one shoulder. "Have we ever heard of anyone going through that stretch at all? I think we had a cow fall in that stream once, and the poor critter died, but no men."

"Ma always said it was deadly."

"She did. But judging from Falcon, standing here alive, Ma might've been trying to scare us into being careful."

Looking stricken, Wyatt turned to Falcon. "We should have kept hunting."

Kevin said, "He must've been shot, then fallen—"

"Haven't you checked?" Cheyenne as good as called them ridiculous. "It's not that hard to tell if a man's been shot."

"He's not that friendly." Kevin gave Falcon a doubtful look. Molly punched Kevin in the shoulder, but she stayed well away from Falcon.

"And we've been really busy," Win reminded them. "Not much time to check for wounds."

"I've never met you people before in my life," Falcon protested. "For all I know, you're the ones who shot me . . . if I've been shot."

Wyatt looked at the filthy, cranky, furry Falcon as if considering checking for gunshot wounds . . . and thinking the better of it. "You've never met us before?"

Cheyenne stomped over to Falcon.

Who snarled.

Cheyenne shoved him, said, "Shut up."

Win had never been more fond of her old friend.

Cheyenne managed to inspect Falcon without touching him. Walking around behind him, she said, "Bend down a little. You've done a lot of bleeding. It's all around your collar back here. I suppose going down the stream like you did washed a lot of it away, then the rain did its share, but there's enough left to tell you are wounded. I can't see how though."

Win waited, wondering when Falcon would drag his knife out and come after them all.

Instead, he said, "I feel a nasty cut back there, right under my hair."

Putting one firm hand on Falcon's shoulder, Cheyenne said quietly, "C'mon. Let me see what happened to you."

He bent forward enough to brace his hands on his knees. Cheyenne pushed his hair aside. She did it with surprising gentleness considering how unhappy she was to have Falcon and Kevin around.

"There's a wound here, possibly made by a bullet. When you fell into the water, the rocks no doubt battered you some," Cheyenne said. "We'll bandage it when we get home." She looked at Wyatt. "Whatever happened, he can't remember nuthin'."

Cheyenne left Falcon's side and grabbed Wyatt's horse.

"You'd better ride, Falcon." Cheyenne led the horse toward him. "You probably need to take it slow and easy."

"Too late to take it easy. I've been living in the wilderness, hunting and fishing and hiding from you for a week."

"Hiding from her?" Wyatt tipped his hat back and scratched his head.

Win felt sorry for Wyatt. Honestly, they weren't making much sense. And he was out searching for them, which was nice of him. And none of this was his fault.

Molly said, "I can give you a ride, Falcon."

But Win could tell her heart wasn't in it.

"I'll ride with you, Molly," Andy offered. "Falcon can ride my horse."

"I'll walk." And Falcon started forward, looking like he planned to leave them all behind arguing over which horse he'd ride.

Molly mounted up, as did Andy, alone on their horses. Cheyenne shrugged, swung up on Wyatt's horse, and rode over to Win. She reached a hand down. "We'll ride then. But we won't just run off in case killers are near and I need to save everyone. I think we need to stick together."

Win smiled at her old friend. "I've missed you."

Cheyenne pulled her foot out of the stirrup. Win stuck hers in, and with Cheyenne giving her a tug, she mounted up, sitting behind the saddle.

"Kevin, Wyatt, you want to ride home?" Molly asked.

Falcon looked back at Wyatt and Kevin. "I think the brothers should all walk. We need to have a talk."

Win said to Wyatt, "We don't mean Falcon can't remember who *hit* him, we mean Falcon can't remember his *name*. And he can't remember any of our names or what brought him to Wyoming."

Cheyenne nudged the horse into a walk, and they started for home.

Wyatt came to Falcon's side as if to catch him if he toppled over. But Falcon just kept walking along behind the horses.

"Winona, or whatever her name is there, said she's heard tell of some sickness of not remembering. I can't remember what she called it, but that's because it's a mighty odd word. Not because of the forgetting sickness."

276

"Amnesia." Win looked behind her and ran her eyes down the row of manhood.

Brothers.

Wyatt, wearing boots and a Stetson. Spurs jingling as he walked.

Falcon, taller than the other two, though they were all of a good height. His shocking resemblance to Clovis Hunt disguised by shaggy hair and a scraggly week-old beard, and his desperate need of clean clothes and a bath.

And Kevin. She gave him a special smile. He was watching her and smiled back. The one that was hers. The best looking, if currently a little battered. A farmer at heart and that suited her.

"I think it's great you're all together again," she said.

The three of them lined up—Falcon, Wyatt in the middle, then Kevin. Walking along at a good pace despite two of them being wounded before the third had shown up to save them after they'd saved themselves.

They looked at each other, and Wyatt said, "Tell me what's been going on. What part does Ross Baker have to play in this?"

Win turned to face forward and said to Cheyenne, "You left riding a horse. Where'd it go?"

"I snuck back with it a couple of days after I left, turned it loose in the corral and got more supplies. Just walked right in, then hiked away. I wanted to be on foot, maybe do some climbing, see some land I've never seen before. And I didn't want to tie my horse up and make it stand, even staked out to eat grass, for several days. I saw signs that someone was wandering around our property and set out to track him. I've been following Falcon ever since, but I never so much as caught sight of him."

Win hugged her and said, "You really have been fine, haven't you?"

Nodding, Cheyenne rode along in comfort.

"I need to tell you a secret. It's something you should know about my pa. You can't—" Win found herself sliding over the horse's rump, landing on her feet. Cheyenne picked up the pace so she was far enough ahead she couldn't hear anything Win said but close enough to rescue them all if needed. It was clear Cheyenne didn't want to hear Win speak ill of her father. Well, the secret could wait. In fact, Win decided right then that the secret could wait until there was no way to avoid telling it. Unless Cheyenne showed signs of eloping, Win would just keep all of this to herself.

Kevin knew. She turned to see the men catching up to her, and she stepped to the side to fall in line with them next to Kevin. He took her hand and she clasped his tight.

Whether they liked it or not, all of them were now family.

THIRTY-ONE

*K*evin, you and Win can have the ramrod house permanently if you're willing to learn to ranch." Wyatt sat at the head of the table and made that announcement.

They'd finally settled into a meal that was going to be too late for noon but too early for supper. They were all too hungry to wait for supper.

Kevin's heart sped up to think of getting his wife to himself. So far, he hadn't managed that.

When they'd first gotten home, they'd gone to work on Falcon. The men had carried buckets of hot water and a big tin bathtub into the ramrod's house. Falcon had cleaned up and shaved, and he'd come up with a change of clothes. The satchel he'd been carrying when he'd gotten off the train had still been sitting in the ramrod's house.

Cheyenne had cut his hair, and he'd let Molly put some salve on his neck wound. While Molly had the doctoring supplies out, she took the stitches out of Win's back and changed the bandage on Kevin's head.

Win had scrubbed the mangy outfit Falcon had been wearing in the woods for a week and sewn up a few tears.

Falcon was looking purely civilized, and he still couldn't remember a thing.

Molly, with some help from Wyatt and Andy, got a meal ready.

Now here they sat eating, and before Kevin's belly was even close to full, Wyatt made his offer.

Kevin looked at Win, who was looking at Cheyenne.

Cheyenne didn't smile, but she wasn't growling.

"It's my plan to find some land here on the RHR that is fit for growing crops. I'm a farmer not a rancher, though I might try and handle a bigger herd, but I'd like to start with six cows like I had in Kansas."

Wyatt snorted.

Cheyenne rolled her eyes and muttered, "Six cows?"

Andy propped his elbows on the table and plunked his chin on his fists. "Farming's no fun, Kev."

"Then the rest of my inheritance goes to you, Cheyenne. I'll give you a real big chunk of one third, sign it over to you. Or . . . as I understand it, we can't make it legal, but I could just leave it alone and let you act like it's yours. We'll figure it out. Then as soon as Molly is old enough to homestead, she'll claim land off the RHR, and we'll let you have the rest of your property. Our pa stole that land from you, Cheyenne, and you, too, Wyatt. I may have a legal claim on it, but it's still pure robbery, and I won't be a part of it."

Falcon said, "What do I need a ranch for? You can have most of mine, too, Cheyenne. I hiked through some beautiful mountain country the last week. And I might not remember my name, but I remember how to build a cabin and hunt for food. I have no interest in being a rancher, so I can take a stretch that's not good for grazing cattle anyway."

"That's not gonna work," Wyatt said. "She can't have two-thirds of it and me only a third."

It reminded Kevin of Win saying she considered Wyatt to being next thing to a brother. A pesky little brother. Kevin was tempted to make him go sit in the corner.

Cheyenne drew in a long breath. A little nod that Kevin could barely see got bigger. "Since the will was read, I've been spitting mad—made worse because the one who did this is beyond my reach." She crossed her arms in a way that didn't look all that friendly, but she didn't punch him, so that seemed like a good sign.

"Thank you for the ranch, Kevin. I accept." She turned to Falcon, who'd stayed on the other side of the table from her. "And thank you, Falcon. I accept your offer, too. And Wyatt, you fool, of course we'll split it in half. Since none of it can be done legally as the terms of the will state, we'll just divide things up like we always have."

She didn't swat Wyatt like he was a misbehaving eight-year-old, but Kevin could imagine her doing it. Nope, Wyatt would've been a bad husband for Win. Terrible. Much better that she'd married him.

"Do you suppose I could take my wife to the ramrod's house and spend a quiet afternoon with her away from all you people?"

He noticed Molly's eyes go wide and sad. He hadn't really meant get away from her. Though he didn't really want her to come.

Andy said, "Don't we have some cattle to brand?"

"The men didn't go out today. It was too muddy," Wyatt answered. "Andy, you can come with me to town."

Andy's brow furrowed. "I'd rather rope calves than go shopping."

"This will be serious business. We need to tell the sheriff about those men attacking everyone. Then we'll need to find their bodies and bring them in."

"I'll ride along," Falcon said. "I know where they are."

Cheyenne shook her head. "He might get lucky and find them, but considering his whole brain is addled, I'd better come, too."

Molly raised her hand in a halfhearted manner. "I'll stay here and make another meal. We'll be ready for a late supper."

Wyatt frowned at her. "You can come if you want to. We'll have to deal with dead bodies and—"

"Just get on with your business." Molly cut him off. "I have no wish to see dead bodies."

Wyatt nodded and most everyone left.

"I'll be back to help you get a meal on, Molly," Win said.

"I just want to spend some time talking to Win, then we'll both be back to help," Kevin assured her.

Molly rubbed her arms as if to warm herself. "I didn't sleep a wink while you were gone. I'm about to drop. I'm going to lie down for a while. Don't worry about leaving me here in the house, completely alone, with all the work."

Molly turned and rushed out of the room.

Kevin watched her go. He heard the hurt in her voice, but he turned to Win and reached for her hand. "I'll talk with her later. For now, I'd like a quiet hour with my wife just to get to know you better and, well," he lowered his voice, "you told me your old secrets b-but I've never told you mine."

Their eyes met. Win squeezed his hand firmly. "Let's go."

THIRTY-TWO

hey stepped into a house Kevin had been thinking was his. Now all he saw were the belongings of a dead man. Ross Baker.

"Cheyenne didn't even talk about shooting Tuttle." Win
looked around.

"No, she didn't." Kevin swung the door shut. "And Falcon
killed Baker and made no fuss about it."

He tugged Win's hand and turned her to face him. "Cheyenne shot Tuttle in the wrist. Who'd think that would kill a
man? Do you think Falcon and Cheyenne are really so tough
they can do that and not be bothered?"

Kevin watched her closely, wishing he didn't have to say what
came next. "Because I know it bothered me bad when I came
home to find my mother beaten to death. Molly halfway there,
bleeding, two black eyes, and her father shot dead." Kevin swallowed hard.

Win's head snapped up, but he looked down at his trembling
hands.

Kevin held them up to eye level and said, "I've never said
those words out loud before. Molly and I swore neither of us
would ever speak of it. I feel like I'm digging inside me for

something buried deep. And the digging is painful. But it's right that I tell you."

Her eyes searched his as she waited for him to finish.

"Her pa was dead on the floor beside my ma . . . our ma."

"Did Molly shoot him or did your ma?" Win reached out and touched his hand, his fist clenched tight, his arms rigid at his side.

"I've never asked. We've never spoken of it. We swore to never speak of it. But it's what has created a connection between Molly and me."

Win's hand tightened. Kevin's relaxed enough he could catch hold, and he held on as if he were a drowning man.

"I hid the bodies." Shaking his head as he relived the memory, he said, "I rode for hours in the night with both bodies draped over a saddle. Kansas is a treeless plain for the most part. I didn't know if I could dig deep enough to keep the bodies from turning up somehow. Finally, I found a stretch of woods that looked like no one wandered there. I buried Ma with considerable care. It felt like a terrible sin to just leave her there in an unmarked grave, but I did it, buried her deep, pulled logs over the grave, prayed over the grave."

His jaw formed a grim line. "And then I rode on. I wanted them a long way apart from each other. I thought that would be better if no connection could be found between them, if they ever turned up."

Win lifted one hand to rest on the side of his face, and the warmth of her touch seemed to drag him out of his dark thoughts.

"I reached the Missouri River. It was coming on dawn, and I didn't want to be seen riding with a dead body, so I tossed Stu Garner in the river. Then I turned tail and rode for home. I had three horses so I could switch saddles and give the horses a rest without stopping. There was plenty of death in Kansas, and it was spring and the water was high. If anyone found him, no one connected him to us."

"When did this happen?"

"Andy was five. Ten years ago now."

"Which made Molly . . ." Win couldn't stand to think of it.

"She was nine years old. Stu Garner meant nothing to me but bad news. I should have killed him the first time I came home and found Ma bleeding. I wanted to a dozen times. But he was careful not to swing on Ma in my presence. Ma always had some excuse. First she said she fell, then when she couldn't deny she'd been hit, she blamed herself. I always thought— hoped—that she didn't want me to kill him because she was afraid I'd hang, but I'm scared that the real truth is she thought she deserved it."

Win went into Kevin's arms, and he held her tight, appreciating her support, her warmth. His words made him feel cold to the bone.

He rested his head on her shoulder and said, "Marrying Clovis Hunt was no great decision on her part, so marrying another worthless man probably said more about her than it did about the men, and I never wanted to think that about my ma."

Kevin fell silent. They stood there in each other's arms. Win now knew his darkest secret. Kevin knew hers.

"Your secret and mine are to hide dreadful acts, but neither of us did a thing wrong."

"And still here we stand." Kevin kissed her neck.

She felt a shiver go down her spine, but a warm shiver that felt wonderful. "Bearing the burdens of others. With no way to change anything."

At last Kevin lifted his head, and Win lifted hers. Their eyes met. An inch at a time, slowly, slowly, Kevin lowered his head until their lips touched.

And Win remembered there was a lot more to marriage than staying away from her father and hiding old, dark, dangerous secrets. There was delight. There was touch. There was passion. There was someone to call her own.

Kevin brushed a wisp of her hair back. "We haven't been married long, Win. Nor have we known each other long. But I am finding nothing but good in marrying you. And I'd like to continue being married in all possible ways. Are you ready for something more than kisses?"

Their talk had been serious, and it surprised her to find a smile. Almost as if a weight had been lifted off her just by sharing her fears about her pa. And she thought Kevin looked lighter, too.

"Yes, we're married, and I know what that means. Yes, I am ready for more."

Kevin smiled. His hazel eyes flashed like liquid gold. He swept her up into his arms and said, "Let's go be married."

THIRTY-THREE

*W*in and Kevin made it to the house in time for a very late supper. They were no help at all making it.

Molly had it in hand, though, and good thing because Wyatt, Falcon, Cheyenne, and Andy came riding into the yard before Kevin got the kitchen door shut.

Rubin, the foreman, came out of the barn, and Wyatt spoke to him for a few minutes while the others put up the horses before going inside.

They all washed up except Wyatt, who seemed to have plenty to talk with his foreman about. The others pitched in setting the table, so Kevin didn't have to worry about Molly scolding him for their absence or asking them what had taken so all-fired long. He sure as certain didn't want to answer that question.

By the time the table was ready and the food was in place, Wyatt was washing up, and they all sat.

Cheyenne said, "Let's say a blessing before we eat. We've had so much upheaval I think we've forgotten to ask the Lord to be with us."

Kevin had said plenty of prayers, but he liked the idea of them praying together as a family.

He looked around the table. Family. His had grown by more than double in a few days. Two of them, Cheyenne and Falcon, had saved his life today.

Three of them, Wyatt, Molly, and Andy, had come searching for them in a towering storm.

One of them had married him. That got a smile out of him.

Had they all been together before today? No, Falcon hadn't met Cheyenne before he went into the stream.

Today was a first. A beginning.

Everyone bowed their heads. Because she was in many ways the head of the house, Cheyenne prayed aloud. Falcon might be older by a little, but it was close, and this was her house, her heritage, and her right.

Kevin could tell she still carried hurts around inside her, but he could also tell she was trying.

Molly. He had to talk to Molly. He'd betrayed his sister, who was also his closest confidant and best friend, for a woman he'd known only a short time. Betrayed Molly by marrying without telling her about it and betrayed her far more than that by telling a secret he'd sworn to keep.

He needed to tell Molly all of that. But for now, despite being left alone in this house while everyone went about doing other things, she was putting a delicious meal on the table. And doing it with a calm and cheerful attitude.

Probably faking it, but she was faking it well.

Falcon was a shock. With the shave, bath, clean clothes, and a haircut, he'd been transformed into a purely civilized man, and Kevin was impressed. He'd have to give the man back his hat, currently hanging over the fireplace in the ramrod's house.

288

This was Kevin's family.

The thought stunned and warmed him. He prayed silently for each of his family members.

When Cheyenne finished her prayer, they raised their heads, and Kevin saw too many serious expressions around the table.

"Tell us what happened today." He looked from one to the other.

"The sheriff rode out with us to bring in the bodies," Wyatt began. "He took Cheyenne's word for everything. He knows her well and has for a long time. I trusted Ross Baker, but he hadn't been with us long, nothing like Rubin. But he was a good hand, a good leader. Why would a man turn coyote like this when he had a good job?"

"The sheriff had heard talk in town," Falcon said. "Tuttle had been grousing some about getting older. He spent a bit too much time, in the opinion of some, at the saloon, and he'd been heard to say being a hired cowpoke is a young man's business. Word is, he and Baker liked the same saloon, and they might've just been men who liked complaining to each other. Except here came Clovis Hunt's new will."

Wyatt nodded. "That's what set them off. It must've been. It was only days after the contents of that will became known that both men vanished from the area. Baker had a good reason, and we didn't even think to question it, though it's a tough time of year to be shorthanded."

"We found out Tuttle took off from your pa's ranch at the same time," Cheyenne said to Win.

"One of them said they tried to kill me in Missouri and that I stole their horses and guns." Falcon rubbed the back of his neck. "I don't remember doing that, but if they took off right away, took the train east, they'd've had time to meet me riding out. I went to the doctor today, and he said he's never seen a case like mine, but he's read of them, and my memory will probably come back. Someday. Maybe."

"You still don't know what your name is?" Kevin had to believe him. Falcon was too straightforward.

"You've told me I'm Falcon Hunt. So I guess I know it. I just don't remember it."

"Well, you have family now, Falcon." Cheyenne met his gaze with her black eyes. "Stay here and we'll be able to help you through whatever confusion lies ahead."

Falcon shrugged one shoulder and didn't answer.

Kevin found himself wondering how to convince Falcon he needed to stay.

"I'll stay until I'm . . . healed, or whatever it is that needs to change for me to remember." Falcon looked up at them. His eyes that strange hazel color the brothers all shared. They seemed to study Wyatt, then Kevin.

He lapsed into silence. Kevin felt like he could hear the beating of his own heart as he wondered what Falcon intended to say.

"I can remember a Bible verse about honoring your father and your mother." Falcon's eyes squinted as if he was trying to dig out more of the memory.

Kevin was surprised Falcon knew the Bible. He hadn't shown much of a tendency to be a man of faith . . . but then, Kevin barely knew him. To forget so much and remember a Bible verse seemed like a good sign.

"It's one of the Ten Commandments. The fifth commandment says, 'Honor thy father and thy mother: that thy days may be long upon the land which the Lord thy God hath giveth thee.' And I remember another verse that says something like, this commandment is the only one with a promise."

"Land," Cheyenne said bitterly. She clenched her fists on the table, and Kevin saw the battle within her for control. To put aside her anger. "Honor your father and live long in the land God gave you."

"It's really about the Promised Land, Cheyenne," Win said softly. "That's the land that God had promised the Israelites."

"And I think it's about heaven," Molly added. "We had a pretty hard life back in Kansas. Hard work every day. Very little time to enjoy life. Before, during, and even after the war, it was a dreadful life. Makes a person try to live a life that pleases God so you can find joy in the next world, because this one is just so hard."

"And, Cheyenne"—Wyatt reached past Andy to rest his hand on one of her clenched fists—"honoring your father and mother is an easy thing for you. Your ma and pa were fine folks. And you will continue to live on this land no matter what my pa did to you."

Cheyenne didn't look that sure.

Kevin added, "It's us that has trouble. Falcon, Wyatt, and me. We're the ones left with the mystery of how God expects us to honor our coyote of a father. A man who, in his last act, stole a ranch from you, Cheyenne, and a nice chunk of it from you, Wyatt."

"Mine was no great pillar of decency, either," Molly muttered. "I think honoring him is going to have to be one of those sins I just have to ask forgiveness for."

Andy's brow wrinkled, reminding Kevin that his little brother really knew nothing about his ma and pa. The telling was too unpleasant. And the youngster didn't seem to remember much on his own, which Kevin found a little strange. Kevin had told Win his dark secret. Would it be right to tell Andy?

Kevin looked at Win, wondering if she'd say the same. But Win studied Cheyenne in a strange way. Kevin couldn't understand it except maybe it had to do with Cheyenne speaking of marrying Win's pa. Why not just tell Cheyenne what Win suspected?

Kevin didn't know why not, and he wasn't going to ask here at the table. In fact, he wasn't going to ask her at all. Not when he was looking forward to the night ahead and wanted his wife to be very happy with him.

Then he remembered something. "When I was growing up, Clovis Hunt was a hero to me. He was off exploring the frontier. Yes, he made life hard for us, but I knew he was a great man, searching distant places, helping to settle the West. When he died, to me, he died a hero. It's only been since I inherited this land that it's really occurred to me not to honor him."

"I wish I could remember anything about how I saw him," Falcon said. "I'm not sure how he was presented to me before I found out he was a lying, cheating swindler. I'll know better when my memory returns."

Kevin looked around the table. "We may never be able to abide by this commandment, and I'm not even sure it'd be right to do so. But—" He held out his hand to Win, who smiled and took it. Then Win held out her hand to Molly, who clasped her hand.

Molly offered her hand to Falcon, who reluctantly grabbed hold. Falcon didn't reach for Cheyenne, but Kevin took Wyatt's, Wyatt took Andy's, and Andy reached hesitantly for Cheyenne. She frowned but took his hand, then looked at Falcon. The slowest of them all, Cheyenne and Falcon closed the circle.

The solemn look she gave tore at Kevin's heart. Cheyenne, of all of them, had been cheated the most.

Or maybe she was the most fortunate with two honorable, loving parents, even though she lost them too young.

Kevin said quietly, "However we manage to wrangle our feelings toward honoring our father, I'm glad to know I've got a family here at the Rolling Hills Ranch. I'm proud to know all of you. I can say with an easy heart that I will honor family."

Every one of them, with one voice, said, "I will honor family."

Andy added, "Can we quit talking and eat?"

Laughter broke out around the table, and they let go of each other. The food was passed, and a bond was formed.

ABOUT THE AUTHOR

Mary Connealy writes romantic comedies about cowboys. She's the author of the BRIDES OF HOPE MOUNTAIN, HIGH SIERRA SWEETHEARTS, KINCAID BRIDES, TROUBLE IN TEXAS, WILD AT HEART, and CIMARRON LEGACY series, as well as several other acclaimed series. Mary has been nominated for a Christy Award, was a finalist for a RITA Award, and is a two-time winner of the Carol Award. She lives on a ranch in eastern Nebraska with her very own romantic cowboy hero. They have four grown daughters—Joslyn, married to Matt; Wendy; Shelly, married to Aaron; and Katy, married to Max—and six precious grandchildren. Learn more about Mary and her books at

maryconnealy.com
facebook.com/maryconnealy
seekerville.blogspot.com
petticoatsandpistols.com

Sign Up for Mary's Newsletter

Keep up to date with Mary's latest news on book releases and events by signing up for her email list at maryconnealy.com.

More from Mary Connealy

To overcome her fears of the outside world, Ursula Nordegren treks down Hope Mountain where she discovers a badly wounded man. Wax Mosby is remorseful over driving out the Wardens, but when he's hurt, the last person he expects to rescue him is a beautiful woman related to them. As they weigh the cost of living new lives, an unlikely bond forms between them.

Her Secret Song, BRIDES OF HOPE MOUNTAIN #3

You May Also Like . . .

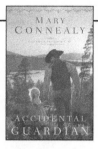

Trace Riley has been self-appointed guardian of the trail ever since his own wagon was attacked. When he finds the ruins of a wagon train, he offers shelter to survivor Deborah Harkness and the children she saved. Trace and Deborah grow close working to bring justice to the trail, but what will happen when the attackers return to silence the only witness?

The Accidental Guardian by Mary Connealy
HIGH SIERRA SWEETHEARTS #1
maryconnealy.com

After being robbed on her trip west to save her ailing sister, Greta Nilsson is left homeless and penniless. Struggling to get his new ranch running, Wyatt McQuaid is offered a bargain—the mayor will invest in a herd of cattle if Wyatt agrees to help the town become more respectable by marrying...and the mayor has the perfect woman in mind.

A Cowboy for Keeps by Jody Hedlund
COLORADO COWBOYS #1
jodyhedlund.com

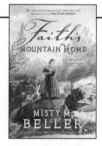

Nate Long has always watched over his twin, even if it's led him to be an outlaw. When his brother is wounded in a shootout, it's their former prisoner, Laura, who ends up nursing his wounds at Settler's Fort. She knows Nate wants a fresh start, but struggles with how his devotion blinds him. Do the futures they seek include love, or is too much in the way?

Faith's Mountain Home by Misty M. Beller
HEARTS OF MONTANA #3
mistymbeller.com

◆ BETHANYHOUSE

More from Bethany House

After smallpox kills her mother and siblings, Gloriana Womack is dedicated to holding together what's left of her fractured family. Luke Carson arrives in Duluth to shepherd the arrival of the railroad and reunite with his brother. When tragedy strikes, Gloriana and Luke must help each other through their grief and soon find their lives inextricably linked.

Destined for You by Tracie Peterson
LADIES OF THE LAKE #1
traciepeterson.com

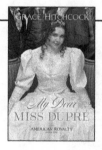

Upon her father's unexpected retirement, his shareholders refuse to allow Willow Dupré to take over the company without a man at her side. Presented with twenty-five potential suitors from New York society's elite, she has six months to choose which she will marry. But when one captures her heart, she must discover for herself if his motives are truly pure....

My Dear Miss Dupré by Grace Hitchcock
AMERICAN ROYALTY #1
gracehitchcock.com

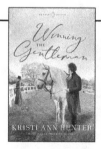

When his reputation is threatened, Aaron Whitworth makes the desperate decision to hire a circus horse trainer as a jockey for his racehorses. Most men don't take Sophia Fitzroy seriously because she's a woman, but as she fights for the right to do the work she was hired for, she finds the fight for Aaron's guarded heart might be a more worthwhile challenge.

Winning the Gentleman by Kristi Ann Hunter
HEARTS ON THE HEATH
kristiannhunter.com

CPSIA information can be obtained
at www.ICGtesting.com
Printed in the USA
LVHW092050030821
694430LV00002B/146